Entanglement

KATY MAHOOD

THE BOROUGH PRESS

The Borough Press
An imprint of HarperCollins*Publishers*
1 London Bridge Street
London SE1 9GF

www.harpercollins.co.uk

Published by HarperCollins*Publishers* 2018

1

HB ISBN: 978-0-00-824565-8
TPB ISBN: 978-0-00-824566-5

Set in Bell MT by Palimpsest Book Production Limited, Falkirk, Stirlingshire

Printed and bound in Great Britain by CPI Group (UK) Ltd, Croydon, CR0 4YY

MIX
Paper from
responsible sources
FSC C007454

For my parents, Tess and Jim

When two systems enter into temporary physical interaction due to known forces between them, and when after a time of mutual influence the systems separate again, then they can no longer be described in the same way as before . . . I would call that the characteristic trait of quantum mechanics, the one that enforces its entire departure from classical lines of thought. Because of their interaction these two quantum states have become entangled.

'The Present Situation in Quantum Mechanics'
by Erwin Schrödinger, 1935

PRELUDE

PRELUDE

4 *August 1977*

At first she thinks it is a cloud, or smoke. But its undulations are too regular, too melodic. As the train closes the distance, the movements become more granular, a lace-like pattern of dark and sky, curving rhythmically in waves and turns above the countryside, and Stella sees it is a group of fast-flying birds. Wingtips almost touching, they move in perfect motion, against the evening sky.

Murmuration. There is magic to it, this seamless dance of small birds weaving a form that exists only in their togetherness. The tree on the horizon, the church, the hill: these things stand still as time moves around them. But this is something more; a new dimension forged in time and motion.

The train arrives. From above, the arches of the roof of Paddington Station curve and roll, ripple marks made by the tide of progress. The concourse teems with life, eddying across the mica-flecked floor. A fresh flood flows from a newly halted train and somewhere within the throng is Stella, returned early from her summer break. She struggles with a heavy bag, nervous for the tiny life pulsing within her, a secret that at this moment is hers alone. In the summer heat the station air is hazy. Specks of smut rise and glisten, and she looks for the face of the man who will meet her, but for now sees only the fuzz of people and particles pushed by the waves of warm air and urgency.

And then, there he is. He moves stop-start through the throb of the crowd, long limbs that don't quite know where to be, long hair falling in his face. John is thinking, she can see, not at that moment of her, but a thought scored through with formulae that could unlock this tangle of bodies, noise and motion. He lifts his head, eyes narrow in the glare of the dipping sun, and sees her silhouette with its halo of gold-lit hair, her shoulders stooped beneath the heavy bag. And though he knows the physical impossibility of it, time for him is suddenly slowed, revealing gaps he'd not discerned before, through which he moves to claim this fresh-skinned woman. They press together and the world around them speeds up once more, gusting fumes and breath and microscopic fragments of life, up, up and into the spiralling dance overhead.

4 August 2007

From below, the arches of Paddington Station reach towards the night sky. Stella sits, silent in her wedding clothes, sipping tea from a paper cup, waiting for the call to the sleeper train. Beside her, John leans back on his chair, his arm resting on their luggage. On the other side of the station, on a bench near a darkened shop front, Stella notices a man in a hat. He looks up and their gaze meets across the concourse. When he nods, Stella smiles in return.

John looks up at the arches of the roof. He knows that they are moving through time and space, spinning on a planet that is orbiting a star – and yet the late-night station seems quite still. A moment later, a clutch of pigeons bursts upwards; his knee knocks the table; hot tea spills. Stella leaps to her feet, skidding in her high heels as John reaches out to catch her a fraction too late. She lands with a gasp on the floor and looks down at her expensive cream skirt, where a murky stain blooms along the thigh. Her ankle hurts. She swallows hard and looks up. For a fraction of a second she sees his face as it once was: wide-eyed and taut with longing. A fine trail shimmers in the light above them and she turns towards the roof, searching for a tiny piece of the young woman who stepped from a train and the young man who was once there to meet her – but all she can see now is dust.

Scalar time passes. The hands on the large clock move. The man in the hat stands and leaves. On Platform 1, Stella takes John's hand as they climb aboard the train and her eyes travel once more around the station, seeking out fragments of her past. She sees herself at twenty-one at the beginning of an academic career. Her violin case balanced on top of a suitcase weighted with books, a knot tightening from her stomach to her throat, her mother and father trotting to keep up as she pushes the trolley through the thronging travellers. They had bundled into a taxi, a sudden rainstorm blurring the windows of the cab as they'd watched commuters and tourists rush for cover beneath the dripping black awnings of Praed Street.

When, later that day, she'd arrived in the pub just off Gower Street with a straggling group of postgraduates, she'd noticed an angular man with sandy-coloured hair and hands that moved with quick precision as he talked. Bell-bottomed brown cords and a murky green T-shirt. Scientist, she'd thought, and turned to go. But her bag had clipped a glass and knocked a pint of bitter into his lap and, to her shame, Stella's eyes had filled with unwanted tears. And then he'd smiled. It was a generous, lopsided smile that made it easy to laugh an apology and offer to buy him a drink. His hand had brushed her arm as they spoke and at his touch she'd felt something pass over her like light. With John the world had felt infused with colour and, as they walked together through the broad white streets of

Bloomsbury, she'd had the sense that London was bursting to life beneath her feet.

More than thirty years on, the station feels the same, despite the screens and signs that jostle for attention. It is, she thinks, as it has always been, a threshold place of beginnings and farewells. Stella looks again at John, who raises her hand to his lips. She finds her thoughts are flying back and forth across the years; moments forgotten for decades rising to the surface, casting ripples that gather and collide, so that everything around her seems coated in a mismatched layer of the past. She can almost smell it as it teeters on the edges of her memory, that nameless musk of youth and sex and hope.

Outside the station, night buses rumble. A rowdy group of students stumbles past St Mary's Hospital. The late-night shops have drawn down their shutters as the man walks past, his hat now in his hand. He sits for a moment on a low wall and wonders, not for the first time, what might have happened that day had he not descended the cellar steps. *There's no use in thinking like that, Charlie*, he says aloud, and after a minute he stands up again and continues to walk.

The students are gone now and Charlie moves quietly in the dark streets, down Sussex Gardens and towards the park. Far away over Oxford Street the city-glow lightens the sky, but the dawn is still a good way off. In the inky still of Hyde Park, the dew has begun to fall. It clings to his heavy shoes and to the cuffs of his suit trousers, which grow thick and cold with the damp. He walks on to the middle of the park, where there is only a suggestion of the city beyond. Here, at the centre, there is almost solitude and except for the orange nub of the tall hotel to the east all is dark. Tired suddenly, he lies in the damp grass and the memories begin, as he knew that they would. But this time they start earlier, in the daylight, in a spot not far from here. He sees it as he saw it then: a young girl running in a thin red dress, the flash of her thigh as the fabric billows in the wind, her hand upon the curve of her belly, a tall man running back towards her. A name. *Stella*. As he closes his eyes, he feels a brief and unexpected peace pass through him and into the earth below.

And then, as they always do, the scenes behind his eyes grow dark. He feels the familiar lurch within and holds tight to his legs to make himself tiny and hard, but the images run through his mind as if on a loop: *a smoke-filled silence, the blue-black glitter of lights on shattered glass, a white hand in the dark.* In the chill night he hears his ragged breath and the creak of his clothes as he rocks back and forth in the grass. He knows this will pass. He remembers how it goes. And yet, it always feels as if this might be the big one, the point of no return. The thought is like a shriek, an involuntary gasp, rushing out of him unchecked.

Is this how it feels to be dying?

A dark chasm of fear looms before him, blank as a dialling tone, and he screws his eyes shut and hums to draw himself back from its infinite, terrifying space.

1.

COLLISION

8 October 1977

To become entangled the two particles must first interact.

McKearnan, L. Quantum Entanglement.
Paradox Publishing, 1982 (p. 2)

1.1

Charlie listened to the angry burr of the dialling tone before slamming the phone back into its cradle. Pushing the hair from his eyes he stood up, took a tie from the wardrobe and lifted a brown corduroy jacket from the back of the door. He shrugged it on, checking the elbows for holes. A yellow crust of egg clung to his cuff and he scrubbed at it with his fingernails, but the stubborn glaze stayed fast to the fabric, so he lit a cigarette instead.

The problem with the same old story is that you've heard it once too many times: a drama that leads always to the bottom of a bottle of vodka. When the phone had rung just after seven, he'd known it would be her. No one else would have rung reverse-charges in such a slurring stupor of obscenities and tears on his sister's wedding day. It wasn't as if you could blame Annie for not inviting the woman. She had been almost unintelligible with rage and drink, and when he tried to calm her she'd turned her venom to him: more swearing, more incoherent keening, something about being just like his father. She'd hung up before he'd had the chance to cut her off, his finger still hovering above the phone's switchhook as he listened to the echo of the open line against his ear.

In the living room, dust floated in the shards of morning light. Outside, a milk float was whirring its tin-pot way along the street, empties clinking, and some time soon, he guessed, the post would arrive. Since Beth had been in France, his weeks were shaped by the post: a day could be transformed by the sight of a handwritten envelope, a foreign stamp. Beth's letters sustained him in a way that a phone call could not, as if the ink held part of her, the deft strokes on the page inseparable from the slim fingers that had made them. Even the envelope could tug his desire as he imagined her tongue passing over its gummed edge.

He heard the creak of a floorboard and the rattle of a pipe from above. Other people were stirring around him, their days easing into the simplicity of this October Saturday. They had not been woken by the phone and the shrieks of his mother. They were lucky.

For a moment he allowed himself to picture what Beth would be doing now, in her flat above the sand-coloured streets of Montpellier. He imagined her asleep, soft tanned limbs curled about one another, dark hair falling across the curve of her cheek as her lips shaped semi-silent words. He closed his eyes, trying to hold onto the image, and a hollow bloomed between his heart and his stomach, a space so tender with longing that he imagined it had actually been carved from his flesh.

The first time Charlie had seen Beth she was sitting by the canal in Camden swinging her legs against the warm stone. She had been luxuriant beneath the early evening sunlight, her taut skin glossy as a ripe plum. As she'd swept her dark hair from her face, he'd noticed her eyes, green with a golden aura around each pupil, a pair of sunflowers floating on the sea. A Jewish princess she'd called herself, laughing over her beer in a pub garden on Haverstock Hill and telling him of a childhood in Hampstead, school days at Haberdashers' and high days and holidays with an extended family that ran into hundreds. 'Though we were not,' she'd said, 'all together at once.' Exotic words and festivals with their own exotic foodstuffs. Honey cake, rich and cloying. The crass heat of horseradish offset by watery-sweet sugared apple. Her body, too, he came to discover was a rare indulgence; the firm heaviness of her breasts, the silken curve of her back, the salty tang of her soft thighs.

On that first evening he had walked her home.

'How gallant of you,' she'd deadpanned as they'd stood in the doorway of her flat, her face half hidden by shadow, a faint gleam of sweat on her forehead. She had turned her eyes up towards him and pulled his hands around her waist. Charlie had longed to say something that wouldn't make him feel like he was speaking from a script shaped by bad films and second-rate novels. But how could he explain the hunger wrestling with fear, the unscratchable itch of his desire? The words that he reached for felt empty and sordid, a cheap imitation of the purity of his feelings. In those eyes and that body he saw his world transformed by a force as elemental as fire. When she'd pressed her mouth to his he'd breathed coconut oil and cigarette smoke and felt his hands shake as they ran the length of her back. She had smiled, her face patrician in the dim light as she'd opened the door and led him to her bedroom where, for a time, Charlie hadn't thought in words at all.

*

There was a crash from the kitchen and Charlie pulled his hand from his trousers where he'd been rearranging himself. A lean man with a cloud of brown hair appeared in the doorway, naked beneath an open dressing gown.

'Sorry, man, I smashed a mug.'

'Limpet! What are you . . .? Shit! Do your fucking dressing gown up, man!'

Limpet tied his belt, put a cigarette between his lips and stood, thin arm outstretched until Charlie slapped a lighter onto his palm.

'Thanks, Chaz.'

'Don't mention it.'

Like Charlie, Limpet had graduated from Edinburgh University three years ago. But unlike Charlie, who was slogging away in the menial backrooms of a literary agency, Limpet slept late, worked evenings in the pub down the road, and played his guitar for most of the time in between.

They sat together, smoking. After a while, Limpet rubbed his eyes and looked at Charlie.

'What's with the suit?'

Charlie scratched at the egg stain. 'It's Annie's wedding today. You're coming, right?'

Limpet drew hard on his cigarette. 'You want a lift?' he asked without looking up.

When Limpet had turned up with his mother's Hillman Imp last month, Charlie had wondered how the old car had made it down the M1. It was so rusty around the door frames and the fender, he was surprised that nothing had fallen off. But the car seemed to be indestructible and Limpet, to Charlie's surprise, turned out to be a keen mechanic, tinkering away with the engine when he wasn't playing his guitar. Still, Charlie was certain that the car was an accident just waiting to happen.

'Hm, thanks mate, but I'm going to take the Tube.'

Charlie liked the Tube. He liked to imagine that all of London flowed through its tunnels: past, present and future. He loved the descent into its warmth and the way he could emerge a short time later in another part of the city. It had taken him years to match the spread of the city above ground to Harry Beck's inspired but misleading Tube map and, like any seasoned Londoner he loved his insider's knowledge of the short cuts and the simplest changes. He adored the smell and the pace of that world underground, the warm blast of air when the train was about to arrive and the giddy rush of the carriages as they drew in just inches from your face. Down below the surface, Charlie found clues of the city's past everywhere: at Marylebone, where the old station name 'Great Central' was tiled along the platform wall; at Charing Cross, where torn layers of posters dated back a quarter century to the Festival of Britain. In the constant motion of the Tube trains and commuters Charlie saw a cascade of lives and times: the tight-lipped Edwardian lady, the bowler-hatted Metrolander, the demobbed Tommy, the East End families sheltering on the platforms, the Mods and Rockers picking fights with each other, the punks picking fights with everyone. The Tube, he thought, was the keeper of the city's secret history, written in the footfalls of the people who'd passed through it.

The jangle of the phone made them jump. Shaking his head, Limpet lifted it from its cradle. His eyes widening as he passed it to Charlie.

'Hello?'

There was a hiss and muffled breathing. Then his sister's voice. 'Charlie?'

'Annie – you OK? – what's up?'

'I – it's – I'm—'

Charlie could picture her holding her hand over the receiver, trying to compose herself.

'Annie, it's OK.'

'I'm frightened, Charlie.'

She was scared that their mother would turn up uninvited to the wedding.

'She might get it into her head to get on the Tube and it's only an hour from home –'

(How can she call it home? thought Charlie. It's never been a home to us.) '– and then she might just show up and Ben will be furious. He's already stormed off God knows where and we've only got a few hours and . . .'

Her voice was growing louder and beginning to race, trying to outrun the tears that were creeping up at the end of her words.

'Annie, Annie. Slow down, shhh.'

Her voice became clearer. 'Charlie?'

There was a cadence to her voice that he recognised from their childhood; the unfailing faith she had in him to find the answer, to fix things when they went wrong. And why wouldn't she have faith? Charlie had been the one who'd taken care of her when their mother hadn't or couldn't. It was he who'd balanced on a chair to cook eggs and beans while Annie played on the kitchen floor, knees grey with cigarette ash, nappy heavy with piss. And later, it had been Charlie who had stood between their mother and angry boyfriends, he who'd run things when she'd left them for days on end. When Annie's periods had started, it was Charlie she'd asked for the money to buy her first box of Dr Whites. And now, he could hear in her voice, she needed him again.

'Annie do you want me to come over?'

'Yes,' she said. 'Please, Charlie, will you come?'

Lying on the sofa, his eyes fixed on a smudge on the ceiling, Limpet seemed to have fallen into a trance. Charlie poked him on the arm.

'Mate, don't you think you ought to go back to bed? You look like shit.'

Limpet bolted upright, his eyes locked on his flatmate. 'When's the wedding then?'

'Eleven. I'll see you there, right?'

'Yeah man, see you later.'

'And Limpet?'

'Yeah?'

'Go back to bed, for fuck's sake.'

The front door opened onto a tiny triangle of green. On a bench in the far corner a sparrow was hopping back and forth, but otherwise the street was empty. In the quiet of the early morning, West End Lane was spacious and peaceful, the windows of the red-brick flats above blanked by curtains as Charlie walked towards Kilburn. Annie and Ben lived above the High Road, down an alley beside the fishmongers and up a geriatric zigzag of rusting iron steps. From outside their front door, Charlie could see a clutch of lime trees peeking out from a garden on the street behind, their leaves sticky in the watery sunshine. He banged the door with the flat of his hand and Annie answered wearing a floral housecoat and clogs. To his relief, she was smiling, a wide grin that showed a dimple in her left cheek. Charlie pulled her into a hug and kissed the top of her head.

'Aren't you supposed to be having a crisis or something?'

She pulled away and laughed, a surprisingly low chuckle for someone so slight. 'Look!' she gestured inside to the kitchenette, her sleeve riding up to reveal a livid bruise on her wrist. She tugged at her cuff and Charlie looked away.

'Ben,' he said.

'He came back!' Annie exclaimed with a shrillness that made her brother's jaw tighten.

A great coal-haired sprawl of a man, Ben dwarfed the chair he sat on, limbs splayed out in all directions.

'Hi Chaz,' he said, 'bit early for a social call, isn't it?'

Charlie glanced at the clock – it had just gone 8 – and grimaced. 'Bit early for anything, mate.'

Annie held the kettle up, brow furrowed but her mouth set in a smile, her spare hand fluttering about her face.

'Tea, dear boys?' she asked. 'Got a bit of a busy day ahead of us.'

Annie's father had left before she was born, just as Charlie's father had done. One morning when Charlie was four, their mother had leaned across the dirty breakfast table, scarlet dressing gown gaping open across her leaking breasts, and said to him, 'You're the man round here now.' Eating his Weetabix, he had looked with intrigue at the baggy skin of the mewling creature she was holding and said nothing. From then on, though, he'd known this baby would be his responsibility; that he would need to protect her from the tidal waves of fury and despair and the many drunken boyfriends that passed through their mother's life.

They had moved with their mother from place to place, the oniony smell of dirty linen and glasses ringed with whisky residue the only constant. And yet there had always been good days. Those were the days when their mother blazed with light, turning on her heel on the way to school and pulling them aboard the number 19 bus, climbing with them up the stairs to the seats at the front where they would see their friends below walking in the opposite direction. They knew better than to question her, for fear that they might lose this moment of brightness, her tinkling laugh. They would go to the zoo or to the cinema, where they'd watch as many showings in a row as they could, legs hooked over the plush of the seats in front. The problem was that there were always more bad days than good. The dark days, she had called them once when she'd tried to explain, 'It's as though all the colour's drained out of the world, Charlie,' she'd slurred from where she lay, 'like it's all made out of tracing paper.' He had learned early on that she was lost to them on those tracing-paper days and so, whenever the darkness fell, he'd taken charge, looking after Annie as best as he knew how.

Charlie swigged his tea while Ben drummed his fingers on the side of his chair. Annie leaned back against the work surface, the tendons in her neck flicking, her hands still fluttering. Charlie noticed the stale odour of dirty clothes; the rumpled bed with a greying corner of the mattress exposed; the sink full of dishes smeared with ketchup and hardening grease. Annie clasped her fingers around her wrist as she spoke.

'What happened there, anyway?' Charlie asked, nodding towards her wrist, trying to keep his tone light.

Ben's face darkened. He stood up. 'Right. I need a piss. We've got to start getting ourselves scrubbed up, Chaz, so perhaps you could – y'know—?'

Charlie looked at his sister's fiancé and gave a faint smile, though he felt his hands tighten into fists. 'What's that now, Ben?'

But Annie interrupted and changed the subject before he could answer, her eyes widening at Charlie as she spoke. For a moment he considered what would happen if he just spoke the words out loud. *What are you doing to my sister?* But her eyes were fixed on his and he could see what she was asking him to do, so he drained his cup, said goodbye and pulled the stiff door open. From the bottom of the steps he looked up to see his sister's head peering over the railings, her pale hair streaming loose.

'Don't forget to be there at eleven!' she shouted.

Raising his arm in a wave, Charlie walked out of the alleyway, swallowing the sudden urge to run back up the steps and take Annie away with him.

1.2

It was the morning of their wedding and fat green lime leaves were swaying by the window, a blue October sky behind them. Stella spoke in hurried whispers, though she could have been as loud as she wanted, since there was no one but John there to hear her. But her voice stayed soft as she pressed her hand against the glass and looked out, misting the pane with her words: *This day is the beginning of a whole new life.*

Outside, Kilburn had woken up. Cars and buses jostled along the High Road. Old women pushing baskets and young mothers pushing prams walked as if still asleep, their eyes cast down, unaware of the rumbling traffic or the loose stride of the young man side-stepping past them. And he in turn did not see them; the old and the baby-laden had no place yet in Charlie's world. Guitar music spilled from Woolworth's and he found himself stepping in time until the sound faded into the noise of the busy street. He looked up as he walked, passing under the striped awning of the butcher's, the red and white swirl of a barber's pole, a line of stone composers' heads above the door of the music shop, their features softened with muck and time.

At Maida Vale, between the strange coupling of high-rise flats and grand houses, he moved south. Traffic fumes caught in his throat and moisture gathered in the curve of his back. A bus honked as he ran across the road towards the Tube station, the driver shouting from behind his cab window. In the heat of the Underground, Charlie waited on the platform, staring into the dark mouth of the tunnel. A soot-black mouse darted between the rails, but otherwise he was alone. He studied the poster on the wall behind the track, an advert for the extended line out to the airport. *Fly the Tube!* it said, and Charlie sighed. As if he could even afford the fare to Heathrow these days. Around him the air lifted, billowing a warm rush of soot and stale cigarettes as the rails shivered in anticipation. The train clattered into view and squealed to a stop, its doors yawning open. No one got off. Charlie stepped into the smoking carriage and dropped onto the blue and red seat, pulling out his packet of Chesterfields as the train drew out of the station.

At Oxford Circus he emerged, buffeted by Saturday shoppers, a rip-tide that threatened to pull him along the swarming pavement. Eyes fixed ahead and hands wedged in his pockets, he pushed against the crowds until he reached the right turn into Denmark Street – *musician's paradise,* he thought, remembering the first time he had walked down here with Limpet. His friend, who rarely seemed impressed by anything, had gazed at the guitars in window after window, taking in with greedy eyes the smooth curves of wood and wire. Most of the shops were yet to open, but outside of Trihorn Music a man was smoking, a silk scarf

tied around the puff of his Afro. Charlie recognised him as
Al, the bassist in Limpet's latest band, and they nodded to
one another as he passed. *Alright, man? Yeah, alright.* A few
doors down, a sign in the steamed-up window of a café read:
Bacon Rolls – 10p and feeling in his pocket for change, Charlie
pushed the door and walked into the smell of smoke and
frying fat.

A few miles north, Limpet was waiting on the platform of
West Hampstead station for the train to Brondesbury. It
would be a brief stop at his dealer's – a small bag of weed
for after the wedding – and then he would head into town.
A short way down the track a train was approaching at
high speed, not scheduled to stop. Inside the train, a young
boy was playing with his new rubber ball. Back and forth
against the wall he threw it, catch and release: a gentle
game for a well-behaved boy. But when the ball rebounded
at an angle and flew from the open window, it entered the
air at the speed of the train, colliding with Limpet's
outstretched hand with enough force to break his meta-
carpal. Clipped around the head by his outraged mother,
the young boy clutched his ear and wailed as the train
sped on, his cry unheard by Limpet, who had fainted on
the platform.

In Paddington, Stella sat in the hospital waiting room with
John, watching swollen-bellied women and stern-faced
midwives as they came and went. Eventually, she stood and
spoke to the lady at the desk, who eyed her middle, still
soft and flat. She wasn't being difficult, Stella said in a quiet
voice, but she had to get married that afternoon, so would

her scan be much longer? The older woman laughed, loud and joyous, and led them to a corner office where a dark-haired sonographer was waiting.

Their little swimmer was loop-the-looping, that was what John said, though from where Stella lay the screen was just a fuzz of green blobs. A good baby, the woman said, you've got a good baby there, and Stella was shocked by a sudden understanding that it was actually a person somersaulting inside her. Through a crack in the blind she could see a needle's width of sky, the loose clouds passing, a tiny bird darting by. Then she was wiping jelly from her stomach and tugging her T-shirt and they were walking past the laughing nurse, who wished them luck, and out into the noisy brightness of Praed Street, where people swooped by as she leaned against John's chest, his hand tucked in the back pocket of her jeans.

At the register office, Annie and Ben stood in front of a wooden desk, a crowd of twenty or so family and friends gathered behind them. The brown carpet tiles rasped and Annie's dress strained against the sharp blades of her shoulders as she wrapped her arms about herself. At the swish of the door, she turned to see Charlie, waving as he slid into a seat just as the registrar began to speak. He'd never understood what she saw in Ben. From the first time Annie had introduced them, he'd known he'd never like the man. Hadn't trusted him then and didn't trust him now. After the vows were said, Ben's hand pressed down on Annie's shoulder as they kissed and Charlie felt again the urge to pull his sister away from that man's grasp. With a shout of 'She's mine!' Ben flung Annie over his shoulder and ran along the aisle between the plastic chairs. As he watched, Charlie felt the growing chatter of the guests recede and in the ringing distance of his mind he heard the words as clearly as if he'd spoken them himself: *it's too late to change things now.*

Afterwards, they stood for photos on the steps, as the Saturday traffic roared down the Euston Road. There wouldn't be any symmetry in those pictures, thought Charlie as he stood alone beside his sister, wishing that Beth could have come back this weekend. Ben's family gathered on the other side. They were big and loud and, judging by the reek of alcohol coming from the two cousins standing closest, more than a little drunk already.

The pub on Marylebone High Street was still quiet as the rowdy party piled in, but soon the cousins were bellowing rugby songs and the room screeched with laughter and chat. It was fun for a while, to be carried on all that noise, and Charlie drank three pints before he started to wonder why Limpet still wasn't there. He apologised his way between a group of older women who were deep in outraged conversation – *Did you hear about the undertaker's strike? Poor Bessie's still waiting for her Albie to be buried. Can you imagine?* – moving towards the payphone by the bar. He dialled, ready with his two-pence piece for when the pips went, but no one picked up. He pushed the coin back in his pocket, noticing how hot the pub had become. It was time he left. Behind him, someone thrust another pint into Ben's hand, who roared with approval, peppering Charlie with spittle-spots as he passed. Wiping his face with his sleeve, Charlie kissed Annie on the cheek and squeezed her wrist. Seeing her grimace, he remembered the purple spread of bruise across her skin underneath, but she waved away his worried look.

'It's nothing, Charlie, honestly.'

Surprised by the daylight, he was blinking back the sunshine when Annie burst out of the pub and caught him by his arm, laughing. 'But *where* are you going, Charlie?'

'Going to find Limpet – he was supposed to be here, but he didn't show. I'm going up to Biddy's to see if he made it to work.'

'Ah, Limpet, my long-lost love. He's a fine man, that one.'

'Annie, are you maybe a little bit drunk?'

She grinned and wound her arm through his, resting her cheek on his shoulder. He turned his head to kiss her hair and then gave her a gentle shove.

'Go on now, off you go.'

She giggled, swaying slightly as she walked back through the door, the beery breeze from the pub buffeting her dress, its filmy whiteness clinging to her like a shroud.

1.3

Hand in hand, Stella and John walked south from the hospital to Bayswater Road, crossing over into the park. By a tall plane tree they turned deeper into the green, to a place where the grass was high and only the tips of the tallest buildings were visible. John set down his heavy bag and spread a blanket on the ground. Tugged by a sudden wave of tiredness, Stella lowered herself next to him. She slid a silky scarlet bundle from John's bag and smoothed it over her knee. It was only a cheap thing, but it pleased her, that red dress. Her wedding dress. She smiled at John, then slipped out of her T-shirt and jeans and pulled the dress over her head.

Now that he was out in the daylight, Charlie realised how drunk he'd become. I'll walk it off, he thought to himself, heading south towards Hyde Park through the tall back-streets of Marylebone townhouses. He ran his hands along the black railings, silting his fingers with city grime, like he had as a kid on his way to school. School had been a sanctuary for Charlie: the one place where he had no respon-sibility for anyone else. He had run there every morning, feeling himself grow lighter as his fingertips had passed along the railings, arriving out of breath with an empty belly, a hungry mind and filthy hands. *Dirty London air*, he said out loud at the memory, smiling to think how free he felt surrounded by the noise and dirt; the kind of freedom you only feel in a place where you know you belong. He was a child of North London: Archway and Finsbury Park and a few places in between, but as an adult he felt as if the whole of the city was his. He tipped his head back and looked at the sky. When the sun shone like this, there was nowhere more full of possibility than London, he thought, rising for a moment on a wave of hope. Perhaps everything really would be alright.

By the time he reached Speakers' Corner, the high from the beer had dissolved and he found himself heavy with fatigue. He weaved his way through the crowd gathered around a man on an upturned box who was shouting about class war and revolution, walking on into the park until he came to a huddle of trees, where the long grass brushed his legs. He lay down, listening to the swill of distant traffic, the hum of planes and the occasional shriek of a bird. He closed his eyes and for a short time he slept.

All across the skyline the swaying leaves shimmered, unsheltered by clouds, unnerved by the sudden, unexpected heat. Stella squinted into the brightness. October wasn't supposed to be hot like this, and yet somehow in the early part of the month, it always was. The amber warmth of a low-slung autumn sun enveloped her as she touched the softness of her belly. *So this is what it means to be entangled.* She thought of the theory John had explained many times before: a collision of particles, an existence transformed so that even far apart they respond to one another. It was barely three months since that evening when they'd sat somewhere not far from here, cap and gown tossed to one side, kisses pungent with cheap red wine. Perhaps it had been the wine, or the heat, or simply the sweet musk of one another. How they had unleashed a need more urgent than their usual caution neither of them could say. But from that collision, their path was set.

Charlie woke with a jolt from a dream-state of falling. Glinting in the grass was a pile of change from his pocket, and tangled among it the chain of a silver St Christopher medal. Annie had given it to him when he left for university – a talisman, she'd said, though it was her, truly, who'd needed protection. And right enough she'd come to stay with him in Edinburgh the first moment she could, climbing onto the train at Kings Cross the morning after she'd finished her last O level. Charlie sat up and rubbed his face, trying to forget about the bruise on Annie's wrist.

John knotted a tie around his neck and lay down next to Stella, watching the flimsy city clouds scudding in the high blue, pressing his palm to hers.

'She's going to look like you, I'll bet.'

'She?'

He laughed again and shrugged. 'Fifty-fifty chance.'

Stella leaned up on her elbow, studying his face as he stared at the sky. Then, with a jerk, John checked his watch and leapt to his feet, all at once in a hurry. Stella clambered after him, but she couldn't keep up. The fabric of her dress

bunched between her legs as she ran and her heart was
pounding as it tried, with difficulty, to meet the competing
demands of her own body and the tiny but hungry one
growing within. Panting for breath, she stopped and pressed
her hand to her belly. John turned and called out. *Stella!* He
ran back towards her, not noticing the dark-haired man
lying on the grass a little way off.

Charlie raised his head to see two people running. A tall,
angular man dashing ahead of a flush-cheeked girl in a red
dress. She stopped a little way past Charlie, her palm pressed
to her middle, but the tall man didn't notice. The young
woman looked quite out of breath and Charlie wondered if
he should help, but as he began to move, the man turned
and called her name and started to run back. Charlie watched
them as they leaned in close, the girl's face softening as the
tall man took her hand. They walked away together and he
gazed after them, feeling a stark aloneness and an ache for
Beth that lodged in his chest.

At Marble Arch, John helped Stella onto the back platform
of a bus as it was pulling away. As they rumbled along the
Edgware Road, with its hookah pipes and coffee shops,
Stella looked out at the jostling crowds of Saturday shoppers, while John glanced at his watch and jiggled his long
legs. Sitting in a drift of old confetti between the columns
of the register office was Liam McKearnan, John's research
partner and best friend, and Niamh, his heavily pregnant
wife.

Niamh hauled herself to her feet and held out a posy of
purple flowers. 'You ready?' she said.

Stella swapped her sandals for a pair of electric blue high heels and grinned. 'Now, I'm ready.'

John held out his hand the wrong way up, so Stella had to turn it over to put on the ring they had bought in Hatton Garden. His skin felt warm and the smooth rounds of his fingernails slid against the flat of her palm as she pressed the gold band into its place on the left. Then Niamh and Liam clapped and Stella and John kissed – and the heels on her blue shoes clacked as they trotted down the stairs and out into the golden blast of October sunshine and traffic noise, clutching the papers of the life that lay before them.

Later, as they walked home beneath the dirty sky of the street-lit inner city, John looked at Stella, his face softened with drink and smiled. 'Mrs Greenwood,' he said, 'I love you.'

Stella pressed her lips against his cheek. 'I love you too.'

John frowned. 'For better or worse?'

Stella nodded. 'Yup. In sickness and in health. All that stuff.'

They both laughed, unable then to imagine their life together as being anything less than golden and fearless.

1.4

Notting Hill Gate was an upended bag of people and buses, cars and bikes, beggars and hustlers. Outside the Tube station Charlie sidestepped a pale and ragged-looking man peddling discarded day tickets. There was another man further down with greasy hair, a jerry can and a story about his broken-down car and a stolen wallet. How Charlie wanted it to be true – to give the man the money and send him home to a wife and his dinner. But that was the romantic in him, always wanting a happy ending. He knew that the only place that man would be going to was a room somewhere with a mattress on the floor, an old belt, a dirty needle. He walked on as the concrete shop fronts became the grand white façades and tall trees of Holland Park Avenue.

A group of teenagers with egg-white hardened hair pushed past him, 'Out the way, hippy!' A skinny boy with a studded collar and army boots sneered and hawked onto the pavement. Charlie sighed and stepped over the globule of phlegm, waiting by the marbled front of an undertakers for the group to move on. Without meaning to, he found himself reading a discreet notice in the window, written in a tight and tidy hand. *It is with regret that due to industrial action we are unable to assist with funerals at this time.* Bloody hell, even the undertakers are striking, Charlie thought. Something must be really wrong with our country if we can't even bury the dead. He watched the punks recede and wondered when this bleakness had set in. In the months since Beth had been in France, he'd seen it worsen, a desperation that was beginning to boil over. Battles were brewing across London, as recession and frustration turned to despair and hate. Skinheads with swastika tattoos, stop-and-search, racial tensions reaching breaking point. *But Charlie,* Beth had written in her last letter, *how could we have forgotten so soon where hate like this can take us?*

Across the street from a green-tiled pub, Charlie heard the sound of fiddle music, a scratched tune that ran like a river, pulsing with his blood and beating with his heart as he waited at the bus stop. In the darkening sky above, he could see the pinpricks of two faint stars and an outline of the brightening moon. The pub opposite glowed warm and he felt a sudden urge to go in, to hear the music, to have another drink – but he needed to go. Limpet should be at work in the pub by now and he wanted to find him. The sound of the violin blew in gusts and he stood quite still and listened until his bus arrived.

Fifteen minutes later, he stepped off the backboard of the bus and onto Kilburn High Road. The street was in its evening half-life; shops shutting up as the pubs began to blink and rouse themselves. Saturday's detritus was littered across the pavement: stray pages of newspaper, fallen fruit from the greengrocer's, dog-ends and dog shit. Pinching his cigarette tight in his fingers, Charlie headed towards

West End Lane and Biddy Murphy's. It had gone 6 o'clock
– Limpet must be there by now.

As Charlie walked into the pub, Jimmy Kneafsey, the
concrete-necked landlord, looked up from his second pint
of the night and nodded slowly in a half greeting. He wasn't
sure about Limpet's friends, they were all so nervy-looking
– skinny fellas with their hair all over their faces – but cocky
too. Strutting about like they were in charge. Here was one
just now, striding in, when that Limpet hadn't even showed
up for work.

'Hello, Mr Kneafsey.'

The old man's steady, smoke-screened stare made Charlie
nervous.

'Are you here with news of y'man Limpet, then?'

'Is he not here?'

'He is not.'

'Christ, he's vanished. I'll go back to the flat, see if he's
there.'

'Right then. On you go.'

Jimmy raised his hand as Charlie walked out of the old
pub, his head bent low.

When Charlie reached the flat, the phone was ringing. He
scrambled to open the door and rushed over to snatch it
up, knocking over a pile of post and a dusty spider plant.

'Shit! Sorry – Hello?'

'Charlie . . . man . . . is that you?'

'Limpet? Of course it's me! Who the fuck else would be
in our flat? Where are you?'

There was a loud noise at the other end of the line as
Limpet dropped the phone.

'Limpet? Are you there? How come you didn't make the wedding? And why are you not at work? Old man Kneafsey didn't look too impressed that you weren't there. What's going on?'

'Oh, man. It's a long story.'

Another pause. Then pips and a rattle of money being inserted in the background.

'Limpet?'

'Yeah?'

'Where are you?'

'The Royal Free.'

'The hospital?'

'Yeah.'

'You're in the fucking hospital?'

'Yeah, Charlie, that's what I was calling to tell you.'

'Well, why didn't you say? Fuck! Are you OK? What happened?'

'Um . . .well, I'm not entirely sure . . . A boxer's fracture, they said. Something from a train – a missile they said, of some sort. Something thrown. Turns out once it leaves the train it carries on at the same speed – like, a hundred miles an hour or something and then – wham! Hits my hand – hurts like buggery and then – well, that's – uh, I pulled a whitey I'm afraid. No idea what happened next – flat on my face on West Hampstead station. Blam. Total wipeout.'

'Shit, Limpet, I'm sorry. Do you want me to come and get you?'

'That'd be good, yeah, thanks. Bring my car?'

'That thing? Fuck, no. I'll take a cab.'

*

Charlie realised too late that he was still wearing his suit as he bundled Limpet and his damaged hand into the back of the black cab, which hurtled down the big hill and into the Saturday night bluster of the Kilburn High Road. Pushing the heavy door into the warm fug of Jimmy Kneafsey's pub, the two young men began to laugh.

Looking up from the bar, Jimmy himself gave them a rare flash of his yellowed teeth. 'Well, I see you'll not be behind the bar tonight then, lad,' he said, looking at the plaster cast on Limpet's hand, which was already greying from ash and dirt.

Charlie leaned across the bar. 'I can help you out, Mr Kneafsey – if you like, I mean?'

Jimmy looked at Charlie and said nothing. Charlie dropped his eyes from the old man's gaze.

'Aye, good man. Round you come then.'

The landlord set two pints on the bar. 'On the house, boys. Don't be getting used to it, though, you hear?'

Charlie liked being behind the bar, its dark wood hiding the chaos beneath: a tangle of old cash bags, broken glasses and half-smoked packets of cigarettes. The night grew brighter and noisier as the pub filled up. Limpet leaned on the bar, talking to people as they came and went, chain-smoking with his good hand.

At half-past ten Limpet punched Charlie on the arm and pointed to the door.

'Ouch! What d'you do that for?'

'It's Annie!'

Through the miasma of tobacco smoke he saw his sister. Her white dress was torn and smeared with something dark, but she smiled and waved as Limpet pushed his way through the pub to meet her, pulling her to him with his cast-free arm and kissing her on the cheek. Limpet and Annie had known each other ever since she'd stayed with them in Edinburgh, the summer after her O levels. Charlie refused to think about whether anything had ever happened between them, and neither Annie nor Limpet had ever told him about the night they'd spent together – just the once, after an evening spent drinking in the festival frenzy of Edinburgh in August. Nothing had come of it, Annie had been due to leave the following day and, besides, Limpet didn't like to let things get heavy. Still, there had always been a gleam of unfinished business whenever their paths crossed. They struggled back towards the bar, arms linked, their bodies pressed together in the crush.

Unlaced by alcohol and noise, Annie and Limpet shouted a conversation at each other by the bar, laughing at Charlie as he confused his drinks orders. He caught snatches of their stories as he poured and served and mopped around them.

'He'd had ten pints and could hardly stand up, silly sod . . . I just left him there to make his own way back . . . no telling when . . . what happened to your hand?'

'Boxer's fracture . . . seriously, man . . . out of nowhere . . . won't be able to play for ages.'

Their heads were almost touching when Charlie slammed two drinks between them, slopping a thick puddle on the bar.

'Hey Charlie,' Annie spoke from far behind her glazed blue eyes. 'Are you OK?'

Charlie cleared his throat, which had grown dry. 'Sorry it took me so long – first time behind a bar, you know?'

'You're doing great, man,' said Limpet, furrowing his forehead.

'Uh, thanks – yeah – sorry about the mess.'

He noticed Annie shift a fraction further from Limpet.

'Charlie!' shouted Jimmy Kneafsey from the other side of the bar. 'Go and fetch another barrel, will ya?'

Charlie raised his thumb and nodded back, touching Annie's outstretched hand with its new gold ring gleaming as he walked towards the cellar steps.

The phone out the back was ringing, so Charlie lifted it as he walked past, but when he put it to his ear the line went dead. Charlie stood for a moment, staring at the greasy receiver, then slammed it back on the cradle so hard that the bells jingled. In the cellar he found the barrel and began to drag it up the steps. This is bloody hard work, he thought, as his arms took the strain; I'm not really cut out for this, a skinny boy like—

The thought was cut short by a beam thrown from the ceiling in the explosion. It sent him tumbling back to the bottom of the cellar steps, where he lay unconscious for the next forty-five minutes. Then a heaviness as he felt himself slowly moving. Darkness and thick smoke, a murky subterranean fog illuminated blue-black, blue-black. His ears rang with a high-pitched whine as he was carried through the charred shell of the bar between the shoulders of his nameless rescuers. A blankness stretched along the line of the blast from a smouldering corner, chairs and tables all pointing the same way, thrown from the charred and empty centre where the bomb had been planted. He tasted blood and dust and smoke as his eyes skimmed the shining viscous patches on the floor. And then he saw the hand, small and white against the blackened bar. The gleam of a gold wedding band. The whine in his ears became a roar and the room spun, a hideous zoetrope of carnage. Charlie turned his face to one side and vomited.

They laid him on a stretch of pavement, a rolled-up coat beneath his head, and a crowd of people gathered around. Between their legs he caught glimpses of the High Road: a police cordon, blue lights flashing, the delicate twinkle of shattered glass, the dimly horrified faces of onlookers. A tall man and a girl in a red dress.

1.5

The noise came from far up the high street, a deep thud that threw sound waves so powerful that they shifted a tide of air with them. Stella and John kept walking. Soon, there were sirens and pulsing blue lights, a glitter of broken glass flung out across the road and the burnt-out sockets of windows gaping. A small crowd had gathered, wordless, by the police tape and they stood to the side of a ruddy-faced man, grey hair greased back, who half-turned and gave the slightest nod before his eyes returned to the smoking carcass of the pub. Stella looked from the chaos to the faces of the people watching. On the other side of the cordon, a woman in dust-caked clothes was holding a lighter to a cigarette with shaking hands and Stella felt a sudden need to help. She stooped to duck beneath the tape but a heavy hand held her away.

'Get back!'

The voice grew louder, 'You all need to get back, go home and get indoors. Now!'

In a tangle of indignation and fear, Stella scowled at the policeman who looked hard back.

'Leave now, miss – it's not safe.'

She drew herself up and bit the inside of her cheek to stop the tears that threatened to spill, speaking to John with her sharpest English accent. 'John, we should go.'

He looked back at her, his face empty. For a second it was as though he didn't know who she was.

Stella caught him by the wrist, her indignation dissolved. 'John?'

He rubbed his eyes, swaying slightly. 'Sorry, Stel, bit woozy. Yes, yes – let's get back.'

Beyond the police tape, two firemen emerged from the black of the pub, a young man draped between them with blood on his face and vomit on his shirt, one leg dragging behind him. A few metres from the building they lowered him to the ground and put a rolled-up coat under his head. Stella's red dress billowed in a gust of wind and she bent to smooth it. As she looked up, she met the gaze of the injured man. His dark hair was matted and his left eye was swollen, but his stare was so intense that for one uncanny moment she could have sworn he seemed to know her.

2.

DUALITY

12 October–18 November 1977

Different models may give equivalent – or 'dual' – pictures of the same phenomenon. It is, in essence, an acknowledgment that each model is incomplete – just one vantage point of many – and that we must rely on multiple, seemingly contradictory models in order to construct the truest picture of reality.

McKearnan, L. *Quantum Entanglement.*
Paradox Publishing, 1982 (p. 25)

2.1

Falling in and out of consciousness, Charlie's body became his whole world: the sharp stabs of horror, the dull drone of shock. When he woke, his mother was at the foot of the bed, smelling of alcohol and a cloying perfume. He opened his mouth to speak and saliva stretched between his cracked lips like gum.

'Where's Annie?'

His mother sobbed and leaned over him. Up close, her face was covered in a fine layer of grease and caked with powder. Lipstick had bled into the creases around her mouth and her eyes were red and clogged with clumps of mascara. She touched his cheek and stared, her eyes empty.

'It's your fault she was there.'

Charlie felt a rush of horror, saw the white hand in the darkened bar as a wave of nausea passed over him. He strained to pull himself up, looking for Annie. And then he remembered. He turned away and pressed his face into the clean chemical smell of his hospital pillow. Even as his mother's voice grew shrill, Charlie did not look up. Eventually a fierce-looking nurse took his mother's arm and led her away, telling her to come back tomorrow when she'd had some rest.

Several days later, he stood in the basement of the hospital, a small bag of possessions at his feet. His legs felt weak as his mother leaned against him, pungent with brandy even at this early hour of the morning. A squat, red-nosed police-woman walked briskly up and introduced herself. Charlie noticed that her lisp sent an erratic arc of spittle as she spoke.

'Straight on, sir, madam. Second on the right.'

They walked along the corridor beneath the Artex tiles and fluorescent tubes. A pair of aproned nurses clipped past them, busy with their shift, their patients. *Their lives won't change a bit because a girl they've never met is dead,* Charlie thought, *today is just another day for them.* They were greeted by a woman who introduced herself as a family liaison officer. She laid her hand on Charlie's elbow as she opened the door.

'She's through here.'

Annie's coffin lay in the centre of the small grey room, a vase of white flowers on a stand beside it. His mother gripped his hand and Charlie felt a surge of cold fear. It seemed as if the room was vanishing, its walls fading into darkness, leaving only that box in the centre and whatever was left of his sister. Sweat prickled across his face and his bowels felt suddenly weak.

Retaliation, that's what the police had called it. The word rang brassy in his head as Charlie stood above Annie's flawless cheeks and pale hair, aware of an incongruous urge to defecate. He gripped the side of the coffin as he tried to piece together the story of how they had ended up here; how he'd come to lose the only person whom he'd loved without question or conditions and whose love for him he'd never doubted. Beside him, his mother's knees gave way and he held her, noticing how small she was: just bones and cloth and the sweet smell of alcohol. He led her to a plastic chair and sat with his arm around her as she shuddered hopeless sobs into his chest.

The twisted shell of the pub had been splashed across the papers, which he'd studied with a grim resolve. Now it reeled across his mind, an endless flow of thoughts he could not quiet, an unstoppable spool of images. He stroked his mother's hair and felt her soften into him, infant-like, as he hummed the half-remembered lullabies she'd sung him as a child. Years later, when he knew much more of daughters and of loss, he would be glad that he had offered her that small moment of kindness.

When he got home, he hung his suit on the back of the bedroom door. In the living room, he picked up the phone and dialled the long string of digits beginning 0033. Beth's voice, when she answered, was bright.

'Charlie! How are you?'

He realised he didn't even know where to begin.

She arrived at his flat the next evening with a bag of dirty clothes and a bottle of Talisker. Charlie pulled her to him, overtaken by a need so urgent that he lifted her skirt and pushed her knickers to one side while they were still in the hallway.

Afterwards, as they lay on the sofa drinking whisky, Beth

took his hand and traced a pattern on his palm, remembering her parents' disapproval the first time she had brought him home. 'No family, no roots,' her mother had said. 'How will he even know how to take care of you?' But Beth had known that her mother was wrong. A passion that burned as bright as this would take care of itself.

As a child, she'd always thought she would become a nurse, right up to A level Biology, when she'd realised that she couldn't stand the sight of blood. The desire to make things right for people, though, had never left her. Not during her degree *(Anthropology?* her father had winced, *What's the good of that?)*, nor during the year she spent working in Camden to save for her time learning French in Montpellier. It was the reason she'd decided to train as a teacher the following year; it was why she wanted to be with Charlie. Charlie needed her more than anyone had ever needed her before.

Being necessary made her powerful. More than that: it made her feel alive.

'Beth?'

Charlie's voice was quiet as he clasped her hand.

'Yes?'

'Do you think it's my fault?'

Beth looked at the fading bruises on his face and the clenched line of his jaw. He was only twenty-five, but he'd been an adult for so long: the person who was always responsible, the one who made things right. And now, faced with a cruel loss and a world he couldn't control, he was trying to seek out some sense, some version in which he could have prevented the bomb that killed his sister and his friend. Beth looked at him, the golden centre of her eyes gleaming in the lamplight and shook her head. 'Charlie, it's not your fault.'

He leaned against the softness of her breasts, her hair falling onto his face and pressed his mouth to hers. Nothing made sense except this.

2.2

15 October 1977

A blue bulb of vein stood out in John's father's neck, his hands thrust firmly in the pockets of his trousers as John's mother cried and stared at the tiny swell of Stella's belly. Picking at the skin around her fingers, a slight tremor in her hands, she didn't look at her son as she spoke.

'But, John . . . what about your research? The post-doc position?'

Stella felt a wave of hot hatred for this weak woman, with her tailored clothes and her pearls and her nervous birdlike hands. *Do you not understand,* Stella wanted to scream, *that this is the 1970s and my studies are important too?* She gripped John's hand, feeling her cheeks burn as they sat down to a roast dinner in the front room. John's mother talked without pause as she handed around the vegetables, while his father sat in silence, grimly slicing chicken.

Stella had never believed in love at first sight. Deep down she knew it for what it really was: a rush of blood to the genitals. But when she'd spilled John's drink in that wood-panelled pub, even in her deepest embarrassment she'd felt something happen to her; it was as if a hidden door had opened. Thoughts came rushing in unbidden; thoughts that to her horror corresponded in no way to the passionate feminist politics she had argued over pints of cheap lager. Like a dark and dirty secret, Stella had become entranced by whisperings of tablecloths and fresh flowers, roast dinners on a Sunday, a warm body in her bed.

They had met again, by chance, in the library. His lopsided smile revealed wonky teeth, his hands were not quite sure of where to put themselves.

'It *is* you!'

Stella had been relieved when she saw that he was pleased to see her. 'Good job there are no liquids nearby,' she'd said, trying to disguise the symphony swelling inside. They'd ended up at the same pub as before and John grinned with delight as she'd paid for two pints before he'd opened his wallet. It was still light when they left and they headed north across the park, walking hand in hand towards the small wooded part in the middle, where they'd sat down and kissed, tipsy in the long grass. He had walked her home later, said he hoped to see her soon.

A few days later she had seen him in the student union. There was a party the following weekend, he'd said. Some friends – here he had gestured around the group of young post-docs with whom he sat – a get-together in his flat, with guitars and a few drinks. 'You could bring your fiddle,' he'd said, pointing at the violin she was carrying. Looking around the gangly, T-shirted group (scientists, all of them, she'd thought with a certain distain), Stella had found herself surprised that John was a musician as well as a theoretical physicist. He spent his days translating the mysteries of the world into the tidy language of mathematics; how then, she wondered, did he suspend this orderly thought and feel his way within the music? For her, music was of the body; it was the world explained as feeling, sound and sense. She'd tried to imagine what that abandonment was like for him. *Sounds fun*, she'd said, feigning nonchalance, and John had watched her walk away, perplexed by the disorder of his thoughts whenever she was near.

The following Saturday, Stella had walked through an early evening Kilburn still thick with people. When she reached John's flat, someone had buzzed her in and she'd climbed the stairs right to the top of the old Victorian house. Through the half-open door, the music came, invisible waves that smoothed the faint chaos of the city-sound outside. She walked into a room full of people and saw John and his guitar in a circle of girls and Stella felt her breath catch short. She was suddenly conscious of her homemade skirt and how the strap of her battered violin case was making her chest lopsided. From the way those girls were leaning towards him, their hair falling loose around their faces, the flushed fullness of their breasts held before them like weapon- onry, it was clear that they knew about sex in a way that she did not. Nauseous with the need to leave, she had thought that she would walk away, but something fixed her to the spot. Guitar sounds rang around her as she lifted the violin from its case, breathing in its scent of wood and resin and tucking it tight beneath her angled chin.

Across the landscape of her brain, small cities came alight. A trail of neuron fire was taking hold, its electric pulses compelling her hands to move, touch, change, strike. All around her as she played, the air leapt up and danced. Invisible waves moved within mathematical space, their liquid peaks melting into one another like ghosts, the confluence of violin-song and guitar jostling and weaving into harmony. And in all this, as unseen as sound itself, something else collided, rising between them with a force both ancient and new-born: the purest of forms, the most primitive of impulses.

From then on they had spent most of their free time together. After a day spent working in the library, Stella would meet John at the physics lab and they would walk together through the park. As the autumn days had shortened, their walks changed course, skirting the edge of that wide, dark space. Along the dim-lit bridleway they shared stories of their research: Stella talking fast and tripping over her words to tell him of the literary works she'd discovered in the London Library; women writers who'd been all but lost to history. She was going to put them on the map, make people hear them, she'd said one night, clasping John's hand tight in her excitement. More steadily, with deep pauses as he sought the right words to use, John had spoken about his work. Quantum entanglement was not something that slipped easily from mathematics into general conversation. But in those early days when every thought was fascinating, Stella had wanted desperately to understand just what it was that filled John's mind when she was not with him. And he, in turn, had felt the tug of two loves and the scalding urge to swallow them both whole.

How did two particles become entangled, and why did they behave in the way they did? What was this spooky action at a distance; and how could it be explained? He'd told her about Einstein, Podolsky, Rosen and Schrödinger – of the bafflement of the first three of those eminent men at what came to be known as the EPR paradox. Quantum entanglement must be an impossible phenomenon, they'd claimed. Because by affecting immediate change in each other, no matter the distance that separated them, the entangled particles broke one of the fundamental rules of relativity: that nothing travels faster than the speed of light. But, he explained as Stella linked her arm through his, over and again experiments had shown that this is how it works. That despite not knowing why, these entangled particles do exist in a state and as part of a system that appears to break the laws of physics. And despite her miserable grade 5 at O level, Stella had understood the fascination of what he was doing: how he was finding the gaps in established knowledge and shaping a new language for what was missing.

John was known to be brilliant, but among his peers he had always been considered a little off-the-wall, particularly when he spoke about this latest project. His controversial hypothesis was the subject of furious debate around the department, but absorbed in love and the mysteries of entanglement, much of this controversy had passed John by. For the rest of that year his research had proved particularly fruitful. Ideas had zipped like potassium across water, flaring for a minute with a brilliant light, then dying back into the dark. And though some evenings he would leave the university buildings desolate and empty of ideas – *How could he explain? They were speaking the wrong language* – each morning, as he'd watched the city moving and pulsing about itself on his way down the Edgware Road, the spark would glow again. There was something in this; he knew there was.

Almost a year from the day that he had sat dry-mouthed

in the Dean's office for his doctoral viva, he had – at his parents' insistence – attended a graduation ceremony. After lunch, Stella had joined them for drinks, laughing at John still in his robes. The conversation flowed amicably with the wine that afternoon and after they'd bade his parents goodbye, John had suggested another drink. The bar was packed with other red-robed PhDs and a few familiar faces had waved and shouted greetings across the smoky room. As the noise and heat began to rise, Stella had slipped her arm beneath his gown and whispered in his ear and soon they were walking into the park, their half-drunk bottle of wine corked with a tissue in her handbag. They'd found a secluded spot and sat down, swigging from the bottle, the rough wine sharp against their throats. The evening light had given the park a golden tone and Stella felt a sudden shot of clarity, as if this moment was destined to become a memory. John had rolled up his trousers and tossed his cap on the grass beside him, looking back at her with the lowering sun in his face.

'Stella?'

She'd moved to sit beside him, kicking off her sandals. Her white feet had burrowed into the rich green of the long grass, a faint tracery of blue veins across them.

'Stella, I really do love you, you know.'

She'd turned then and looked at this man, the angular slant of his shoulders brushed by his light brown hair, the wide hands that were clasped at either side of her waist. His face was tense, as if struggling with a devilish maths problem and she'd smiled at how much that must have cost him to say.

Pushing him gently to the ground, she'd leaned across him. 'I love you too, John.'

Ten days later, they had stood at Paddington Station waiting for Stella's train to Bristol. John pressed his face into her gold-streaked hair in a last embrace.

'It's only for two weeks,' she'd whispered, trying to ignore the tug within her throat.

They'd kissed and then she'd run, waving as she climbed aboard the train, thinking only of home and her parents and the rolling green landscape that would soon unspool to take her there.

Her father had been waiting at Bristol Temple Meads, car keys jangling in his hand. She'd slipped her arm through his and they had walked together out of the grand old station and into the cloudy warmth of that late July evening. At home, her mother had held her tight and kissed her cheeks.

'My baby's home!' she'd laughed, appraising the young woman before her, with her stack of books and washing. Later, in the kitchen, they had sat down to eat together and talked about her brother and his year in France, her research and the writers she'd uncovered in the archives, the house repairs – an endless litany of things to do.

'Victorian houses,' sighed her father as his after-dinner cigarette glowed bright.

The week had drifted past. Stella ate and slept and read. She walked with her mother to the shops and helped in the garden, sweating in the muggy heat of the overcast summer.

Around her everything had seemed quite as it should be. And yet. There was, she noticed, a shift she couldn't quite describe: an unlatching, or perhaps an ebbing away. She would find herself suddenly tired, a lethargy that made her trail off in conversation, an absence that overtook her. But then, she thought, those weeks before the holidays had been frenetic, carved in sharp relief by adrenalin, hunger and a biting sense of time running out as she'd scrambled to finish her literature review. She'd been rushing for weeks now; it was no wonder that her period was late. She'd stared again at the whiteness of her underwear as she'd wiped herself and dropped the tissue in the toilet, wondering when her cycle would be back to normal.

She'd slammed into the thought as if it were a wall.

For a moment she'd been frozen, her head a rattling void. Then she'd run down the stairs and out of the heavy front door towards the doctor's surgery. Her hands had shaken as she made the appointment with a stern-faced receptionist, who'd eyed her naked fingers with small ungenerous eyes.

Days later, when her parents were out, she'd held the paper slip while sitting on the landing floor, staring at the red stamped letters – POSITIVE – in their neat white window. Eventually, soundlessly, she'd walked into the bathroom and flung the paper into the toilet. Leaning over the washbasin, she splashed her face with water. Straightening up, she stared at her reflection. In the mirror she saw the same face, startlingly unchanged from yesterday. Stella felt the wet skin on her bare neck tighten into goosebumps and heard her breath crashing in her chest. How could they have let this happen? *Stupid stupid stupid.* But as her breathing had slowed, in amongst the panic and the fear she'd sensed

a glimmer of something else, a gentle rise inside herself,
like the faintest strain of song. She'd phoned the lab and
told John she was coming back, then called her mum at
work. It had been impossible to ignore the note of disappointment in her mother's voice, but she'd promised she'd
be home again soon. She'd scribbled a note for her father,
pushed her clothes in a bag and called for a taxi to take her
to the station. The whistle had gone as she'd been running
down the platform, and she'd had to tug at the door as the
train started to move, jumping onto the step and slamming
it shut behind her. The late-afternoon landscape unfurled
as the train had picked up speed, and Stella had watched it
with her head pressed to the cool glass, feeling her plans
for the future slipping further away with every mile that
passed.

An hour and a half later she'd descended cautiously from
the train with the early evening sunlight behind her, her
bag heavy on her shoulder. John had emerged at last through
the rush of commuters, his face creased in thought, and
she'd felt a rising flare of love for this earnest, angular man.
He'd picked her up in the middle of the concourse and spun
her in his arms.

'Let's go for dinner, shall we?'

Stella had nodded, putting off the revelation. Instead of
going north to Kilburn, they'd headed south and emerged
at Piccadilly into its circus of vulgar lights, passing home-
bound office workers streaming down the steps into the
station, tourists struggling with their maps and finely
dressed theatre-goers gliding through the crowds to
Shaftesbury Avenue and Haymarket.

John had led the way across the busy road, past the liveried doormen of the Piccadilly Hotel and up a narrow side street where he stopped outside a grubby-looking café.

'It doesn't look like much,' he'd said, 'but we might just see someone famous. It's where all the actors eat between their shows.'

Stella had nodded and tried to smile as they'd sat down at a sticky-topped table and ordered pie and chips. Leaning across the table, John had held her hands between his as he told her about his research and all its latest findings. So much had happened, he'd told her, speaking so fast that Stella had struggled to follow. Eventually he'd paused as the waiter had clattered their steaming plates of food in front of them and Stella had taken her hands from his.

'John.'

There had been a note to her voice that he'd not heard before.

'Stel? Are you OK? I'm sorry – there's so much happening, am I going on too much?'

He'd lifted his eyes to hers, but she did not return his lopsided smile as she raked her hair from her face with both hands.

'I need to tell you – that is, God, I don't know how to say – it's just – I'm pregnant, John.'

He'd stared at her, his face blank, his eyes distant. 'Oh . . .'

In two words, the world as he knew it had been transformed. The future, which until that moment had existed for him only as a concept, became something material, a bulb of cells multiplying within Stella's soft pink flesh. He looked down at the untouched pie and chips and remembered that first sharp moment when he'd seen her, flushed and stuttering because she'd spilt his drink. He'd known, of course, the biology of his need: the pheromones and oxytocin, the elemental programming that sustained the human race. And yet, somehow, he'd understood in that first rush of desire the same truth that he saw now with this baby; that – expedient as they were – these basic functions of human life were each a kind of a miracle.

'John? Aren't you going to say something?'

He'd felt the twang of anxiety in Stella's voice and looking up he'd been perplexed to see tears in her eyes. He'd asked her what was wrong and when she'd answered he had laughed, amused by how illogical she could be. Of course they would get married – this was their own little miracle! They'd kissed across the table, certain that life was good.

But now in Finchley, it all felt far from miraculous. Around the table, John tried to catch his father's eye, but both his parents were concentrating hard on the remains of their Sunday roast.

'So you see, Mum, Dad, we didn't want a fuss.'

His mother looked up, smiling with her lips pressed into a tight line. 'Yes, darling. We understand.'

But Stella could hear their disapproval in the silence on either side of what they said. She turned words over in her head. *At least tell us you're angry!* But she knew she wouldn't be able to bring herself to say them aloud.

John's father coughed, looking at each of them in turn as if to signal that the wedding conversation was at an end. 'What about the bomb near you, then?' he said, shaking his head. 'It's a terrible thing to say, but I don't even get shocked by that sort of thing any more.'

It was true, Stella thought. There had been so many

bombs going off over the past few years, she too had begun to feel immune to the horror until she'd stood up close to that unnatural scene of charred walls and blown-out windows and bloodied survivors.

John nodded at his father, accepting the change of direction. 'It was awful. Like a war zone, but just there on our doorstep. And those people – do you remember, Stella, that guy they brought out?'

Stella tried to blink away the image of the man as he lay on the ground, his eyes fixed on hers from his blood-streaked face.

'Oh, how horrible!' John's mother clasped her hands together.

Stella turned to her new mother-in-law. 'It was horrific, Mrs Greenwood.'

She'd expected to be corrected, *It's 'Mum' now, Stella.* But the older woman said nothing as she gathered their plates and left the room. Stella noticed that the feeling in the room had changed again.

John's father leaned forward. 'We don't have money, you know, Stella. There's no gold to dig here.'

John blinked, unsure if he'd imagined the words. But Stella's flushed cheeks and her tightening grip around his wrist told him he had not.

'Mr Greenwood—' Stella began, a waver in her voice.

But John interrupted. 'Dad! Where did that come from? What are you thinking?'

His father scowled. 'What am I thinking? What are *you* thinking? Knocking up a girl you hardly know, getting married on the sly, breaking your mother's heart while you're at it, it's—'

'Stop! Please.' Stella stood up. 'John, I'm going to go—'

John's mother had brought in a trifle from the kitchen. 'Won't you stay for dessert?' she asked Stella, who laughed despite herself.

'Oh, no, we'd better not. Thanks very much for a lovely lunch.'

The words seemed to exist in a world apart from the strange chaos that her body had become; it was as if she were reading them off a card. John kissed his mother's cheek, then took Stella's arm and led her out of the house.

'Well,' he said as they walked to the Tube, 'that could have been a lot worse.'

Stella looked at him and he broke into a wide grin. She punched him on the arm, not quite hard enough to hurt.

'You utter bastard,' she said and they both started to laugh.

2.3

More than a month after the papers and almost all of London had forgotten the attack, Charlie stood in an unfamiliar church and waited to bury his sister. Ben was in the front row, weeping into his hands, which were mottled red and white like raw meat. But for those huge hands, it was almost possible for Charlie to feel sorry for him. At the front of the church, the priest mumbled the mass, his voice almost inaudible except for the occasional sudden spike in volume that seemed to take him by surprise every time it happened. Charlie stared at the wooden box with his sister inside. It baffled him that all that life could just have vanished. Vaguely, he recalled that energy could not be destroyed, only transferred. So where had Annie gone? It was impossible to believe that she had simply ceased to be, however unknowable the alternative.

His mother leaned against him, shell-like and smelling of drink. Charlie shifted in his seat. Beth had offered to come back, but he'd told her she should stay in France; in part because he wanted her to finish the final days of her course, but mostly because he was afraid of the scene that his mother would make at the funeral. But when he'd met his mother at the Tube at Kilburn Park he'd realised there was nothing left to be afraid of: she had become a shadow of a woman. The figure from his childhood had gone. The flashes of glory, the fury and despair were all just memories now.

The priest was flicking arcs of holy water across the casket. Ben shuddered, blew his nose into a large grey hanky and took a surreptitious swig from a small brown hipflask.

The priest continued: '. . . but to command thy holy angels to receive it, and to bear it into paradise; that as it has believed and hoped in thee it may be delivered from the pains of hell and inherit eternal life through Christ our Lord. Amen.' His final words reached a wild crescendo and Charlie flinched as he muttered 'Amen' along with everyone else.

The pub afterwards was packed with black-clad family members and nervous-looking friends of Annie, awed by their first funeral, uncertain how to behave. Charlie watched as Ben shook their hands, accepting the drinks pressed into his, as his eyes grew vacant and his mouth set hard. The voices grew louder and blurred with drink so that the room seemed to become a singular bellow, a bright and clanking hub of life.

A hand fell heavily on his shoulder and Charlie turned. Ben's eyes were small, his face flushed and cruel and when he started talking it seemed as though he was already halfway through a conversation.

' . . . but Charlie, right, the thing I want to know is, yeah, why was she even in that pub on our fuckin' wedding night? I was entitled to a few drinks with my mates, y'know? But then she's gone and I says to Roddie, "Where's Annie got to?" and Roddie was giving it all "You've had too much

mate" and "I think it's time we got you home", so I smacked
him – ahaha! – I mean, for fuck's sake, it was my wedding,
yeah? And then someone nuts me and the next thing I know
I'm in a police cell on the Edgware Road an' it's all chaos
cos some terrorist fuckers have bombed a pub. But what I
want to know is *why* was she at that fuckin' pub?'

Charlie winced as the hand gripped tighter. Ben's face
was damp with sweat and a streak of snot glazed his upper
lip. Three drinks in, Charlie was less drunk than Ben, but
he wasn't sober. He felt the thud of his blood through his
body as he listened to his dead sister's husband slur and
rant. As gently as he could, he lifted Ben's hand from his
shoulder. He tried to look his brother-in-law in the eye but
Ben's gaze was hooded and unfocused.

'Ben, she's gone. It makes sense that you're angry. We're
all angry.'

His head slammed back sharply as the two huge hands
pinned him against the wall. Someone, perhaps his mother,
gave a hoarse shriek and the pub fell quiet, watching.

'Fuck, Ben, what are you doing?'

There was at least two stone in weight between them.
Charlie's bones were balsa-light beneath the tight-packed
bulk of those straining arms. A muscle in Ben's jaw flexed
and a ferocious roar ripped from him. 'Why – was – she
– there?'

Ben's contorted face receded from view as images flashed
in front of Charlie's eyes: pale hair streaming down, a livid
lick of bruise, a hand against burnt-out blackness. He realised with sickening clarity that Annie wouldn't have survived
this man. There was another roar, but this time it came
from Charlie as he brought his forehead down against the

bridge of Ben's nose. Blood spilled and Charlie ducked away from the hands that had lost their grip on him, grabbing a bottle and smashing it against the edge of a table. Looking up, Ben saw the glint of glass as Charlie's arm thrust towards him, but there was no time to shield himself before the jagged edge connected with the soft flesh of his neck.

Afterwards, Charlie remembered that the noise began only when he hit the floor. In the moments before, the pub was entirely silent, a collective held breath. There was a high-pitched ringing in his ears, then a bursting of voices, as if he'd suddenly surfaced into sound. Ben was looming above him, a thread of blood along his neck where Charlie's hand had swooped away at the last minute. Two huge cousins held Ben's arms and someone's knee pushed Charlie down, his face twisted into the beer-sodden carpet. His mother emerged from the gathered crowd and with a sharp word to the owner of the knee, pulled Charlie up and pushed him with surprising force towards the door.

'Just go.'

'Mum, he hurt her.'

His mother stared hard at him, a stripe of white roots visible along the scalp of her dirty yellow hair, a greasy glass of vodka tonic swaying, iceless, in her hand. Her rheumy eyes glistened and her thin mouth twisted into a joyless smile. 'That's life, kiddo.'

With a swig of her drink, she pushed the door open. Charlie looked at her for a moment, then, without another word, he walked through the door and into the busy street.

Life on the High Road had carried on as usual since the police cordon had come down a few weeks ago. The shoppers and the traders went about their business as usual, passing without a second glance the boarded-up windows behind which his sister and his best friend had died. Charlie felt his fury burn. How dare they act as if nothing had changed?

At the off-licence he bought a quarter bottle of whisky, the shopkeeper eyeing his injured face as he handed over the change. 'Looks sore, mate.'

Charlie stared, wordless, until the older man looked away. Then he walked out of the shop, drinking his way through half of the bottle before he reached the top of West End Lane.

The next morning, as Charlie slept on the sofa where he had passed out the night before, Beth stood in her flat in Montpellier, smoking the last of her cigarettes. She turned her father's letter over in her hand. His pen had pressed so hard that mirror images of the words were embossed on the other side of the paper; but then, her father had always been a man of strong feelings. That's why he had offered the money – so much money that her mind still swirled at the thought of it – for her to move to Paris and study at the Sorbonne. Not only for the prestige, but because he wanted her away from Charlie. *He's dragging you down,* her father had said after she'd refused his offer and told him of her plans to teach. She read the letter again, then bit her lip and tore it into pieces. It wasn't as if she hadn't tried to break herself away. She thought of the student from Marseilles she'd met weeks ago, and how her desire had extinguished the moment they had kissed – his smell and taste so *wrong*. When she was with Charlie the world felt full of fire and promise. She craved it with an addict's passion.

Outside, the airport taxi blew its horn. She knew where she needed to be.

From above, London spread out grey and green, a sprawling mass of conurbation. The plane turned and banked and Beth felt the sweat soaking her underarms. How contrary to all common sense to trap yourself inside a metal tube and launch into the air. She'd had a maths teacher once who'd tried to explain the magic of flight, the way the wing was shaped to make the air move faster below and create lift. But then, as now, all she could think was that none of it made sense: not the maths or the physics or the desire to travel at a height of 36,000 feet. Below, the silver band of Thames snaked through the miniature city. As the plane circled a descent Beth followed the river's path, her eyes passing over a stretch of embankment near Hammersmith where, if she could have seen that far, she would have discovered the dishevelled shape of Charlie, drinking beer from a can and looking up at the sky.

When the can was empty, Charlie retraced his steps towards the Tube. He had come here on a whim, remembering the day he'd stood on these banks to watch the boat race with Beth and her school friends. They had bought two rounds at a time in the overflowing pub, their public school voices full of confidence. Charlie had marvelled on that bright spring day at how they seemed ready for anything, so blithe and unafraid. Around him now the light was fading and a November wind whipped off the river, stinging the cuts on his face. At the foot of a block of flats an unruly group of children were playing on a bald patch of earth. There was a shriek and Charlie saw a young girl clutch her cheek as her mother dragged her away by the wrist, the woman's voice an angry slur. He thought of Beth and how different it must be to choose your own responsibilities, instead of having them thrust upon you. He was glad she'd never known the bitterness of looking after someone that you sometimes hate, and yet it was a gap that stretched between them. How could she ever understand a life like his? And yet, an hour later, when he saw her sitting in the doorway of his flat, a sudden realisation passed over him like wildfire. Their difference didn't matter; she was the only way he could survive.

Beth was startled when she saw his battered face. She touched her lips to his eye, his cheek, his forehead, his mouth.

'Charlie, what happened?'

He shook his head as he held her. 'It's a long story. Let's go inside.'

The next morning, as the sun filled the bedroom with a cold white light, Beth leaned over him, her dark hair brushing his face. 'Charlie, wake up!'

The room smelled of coconut oil and smoke and sex. He ran his fingers along the silky curve from her breastbone to her hip and she closed her eyes and stretched. He looked up. Beth was here. Not in France, not with her parents, but here in his bed. She had chosen him.

He pressed his mouth against her neck. 'Beth?'

The soft rise of her breast brushed his arm and he felt himself grow hard again.

She smiled, hooked her leg across his hip and rolled on top of him. 'Mmm?'

He kissed her again. 'Will you marry me?'

She looked down at him and laughed. 'Are you serious?'

He sat up and wrapped her legs around his waist. She smiled and raised an eyebrow, but her eyes were bright with tears. Charlie took her hands and kissed them. 'Please? Please marry me.'

Beth leaned against him, her tears dampening his shoulder. 'Oh, my love. I thought you'd never ask.'

3.

SUPERPOSITION

1978

. . . the condition of existing in all possible quantum states at the same time, manifest only when a particle is unobserved. A favourite example of this phenomenon is Schrödinger's cat — that unfortunate beast who, until observed, is equally as dead as he is alive.

McKearnan, L. Quantum Entanglement.
Paradox Publishing, 1982 (p. 42)

3.1

On the morning of their wedding, Charlie didn't have to worry about his mother making a scene. There was no early morning phone call, no senseless anger. There was only the quiet burr of traffic from two streets away and the clink of bottles and glasses in the kitchen. Charlie lay in bed watching the sky moving in the mirror on Beth's dressing table. Strange, he thought, how the view he knew so well became exotic when reflected in the glass: an uncanny glimpse of the familiar, forever unreachable.

Beth stood in the doorway, dark hair tumbling down the back of the brown and gold dress she'd made herself. She was wiping her hands on a tea towel, the smooth skin of her forehead creased into a question. 'Are you going to phone your mum?'

He considered the question. Was it worth it, really? After the funeral, his mother's phone calls had grown more frequent for a while, berating him at all hours for the fight with Ben, for Annie's death, for all the negative aspects of his character that she could dredge up in her drunken state. After a few weeks, she had gone silent, until a month ago, when he'd had a call from her local police station. She'd been found wandering in a T-shirt and slippers, confused and disoriented. They'd assumed at first she was just another drunk, the officer had said in an apologetic voice, but then she'd had a seizure in the back of the police car and ended up in hospital. Could Charlie come to collect her? Typical, Charlie had thought. But he'd gone, because who else was there?

Now, his mother mistook him for his dead uncle, if she recognised him at all. When she did know who he was, she would suddenly remember Annie, each time experiencing anew the full force of her grief. Charlie almost preferred to be forgotten than to see her suffer like that. He looked back at Beth, who was watching him, waiting for an answer.

'I don't know.'

She sat next to him on the bed and he smelled coconut and soapsuds as she pressed her cheek against his chest.

'Oh Charlie, I wish I could make it better for you.'

'I can think of one way,' he said as he reached for the heavy softness of her left breast.

She laughed and flicked the damp tea towel as he lunged. 'Get off! My parents will be here any minute!'

Their honeymoon was a barge trip in Warwickshire, saved for from Charlie's meagre salary as a junior agent and Beth's teacher training grant. They returned to London a week later, to the flat in West Hampstead that Charlie had once shared with Limpet, the second bedroom now piled with the manuscripts that he brought home from work to read. At night, after he'd finished reading, he would sit among the pages of other people's words and write his own stories, the words expanding inside him as he struggled against their relentless flow, siphoning out what he could onto the page. Coffee-stained and smudged with cigarette ash, his papers had grown to a modest pile alongside the reams of submissions from the agency. He didn't know why or what he was writing for, only that it was inevitable and a relief, like piercing your nail to release fluids from a swelling finger. What flowed out was not necessarily good, but it needed to happen. Often Beth would find him asleep at the desk, his typewriter for a pillow, key marks dented across his cheek.

One morning many weeks later, Charlie awoke in the study and staggered to the kitchen, where Beth was sorting the washing in the middle of the floor. He had been up most of the night writing, and yesterday, reading through the pile of submissions, he'd found Alexa Godfrey's manuscript. He had a good feeling about this one.

Beth looked up at him and smiled. 'Here,' she whispered, 'this came in the post.'

She handed him a slip of paper from the hospital with a plus sign stamped in red. Positive. He looked at the slip and its red-stamped cross, her face and its smile, and those sunflower-centred eyes.

'A baby?' he asked, unsure if this was real. 'We're going to have a baby?'

'Yes we are,' she laughed, 'we're going to have a baby.'

He sat with a thud on the floor, wrapping his arms around her legs and crying into her red wool tights as Beth laughed and tugged at his hair, saying *Charlie, Charlie, Charlie*, while they kissed between their tears and the dirty laundry.

*

When she lost the baby a few days afterwards, Beth didn't eat for a week. Charlie brought her everything he could think of: toast and finely sliced orange, Turkish delight and salted cashews, bagels and Bakewell tarts, baklava and hot milk with honey. But she simply couldn't swallow; it was as if her throat had closed over. At night she would sleep with her back to him, unable to bear his touch for longer than a few minutes. Five days after the blood had stopped, she took his hand and looked at him. Her face was grey with fatigue, her cheeks hollow, eyes dim. 'It was all I ever wanted.'

He held her, grateful that she let him, and tried to ignore the searing ache within his own chest. 'I know, love. I know.'

She sighed and peeled herself out of his arms. 'I'm sorry. I'm just so tired.'

He led her to the bed and pulled the blankets over her as she lay looking at the whorls of plaster on the ceiling. In the darkened hallway outside he sat on the floor and cried, pressing his sleeve to his face so that Beth wouldn't hear.

He left the flat almost without thinking; it was as if his body had decided for him. In the corner shop, the lights made him squint and itch to be back in the dimness of his flat; but once he had the cool weight of the bottle in his hand, instead of turning onto the little patch of green, Charlie found himself walking up the hill towards the tall houses of Hampstead. When he reached the spread of the Heath half an hour later, most of the vodka was gone. Lights checkered the darkness: a bedroom, a stairway, a woman at the kitchen window. But in the centre, beneath an uneven horizon of trees, there was only blackness. Charlie drained the last of the vodka, dropped the bottle into a bin and walked into the dark.

On a bench, someone was smoking. At first, Charlie saw only the tip of a cigarette, but as he approached he made out the figure of a man leaning slightly forward, elbow propping up his chin. Charlie felt the heat of a gaze across him as he passed, though he couldn't see the man's face. Further on, another figure turned from a spot by the bushes. A series of ragged gasps came from deeper in the darkness. Charlie looked away, stepped off the path and climbed a bank, clinging to branches as his feet slipped against the muddy ground, emerging at last at the top of a hill. London lay in the middle distance, a system of lights and dark patches of buildings cut through by cars and buses and underground trains. From where he stood, Charlie felt the vast gape of his own insignificance within the city; a tiny cog in a machine that would long outlast him. Crouching down, he closed his fingers around a clump of grass and ripped it from the ground. It smelled of earth and rain. *I am a part of all this.* He shut his eyes, but the images came anyway: shattered glass, the turning lights, a white hand in the darkness.

3.2

March 1978

On the day of Stella's twenty-second birthday, her grandmother died. Stella had never liked birthdays. As a child she would hide beneath the kitchen table at the first bars of 'Happy Birthday to you'. So, as an adult, she decided to do away with the whole thing and after the age of twenty she gave up on cards, cake and forced jollity. By then, anyway, she thought of herself as old – she'd always had a depressive streak, her mother said – and so the passing of another year never seemed like something worth marking.

The family migrated west to Wales for the funeral. She was thirty-six weeks pregnant by then, but she braved the uncomfortable journey to say a last goodbye. In the smoke-filled kitchen of her aunt and uncle's house in Carmarthen she'd sat, feeling fat, in a corner, watching her uncles drink beer out of tin cans, bellowing old Irish songs as they conducted with their cigarettes. Her ankles were heavy and her belly stretched like a drumskin, the baby wedged tight up against her ribcage. Exhausted, she looked about the bright room. She longed to lie down, though there was no comfort to be found even in that now. Her grandmother would have loved this, Stella thought, though she'd have told the uncles off for their drinking. But the chaos and cacophony, the shrine of photos on the piano, the singing, and the fact that she was centre of attention, all that would have delighted the old woman.

The next morning, among the sore heads and empty bottles, Stella ate bacon and drank strong tea. The uncles were silent now, hushed for their mother as they used to be in the days when she would blaze and row with them. The rattle of the kettle and the chink of glass and cutlery were the only sounds in that crowded kitchen, until Uncle Michael walked in, snorting back the tears that were streaming down his blotched face. Stella watched as her mother took his hand and led him to the table where he sat and sobbed between mouthfuls.

As the baby rolled inside her, she understood that she was becoming many versions of herself: mother, daughter, wife and woman. When no one was looking, she supposed she'd be all of those at once – the way light unobserved was both particle and wave, or Schrödinger's poor old cat was both alive and not alive. And when people looked at her, like light or that unfortunate cat she supposed that she'd take one form or other, determined in a moment by the act of being watched.

The rain lashed against the car windscreen as they drove to the church. By the altar she saw the coffin, bedecked in purple cloths, banal as a trestle table. Mass began. Stella stood, sat, listened and responded, mumbling through the hymns – 'The Lord's my Shepherd', 'Bread of Heaven' – until it was over. At the crematorium, she watched the wooden box glide towards the curtains and then continued to watch as, to her horror, it stopped halfway through. The back end of her grandmother was left protruding from the vulgar green drape like baggage at the airport. The baby pushed and turned, fed up with its cramped surroundings, and she watched the nodule of a knee or an elbow slide across her belly as the priest talked on and a small child started screeching. The coffin gave another judder and slid forward an inch, the curtains still a foot short of its end. Music played and a poem was read, but Stella could think of nothing except the non-committal coffin. She stood and waddled to the front of the hall, tugging one curtain and then the other until it was covered properly. Then she walked back down the aisle, out into the car park and, looking up to the green-grey outlines of hills sheathed in mizzling rain, she wept.

The old house still smelled of frying and cigarettes, even after the rooms were emptied of everything except the ghostly lines of the pictures that had once hung upon the wall. She thought of the school photos and samplers, the sacred heart of Jesus. She thought of the endless comings and goings of uncles and aunts and cousins and neighbours, the smoke and the noise that had always surrounded her grandmother. Always the phone at her side and always her tea in a cup and saucer, a cigarette held in pink polished nails, stray rollers and tissues – and books everywhere. So many books. As a child, Stella would take piles of them and hide herself in the attic, sitting on stacks of old newspapers, away from the din. There in the dust with the murmurs of chaos below she could find her way into Narnia or lands where dragons flew, or the minds of people from far-off times. And then later, when the house was quieter (for it was never very quiet), she would creep back downstairs to speak of all she'd discovered. And her grandmother would hand her toffees and listen as if this was the first time she'd ever heard those stories.

Stella was pleased at last to feel the gentle release of being alone. Her fingers rasped along the wood-chip walls as she heaved her body up the stairs. The steps to the loft were hanging down and, without thinking, she began to climb up towards her old hiding place. Her muscles complained and she didn't get far before it became clear that she was never going to fit through the attic door. But she wanted one last look before the house was sold, so she kept on climbing. Balancing at the top of the flimsy ladder, she craned her neck to look inside and saw at the far end a narrow slice of light that fell across a tangle of cloth. A pale coloured cardigan of her grandmother's was crumpled in the corner, its sleeves wrapped around the familiar corduroy of a gardening jacket that had been her grand-father's. Nothing else remained. Stella climbed down. Pulling the front door shut, she looked up at the bold letters of the sign that said 'Sold' as she walked over to where her mother was waiting to take her home.

Her waters broke the next night, just a few hours after she'd arrived back in London. It was all so fast, not at all like it was supposed to be. The ambulance operator asked if she might put her husband on the line and she watched as John's face froze.

'What did she say?' Stella asked, when she could.

John held her hand as the next contraction came. 'Well,

try not to panic, but it looks as if I'll be delivering this baby.'

They wrapped her in their best bath towel and sat beneath a blanket on the bathroom floor to wait for the ambulance, too afraid to cut the cord from the meaty mass that had emerged after.

'Hope,' John whispered as he stroked the matted dark hair. 'Can we call her Hope, Stella?'

Stella looked at the perfect buds of her baby's lips, her small unseeing eyes, the blood and strange white curd smeared on her dark hair. She wrestled then with something that felt like a death, astounded that this day was the beginning of her daughter's life, but also understanding with a startling new clarity the finitude of her own existence. She held her breath, then let it flow, watching the curl of the baby's delicate fingers and the rise and fall of that miraculous chest.

'Yes,' she whispered. 'Yes, let's call her Hope.'

No one had explained it would be so hard.

Or at least, the words may have been said, but how could she have understood, then – *before* – that some days it would feel as if she might never know herself again? That you can in fact be too exhausted to sleep and that tiredness is not a feeling but a way of seeing the world. That some part of being a parent is a bereavement, grieving the loss of a life that is light to the touch, weighed down as you now are with fear. Fear that the baby will die in any one of a million different ways. It's incredible, Stella realised, how many things can kill if you really set your mind to it – grapes, dressing gown cords, central heating. Everywhere, there's death.

Nobody said that Stella's body would continue to be beyond her control; nor did they tell of the night sweats and the clots of blood like kidneys and the milk that sprang like needles at the sound of every cry. She hadn't guessed that there could be a place where nothing matters, not even her own nakedness, or that sitting in a bath could feel so hard.

On the first day she and Hope were left alone together, Stella felt the world grow vast and frightening, filled with potential disaster, so she stayed as still as possible, hoping that the hours might pass more safely that way. She ignored the postman when he knocked and the health visitor too. The telephone rang and rang, but she stayed wrapped in the bedclothes, Hope sleeping and feeding beside her. After what seemed like hours, there was a key in the lock and a flurry of feet on the stairs. The clock on the wall said quarter past one. It was lunchtime, then? The door of the bedroom burst open.

'Stella!'

John's face was pale and frantic. 'My God, I've been so worried – why didn't you answer the phone?'

He flopped onto the bed like a broken toy. Stella held Hope close, smiling at her tiny kissing noises, breathing in her yeasty milk-clean smell, and opened her mouth to speak, but only tears came out. He held them both in his arms and they lay, all three, dappled in the afternoon light as it fell through the trees by the window.

Days, then weeks, passed. Stella remained as tightly primed as a wild cat, ready to pounce, awake at the slightest sound.

To the outside world, Hope was an unremarkable infant, sleeping and not sleeping as a baby will. But with every day that passed, Stella felt the fear inside her rise. *What if I get this wrong?* It was dizzying to think that she could shape a life so completely, that everything depended on her. And then there was colic, a word she only learned after two weeks of almost constant crying. One morning, after another night of fractured sleep, Stella looked down at the little body rigid with fury and wind and she felt a wave of heat rush through her. At that moment, she knew nothing except her daughter's scream. Taking a deep breath, she picked the baby up and rubbed her back. The crying carried on. She checked her nappy, then put Hope to her breast. The baby suckled for a moment, then began to choke as the milk flowed faster than she could manage. A howl of rage shook through her and Stella held her at arm's length and shouted as she put her in the cot.

'I'm sorry, Hope, I don't know what to do!'

She hadn't meant to scare the baby, but her voice had been so loud and the movement to the cot not rough, exactly, but not quite gentle either. For a few seconds Hope was calm and in the quiet Stella began to panic. *Oh my God, I've hurt her.*

Food and sleep grew difficult, as did people. Stella found that she couldn't bear to see her friends: their simple chatter, the way they moved unhindered, their preoccupation with the nothingness of daily life. Even the smell of washing powder and shampoo enraged her. The days became excruciatingly long. A sudden breakthrough in John's research meant he was in the lab until after 7 every evening and

Stella battled with a creeping sense of loneliness that she didn't want to look in the eyes, for fear of what might happen.

One day, when Hope was six weeks old and still screaming for hours on end, Stella decided to go to Bristol. Her parents would know what the secret was. The train when she boarded was heaving with people and she shook as she struggled through the carriage. There was a free seat beside an old woman and Stella lowered herself gratefully into it, holding Hope tight, willing her not to cry. Their legs bumped and the old lady started to speak. *Oh Christ,* thought Stella. With a deep breath to summon her strength, she looked up at the talkative old lady and smiled. The woman took a packet of digestive biscuits from her bag and offered one to Stella. Hunger blossomed like a blood-spill as Stella's veins flooded with sugar-fired warmth. Another and another was offered and eaten, while the old lady watched the hungry-looking young mother devouring her biscuits as she talked on. Stella nodded at the woman's stories and carried on eating, dusting Hope's downy head with biscuit crumbs. At Chippenham, Stella watched through the outline of her own reflection as a tattooed man in a polyester jacket helped the old woman onto the platform with improbable gentleness and kissed her on her wrinkled forehead.

She climbed down at Temple Meads, baby in one arm, buggy in the other. Her dad was there to meet her, grinding his cigarette beneath his shoe and raising a hand in greeting. Laden and ungainly, Stella walked nonetheless with a new lightness along the curve of the platform, buggy and baby bouncing. They drove home along the streets that Stella had known since childhood, the windows of the houses glinting in the evening light. Everywhere she looked in this city was inscribed with her past, the pavements marked with footprints of her former lives. The car climbed to the brow of a hill lined with crumbling Georgian terraces, Bath stone decayed like the teeth of unloved children, and paused at the top as the traffic slowed. The imperfect houses were smoothed by the glow of the late-day sun as Stella began to hear the whispers of a lifetime's worth of dreams.

For three days she paced, awake and joyous, walking the streets around her parents' house while the baby slept. She watched three sunrises meander above the park and sink below the hill. She discovered signs everywhere: shapes that embodied the meaning of life, numbers that held the divine. The third day was mostly a blur – emotion star-bursting against a deadening tiredness. She could barely speak. Words formed a stream of hot and cold nothingness, a static fizz she couldn't really comprehend. Time slowed. The ice-sharp clarity thawed and she was left like a nub of melted snow, greyed and unsteady. That night, her mother sponged her like a baby in the bath, then led her to her childhood bed and stroked her hair until she finally fell asleep.

In the dim morning of the fourth day an engine stuttered then stopped in the street outside. A car door clunked open. The front door creaked and low voices slid upwards from the hallway. Hope's cries sent an eddy of movement upstairs, and when Stella sat up, John was at the end of her bed, baby in his arms, the early morning sun falling on his face like a benediction.

The road was quiet on the journey back to London the next evening. Hope slept in her carrycot, lulled by the low

thrum of the engine, as Stella looked out at the dark hinter-
land of the motorway at night. John spoke as he drove, his
voice low, his eyes on the lights of the cars ahead, safe in
the traveller's freedom of between-time. He talked of finding
a place outside the city, somewhere they could go now and
then, when London life became too much. A place beside
the sea.

'Because the sea,' he said, 'reminds us of how small our
problems really are.'

Then he began to sing:

*I must go down to the seas again, to the lonely sea and the
sky,*
And all I ask is a tall ship and a star to steer her by.

Stella thought of her work, of the world of ideas she'd
abandoned as the baby grew inside her and even in the tar
of her exhaustion she felt something gentle, a kind of hope.
The passing lights moved across John's face as he drove
steadily on, travelling always in a straight line, confidently
into the dark.

3.3

May 1978

Charlie arrived early at the office, dropping a block of submissions on his desk. He liked to read through the slush pile before the day began and his in-tray grew full of filing and letters to type. That was how he'd found Alexa's manuscript a few weeks before: his first author. At 9.30, the small office began to fill, coats were hung up and fresh coffee brewed. At 10, Genevieve arrived with a rush of cold street air and rich perfume.

'Charlie?' she called as she removed her shoes and curled her stockinged toes in and out, one foot at a time.

'Yes, Genevieve?'

'We need to run through the list for tonight's launch. Do you have it?'

'Just a sec.'

Charlie took notes as she rattled off names and instructions, barely pausing for breath. From 10.30 the phones rang non-stop, the fax spewed paper and people ricocheted across the office, talking loudly in half-formed sentences. Words everywhere. Charlie tried to imagine how life could get noisier than this. Years later, in the silence of a pub where people sat cocooned in their separate smartphone worlds, he would smile to think how life had grown so quiet. But today the office thundered with a tide of other people's words and he let the rising volume carry him along.

'Charlie!' He flinched at being caught dreaming.

'Yes, sorry – um – how can I help?'

Genevieve looked at him, her eyebrows slanting in concern. She pursed her coral pink lips. 'Are you getting enough sleep?'

Off-guard, Charlie stuttered, thinking of the path he had walked with a bottle of vodka last night, down to Regent's Park and back again, climbing into bed beside a sleeping Beth after 3 a.m. 'Ah – yes, yes. Bit of a late night last night, that's all.'

But Genevieve had lost interest. 'Good good. Anyway. Can you copy these? Thank you, darling.' She turned in a swirl of silk trench coat and left the office for lunch.

Walking home that evening between the steep terraces of red-brick mansion blocks, Beth felt herself grow heavy. How encumbered she'd become. She cut over a graffiti-daubed railway bridge and carried on towards the flat, sapped by a deadening tiredness. The hallway was littered with empty beer cans and a trail of coal dust that stretched along the stairs. As she closed the front door, she looked up at the electricity meter. A couple of wires dangled down from the device that their neighbour had pushed into the coin slot – a 'jumper' he'd called it. It was a clever contraption made of copper and plastic tubing that caused the current to keep flowing without a steady stream of ten-pence pieces, but it made Beth anxious. She checked, as she always did, for scorch marks on the casing. She'd heard stories of jumped meters catching fire – just the other day in fact, a squat on Villa Road had burned down. She'd passed it the same evening on her way home, its damp ashes still smouldering.

She let herself into the flat. The kitchen smelled of last night's stew, clinging to the dirty dishes stacked beside the sink. She placed a pile of marking from her bag on the cleanest-looking patch of sideboard and went into the bedroom. Days-old washing hung on the clothes horse; piles of books littered the floor; a hillock of shoes had gathered in the corner by the window. She peeled off her dress and tights and sat on the edge of the bed in her underwear, one foot raised onto its opposite knee, as she rubbed at the ache from having stood all day. At the agency Charlie was flourishing, his evenings full of dinners and parties. Beth tried to staunch the rising flow of her resentment: this was his work, after all. But with every month that her period arrived she felt a new layer of sadness pressing inside her, calcifying into a brittle anger. Sometimes, when Charlie rolled into bed smelling of wine and cigarette smoke, she would touch his back, her fingers brushing down the jutting bones of his spine and he would turn to her, stroking her soft thighs, kissing her with his bitter breath. But then she'd feel herself grow tense, her quiet fury flaring at his touch, the unsaid things polluting her like poison.

In Soho, Charlie was on his second glass of wine, the sharp edges of the day smoothing off as he spoke to a succession of beautiful women. He looked around the room at the people laughing and the drink flowing and felt himself becoming the Charlie that people were expecting: witty and playful, always up for another, the life and soul. He took a third

drink from a passing tray, draining the glass in two long
draughts as he headed over to introduce himself to the
slender girl with red hair who had just become his first
client.

Charlie and Alexa met again the following afternoon, in a
cellar bar off Greek Street where they served sharp white
wine in squat glasses and clay bowls of salted peanuts. Alexa
arrived on time, her hair twisted at the nape of her neck,
arms like willow switches from her loose black dress. Her
white skin glowed against the warmth of the Soho afternoon
and Charlie was overwhelmed with an urge to wrap her in
his jacket to keep her alabaster flesh from smudging. A smile
spread across her face.

'Charlie?'

He grinned and raised his eyebrows. 'The very same.
Hello again, Alexa.'

'Hello again, Charlie.' Her face was still when she spoke,
the words unhurried, her wide-set eyes a clear, arresting
blue. He found it was impossible to look away.

'Shall we?'

They descended the stairs into the dark bar, where a
skinny young man stood twisting a cloth in a glass. But
apart from him, all the tables were empty at this hour.

Charlie glanced around and shrugged at his new author.
'Funny sort of time to come to a bar, isn't it? Sorry about
that.'

She touched his arm and his body seemed to burst alive.
'That's quite alright. I can be very amenable to an afternoon
drink in the right circumstances.'

Outside, the street began to darken. But in the bar, fresh

drinks lined up beside three rounds of empty glasses; it was warm and smoky and timeless.

'Charlie?' Her fingers closed across his hand and he stopped talking. The slow smile spread once more across her pale face. The bar was full now with after-work drinkers and Charlie had to raise his voice against the chunter of their tangled conversations.

'Yes?'

He felt the press of her thigh against his beneath the table.

'Shall we continue this at mine?'

For a moment he sensed all the unspoken things; the many absences that circled his life. He thought of Beth, waiting in their small flat for him to come home. Of her quiet sorrow when her period had arrived a few days earlier. He knew that he should get up and leave, say goodbye to Alexa and promise her a phone call. But he was caught by something strange and powerful, a compulsion that pulled against sense and yet seemed to be the answer to everything he lacked. A way to step outside all this sadness.

Alexa's cheeks had pinked at his silence, a tiny chink of uncertainty, but her hand had not moved from his. He lifted it and kissed the soft warm skin, then pushed his hair back, letting out a slow breath. 'You know,' he said, 'I like the sound of that.'

Beth was long asleep by the time that Charlie came home, so she didn't hear the shower running or the furtive rustle of the laundry basket, though she dreamed of walking through long grass in the rain. That night, Charlie didn't dream at all, but the following night he woke in the depths of a fear so vast that he'd sat up gasping for air. The terror thumped through his whole body and even with his eyes screwed shut he couldn't stop the pictures from scrolling: *red hair falling loose, a pale curve of back, the unfamiliar lines of a stranger's bedroom* and beneath these, jagged fragments piercing through: *a smoke-filled silence, the blue-black glitter of lights on glass, a white hand lying in the dark.*

Beth groaned. His muscles twitched. In the darkness of the bedroom Charlie pulled on his clothes, creeping out of the flat and into the comfort of the anonymous night.

3.4

A bead of blood rose on her finger as Stella gathered the pieces of broken plate. She'd missed when she'd thrown it, naturally, and John had stared at the remains of the chicken stew as it dribbled down the wall, a look of mild confusion on his face. She'd said his name, her voice barely scratching the air, but his hand had dropped to his side and he'd turned and walked out of the flat, scooping his keys from the table by the front door as he'd left. In the bedroom the baby cried out in her sleep.

'Shh, shh, shh,' muttered Stella as she sucked her bleeding finger, a mantra more for herself than for Hope.

When had her temper grown so short? She was sure there'd been a time when she'd at least been patient, even if she could never be called laid-back. The relentless whir inside her head made it hard to simply be; there was always something that needed to be done. The difference was that, nowadays, instead of research and writing it was washing nappies and feeding the baby. John would have gone back to his office in the physics department, without a doubt. She imagined him cycling back there through the evening streets, witness to the freedom that other people wore so lightly. Heading south this summer's evening, he would pass young couples ambling along the pavements of Maida Vale, heat rising through the flimsy soles of their shoes; or outside the pub in Little Venice, sipping beers in the warm dip of the evening sunlight, painted houseboats bobbing on the water.

Arriving at his office, John sank into the safety of his work; a world where – even if he didn't yet know why – things were predictable, measurable. Sure, he was engaged in a project that some were saying would upset the establishment, but wasn't that the point of science? To seek the truth by disproving false assumptions. Across his desk and the blackboard above it, strings of algebra sloped in his uneven hand. A scientist's handwriting, Stella had said with a laugh, when she'd first seen it. She had a rich and throaty laugh.

These days, though, there never seemed to be much call for laughter; it was all they could do to make it through the day without a fight. A thrown plate was a new twist, though, and all because he'd missed the baby's bedtime. Such a waste of what smelled to be a tasty dinner. It simply didn't make sense to be so angry with him for not being there and then to send him away once he'd arrived, with a plate flung at his head for good measure. It's not as though he could help it. She really didn't seem to understand that things were progressing at such speed with the entanglement research – it was imperative that they wrote up their findings before the Cambridge people got wind of the project. Second place is no place when it comes to breaking new ground, as his dad had always said. Sighing, he laid his head on the desk, listening to the gurgle of his empty stomach.

In the flat, Stella scrubbed at the grease mark that looped along the wall. Her head burned with tiredness as she tried to remember the thread of the argument that she'd been planning for her dissertation little more than a year ago. *Speaking the Silence,* she had called it and felt so pleased with herself at the time, with the idea that she might be casting a net into the unseen and dredging up gold, finding the stories lost to the roar of white male voices. There was one woman who'd particularly stood out. A maid of all work to a London family, self-educated, writing in secret until the lady of the house had come across a piece that she had written: 'When I am Invisible: or tales of a life half-lived'. Against the odds, this woman had become the young serv-ant's patron, presenting her to fashionable friends – tastelessly perhaps by modern standards, but giving her a voice that for a moment could be heard. A voice crying out: I am real, I am here. Stella paused, stepping back to see if the mark on the wall had gone. A faint outline remained, but nothing that a bit of sugar soap tomorrow wouldn't sort out.

In her cot, Hope slept with her arms thrown up above her head, the rounds of her cheeks flushed red, her eyebrows raised in faint surprise. Laying a hand on Hope's cheek, Stella felt herself relax. It was her relief and yet her torment, all this love. She pulled the door ajar and went into the living room, twisting the dial on the television and settling herself on the sofa with a plate of cold chicken stew.

She dozed off in front of the TV, waking later to the clunk of the main door and the clank and tick of a bike: John was home. Stella stared at the back of their apartment door, picturing him carrying the bike upstairs on the other side. Beyond that door, she knew, life was still untethered, a whole world of people moving past each other. It was a world that John could step into whenever he chose, the ties of his home life dissolving behind him. His key rattled in the lock. Stella turned and padded quietly into the bedroom.

'Stella?' John's voice from the hallway was gentle. 'Are you OK? Can I make you some tea?'

Lying in the dark, Stella pretended to sleep.

The next day he brought her breakfast in bed, sitting beside her in his work clothes as she struggled awake after a night punctuated by Hope's feeds. One side of Stella's face bore the imprint of the pillow's edge and he reached out, tenderly touching the crease along her cheek.

'I love you, you know, Stella. I really do.'

Hollow with exhaustion, she looked at the man in front of her, with his lopsided smile and his light brown hair grown too long. She hadn't realised she was about to cry, but her voice wavered and tears spilled down her cheeks, coursing trails of yesterday's mascara with them. She pushed her hands into her face, trying to find the words to make him understand what it was like to be imprisoned by the thing you love the most. Since the summer's evening when she'd told him she was pregnant, she hadn't doubted that she wanted to have the baby. And yet right now she felt cast adrift, trapped only in one state, when really she was so much more. *Mother*, yes, and *wife* as well; but *lover*, *writer*, *woman* too.

'I can't explain,' she said as her body folded in upon itself and the sobs kept coming.

In theory, John knew what he ought to do to make her feel better. But when he tried to take her in his arms she swore at him and pushed him back. He stood up. From the other room the baby started to wail.

'Shall I fetch her?' John asked.

Stella screamed, burying her face in the pillow to muffle the sound.

Unsure of what he should do next, John watched his wife as she pressed herself into a ball among the bedclothes. From the next room Hope's cries were growing more intense.

He cleared his throat. 'I'll get the baby.'

Hope's shrieks were becoming vibrato, but when he scooped her up, to his surprise, she quietened down. He walked back to the bedroom, where Stella was now sitting up.

'John, I'm sorry. I – I don't know what's happening to me.'

'It's OK. It'll be OK. You're tired, is all.'

She looked at him with Hope perched in his arms and shook her head. 'It's not because I'm tired. It's because I'm stuck. Stuck here just being a mother.'

'But Stella, a mother is an important thing to be—'

'That's not what I mean!'

John glanced at the clock and his face clenched. He held the baby out to her and sighed.

'Look, I'm sorry but, here – can you take her? I've got to leave or else I'm going to be late.' He leaned over and kissed her, placing Hope on her lap and breathing in the baby's tang of milk and urine.

'I'm never going to do it, am I?'

'Do what?'

'The PhD. It's never going to happen. Not when you're always so busy – I mean – I don't . . .'

But John was already halfway out of the door. 'Stels, can we talk about this later? I've got to give a lecture at 9.' And without waiting for her answer, he wheeled his bike out of the flat.

Stella listened to his footsteps fading down the stairs, dissolving into the world beyond.

Later on, when Hope was napping, full once more of milk, Stella took down her battered violin from the shelf above John's guitar and the record player. She wiped the thick blanket of dust from the wood and pressed the strings beneath her fingers. Still wearing the old T-shirt she slept in, she pushed the instrument under her chin, flexing her fingers up and down the neck. A bloom of morning sunlight lit the room and she closed her eyes, feeling it warm her skin. Breathing slowly, she lifted the bow. The first few notes were scratchy and self-conscious, her chin was sore, her arm ached. But slowly she found her way into the music that she was making, a clean and mournful song that held love and loss, birth and death, a beginning and an end.

3.5

July 1978

Charlie was leaving the office as Beth turned the corner. She watched him pulling on his coat, a cigarette dangling from his mouth — a flashback to a man that she'd once known. A young woman — blonde, underfed, bright red lipstick — was talking to him with such intensity that for a fleeting second Beth felt like an intruder. Charlie looked over as he zipped up his jacket and, without missing a beat, he stretched his face into a wide grin, lines fanning out around his narrowed eyes. Such a consummate performer, Beth thought, feeling an inexplicable pang of pity for the younger woman whose face was not so well practised in the art of deception.

Charlie waved the blonde girl on and held his arms out wide.

'Beth, you're here! Happy birthday, darling.'

He spoke with a slight slur and as he drew her into his arms she could smell the vodka on him. A red metal cap peeked out of his inside pocket.

'You're drunk, Charlie.'

'What are you talking about? I'm not! Just had an after-work snifter, is all. You know it's practically obligatory.'

He pulled a face, but Beth didn't smile.

He gave a harsh laugh and turned up the collar of his jacket. 'I've booked us a table just around the corner – lovely place, you'll adore it. French, very romantic.'

Their eyes met and she saw that his were already glassy with drink.

Charlie leaned against a bin, lighting another cigarette, his hand cupped around the flame as he pulled the smoke into himself. Beth took a deep breath, deciding to find the good, to make this evening work. After all, he had booked them a table somewhere romantic (though she knew, of course, that it would have been his assistant, not him, who had made the call). She heard the metal scrape of a bottle-cap and saw Charlie tip the clear liquid to his mouth.

'Could you at least get rid of that?' Beth heard herself say in a voice that was her mother's.

Charlie flashed her a dark look, swigged again, then tossed the bottle in the bin. 'There you go,' he said in a tone that made Beth flinch.

A young couple pushed past them and Charlie muttered in annoyance, but deep in conversation the two young people didn't hear.

Beth took his hand and kissed his cheek. 'Shall we start again?'

'OK.'

'OK, well, where are we headed now then?'

Hand in hand they walked through the thrum and bustle of early evening Soho. At a dark-painted restaurant with candles glowing in the window, Charlie stopped and made an elaborate bow. '*Madame* – if you please.'

Beth took his arm and they stepped inside. The air was hot and fragrant, the tables packed tight. A waiter pulled back chairs – 'The window seat, Monsieur, as requested' – and they ordered a bottle of Fleurie. In the candlelight Charlie's eyes were dark, the angles of his face more pronounced. It was funny how the drink did that; the slight changes that could make him someone else. Beth laid down her fork and leaned towards him so the light fell differently across his features and there he was, her Charlie, the person she recognised.

They were on their second bottle of wine by the time dessert arrived. She saw him watching as her breasts strained against her dress and a small smile slid across her face.

'Tell me more about that author – the arty one,' she touched his hand as she spoke.

Charlie lifted his glass and drained the wine in one long draught. 'Roger? Old Ro-jay? He's had quite the life. God, some of the stories he comes out with – there's a whole world out there that we don't know about, Beth.'

He poured more wine and as she lifted her glass Beth realised how drunk she'd become. 'Out where?'

'Here – London. There's another version of this city, you know. One that comes out after dark and is full of sex and iniquity.' He held her gaze.

Her body seemed to grow fuller, warmer as he looked at her. She pressed her thigh against his and he stared at her with such intensity that the room faded around them. Her mouth was dry as she reached for the last of her wine.

'Charlie?'

'Yes?'

'Shall we get the bill?'

They were both unsteady on their feet as they left the restaurant, arms tight about each other. The city had awoken into its vibrant night-time self, the lights along the street glowing brighter than before. Around them, Soho ducked and weaved: a pale girl in an upstairs window, a drag queen smoking by a stage door, an unremarkable man walking out of a sex shop. But hazy with wine and her flaring desire, Beth noticed nothing but Charlie.

When they reached Dean Street, he pointed to a handsome old pub. 'Let's have a nightcap?'

She wrapped her arms around his waist and murmured in his ear. 'But I don't want another drink. I want to fuck.'

Beneath the streetlight, his face seemed to sharpen. He looked at her with a hunger that she didn't recognise as his fingers clasped tight around her wrist. 'I want both. How about we go up there?' he said in a low voice, pointing to an alleyway between two shops.

A potent mixture of anger and disgust made Beth feel suddenly sober. 'No way – God!'

'Aw, come on – don't be a prick-tease.'

Once, that would have made her laugh. But this sinister version of her husband didn't seem to be joking.

'No. Let's just go home.' She unpeeled his fingers from her arm and began walking.

'Come on! Don't be like this.'

He grabbed for her hand, but she pulled it away and kept moving.

She turned down a side street and he ran to catch up with her.

He caught her wrist. 'Slow down a minute, Beth. Let's just—'

'I don't want to! Let go of me!'

He wrenched her arm hard then, twisting it, and she let out a cry of pain. She looked at her arm, then at Charlie, her face cracked wide open with shock.

'Oh my God, I'm sorry, I'm sorry.'

A livid mark wreathed her wrist.

She stared at him, her fingertips moving from her forearm to her parted lips, pressing her eyes shut as she spoke with quiet precision. 'I'm leaving now.'

Across the street, music blared from the doorway of a bar and Charlie staggered in, the bouncers casting a doubtful glance, but waving him through. In a dark corner he drank until the room span, but even then the images still came.

He woke up on the sofa in their living room, with no memory of how he'd got home. His wallet and pockets were empty of cash and a half-drunk can of lager sat on the coffee table. His body hurt all over, as it had after Annie's funeral and his run-in with Ben. He wondered whether he'd been fighting last night. Then, in a vertiginous sweep, he saw it all in montage: the warm restaurant; walking through Soho; the glow of the pub; Beth's look of disgust; the purple welt on her wrist that he had made. He thought of the things that she didn't know – the secret phone calls to Alexa from the payphone near his office, a second meeting, a third, all with the same desperate ending. He told himself he was in the thrall of forces beyond his control; that it meant nothing; that what Beth didn't know couldn't hurt her. But in the silence of his own head, he knew these were lies so flimsy that they couldn't withstand even his own biased scrutiny. Was that who he'd become?

He pulled his knees into his chest and screwed his eyes shut. Beth found him an hour later, still curled up in a foetal position. The mark on her wrist had faded to two violet fingerprint bruises.

He reached out to touch them, but he couldn't raise his eyes to her. 'I'm so sorry.'

She spoke in an even tone. 'You need to sort yourself out, or I'm going to leave.'

He nodded to show that he understood.

Outside the window the sky was layered in thick clouds that dulled everything below. Beth watched them move slowly across the sky and wondered what would happen if the world stayed this grey forever.

3.6

August 1978

'Ah!' said Stella. 'Here we are.'

The stone face of the college loomed above them, a line of mullioned windows along its front. John peered into the quad through the huge studded door. A baize-smooth lawn was overlooked on all sides by high sand-coloured walls, with low stone arches at intervals around its edge.

'That was my room,' Stella pointed to a window, three across from the far right corner, 'in the first year, at least. That was the girls' staircase.'

There hadn't been many women there then, she laughed. The college had only gone co-ed a few years before, much to the distaste of some of the older dons.

She lifted Hope from her hip and handed her to John. 'Here, you take her through while I go and speak to the porters. I'm not sure what they'll think about having a baby in the place.'

A contemporary of Stella's, now a junior lecturer at the college, had offered his room as a place to stay for a weekend while he was away for the summer. She had accepted at once. Time away together would be just what they needed.

As Stella talked with the porters, John sidled into the quad with Hope and their bag of belongings.

'This way,' Stella whispered as she returned from the lodge, lifting Hope from John's arms and heading towards one of the arches.

It was strange to be back, she thought, as she stood a while later beneath the domed shadow of the Radcliffe Camera. It was as if she had been split in two. Here she was memory: the hopeful finalist looking ahead to the bright path of her future. Here she was shadow: the new mother wondering if she'd ever find that path again. Funny to think that if she had stayed at Oxford, as her tutor had wanted, she would have never met John. Closing her eyes she could hear the old don's voice. *You'll regret it if you leave, Stella.* But of course she didn't – couldn't – regret all that had happened since.

John was standing by the railings with Hope in the crook of his arm, his other hand shielding his eyes from the glare of the dropping sun. 'Stella? Shall we go and find somewhere to eat?'

She walked towards them, slipping her hand into his and leaning in to sniff the scent of Hope's warm head. *How lucky I have been*, she thought, trying to ignore the echo of her tutor's warning words.

In a pub by the river Stella sipped a shandy as she fed Hope beneath her T-shirt, her bright mood slipping away. From across the table John noticed how thin her face had become, the dark rings beneath her eyes, the tense grip of her jaw. He wished he knew what to say, but words felt dangerous nowadays; a misplaced question could light a fuse and Stella

would flare with a sudden chaos of emotions that he had
no idea how to tame. Easier, he thought, to weather the low
than risk a tempest. God, that sounded like something his
father would say.

He placed his hands upon the table. 'Right. Won't be a
sec – just got to use the phone.'

Stella lifted her head, her mouth tight with disapproval.
'Why do you need to do that?'

He considered a lie for a moment, but then he reasoned
she might think he was having an affair. Better to tell the
truth and hope that her rational mind would prevail. 'I've
got to phone the lab. Check on a few results.'

Her mouth opened, then shut. She pulled her free hand
across her face and let out a sigh. 'Isn't it a bit late in the
day? No one's going to be there at this time, surely?'

'Oh, quite a few of them will be – it's at an exciting stage.
It looks like we're about to disprove the local hidden variable
theory, which . . .'

A flash of anger passed across her face, but faded into a
look of resignation he'd not seen before: flat and empty, as
if she'd been deflated.

'OK. We'll wait for you here.'

Inside the pub, the barman pointed him to a payphone
and he slotted in two coins, dialling the number he knew
by heart, grateful to have avoided a row.

The conversation was brief, results so far inconclusive,
but when he returned, Stella was wrapping Hope into the
sling. She didn't look up.

'Nothing to report. It's quite frustrating, actually – I was
really expecting something to come of this version, but it
looks as if we'll need to rethink the parameters, or maybe

the entire hypothesis, which would be a complete pain. Oh
– Stella? What is it?'

She had sat down with a thud on the wooden bench, her
arms around the baby. At his question she looked up at him
blankly, the empty expression deadening her eyes. 'I thought
this was a good idea, but it's not.'

'What's not? Stel?'

She grasped his hand, shaking her head from side to side.
'Coming here, to Oxford – it feels all wrong – it feels sad.
All that promise, all those hopes and now what am I? Your
housewife, that's what. Always in the shadow of your bloody
work. It's not what I signed up for, John.'

Clasping her hand he knelt down in front of her. 'Stella,
you won't always be at home. As soon as Hope is old enough,
we'll find a childminder and you can get back to your thesis.
I promise.'

He saw her soften slightly and she leaned into his chest,
their sleeping baby between them.

'Promise?'

'I do. Now, come on – let's go back to the college. You
can tell me stories of your blue-stocking past. Or was it
naughtier than that?' He lifted his eyebrows, trying to make
her laugh.

Stella smiled weakly, but shook her head. 'No. Let's go
home. Back to London.'

He thought of the short trip back on the train, the
warm slice of underground from Paddington to Kilburn
Park, a stroll along the High Road to their flat. It would
give him tomorrow. Perhaps he could go into the office.
Sundays were his favourite day for working and there was
so much he needed to get done. Now wouldn't be the

right time, of course, but perhaps later he would talk to her about it.

'OK,' he said, as they stood up.

They walked out of the pub and flagged down a cab, pausing at the college to collect their bag on the way to the station.

Passing through the back-end of Ladbroke Grove, where high-rise apartments loomed above the train track, John mentioned he'd like to stop by the office the next day.

Stella turned back from the window. 'Are you joking?'

John smiled and shrugged, trying to buy time.

'It's not funny, John! How can you even ask?'

'But what? I just thought since we're going to be in London that I could use the time constructively.'

'*Constructively?*'

Exasperated, Stella took him by the shoulders, looking hard into his face. 'But can't you see,' she asked him as the train drew into Paddington, 'that I need you to stay with me?'

Stung by her anger and unsettled by the whip of her emotions, John closed his eyes. Why didn't she understand that he had to do this? It was not a choice. His research was at a critical stage where every second counted; he had to make sure it was right. Why couldn't she see?

Hope started to wail as the train jolted to a halt.

The station was noisy and hot. Between her sandal straps, black grime caked Stella's sweaty feet as she struggled along the busy platform with Hope clutched to her chest. A rush of new passengers surged towards them and John took

Stella's hand, leading her through the melee. One of the worst things about being short, she thought, is that in a crowd everyone assumes you're a gap and heads your way, so that you end up knocked this way and that like a pinball on the bumpers. Grateful for the clean path John's height cut through the mass of people, she held his hand tight and when they emerged into the concourse she wrapped her arms around his waist, standing on tiptoe to kiss him above the baby's head.

'We're going to be OK,' she said with a faint smile. 'It's supposed to be hard.'

Looking down at his small family, John nodded. He knew somehow that Stella was right, that they would work it out eventually; but even so, he couldn't help but wonder how long it would take for him to navigate this strange new terrain.

Waiting beneath the pigeon-fouled fronds of the clock, Charlie saw them: a sandy-haired man and a pale woman wearing a baby in a sling. He watched as they spoke, noticing how their serious faces softened for each other. He imagined their roots running deep beneath them, a shared life that secured them to each other, a child they both loved. From where he stood it looked simple, a world apart from his life now, where each day was coiled with guilt and fury and each month brought new loss. An image of Beth weeping on the bathroom floor flickered into his mind. His stomach turned as he felt the rush of an urge to go back home to her, to overcome this reckless need for otherness. When Beth had chosen to be with him despite her parents' objections, she had made it seem effortless, as if she'd always

known where she belonged. Charlie watched the crowds of
people weaving through the station, a chaos of bodies and
movement in which everyone but him seemed certain of
where they were going.

The young couple descended the steps to the Tube. The
minute hand on the station clock clicked. He would go. Lifting
his bag onto his shoulder, he turned to see Alexa walking
towards him, Titian hair loose, her expression serene.

'You're leaving,' she said. A statement, without reproach
or panic.

'No, I just – uh. Oh, you look so beautiful.' He caught
her waist in his hands. She was like a slender stem, firm
but tender. He held her closer, feeling her thin body against
him, so different from Beth's warm curves. *It should be simple.*
But it was not. His body seemed to be thinking for him as
he pressed his mouth to hers, gently at first and then with
a growing hunger.

'Charlie?' Alexa leaned away, a rare flush of colour in her
cheeks. In the pale blue of her eyes, Charlie saw a world
transformed: loss and pain dissolving to a singular point of
perfection. She kissed him again and he felt everything else
slide away: the young family he had seen, Beth and the
future, the many losses of the past. His thoughts spun and
receded, lifting high into the air and into the swirling station
dust. In that moment he wanted only the blankness that
Alexa brought: a togetherness unsullied by the thousand
tiny disappointments of everyday life.

3.7

October 1978

Beth had always supposed that suspicion was a gradual arrival, a crescendo of many wrongs. But when she found Alexa's note, she discovered it was more like a collision. A sudden and irreversible reconfiguring of the world. A folded square of paper slipped in Charlie's jacket pocket. Intimate words signed off with: *Your Alexa x*. Winded, Beth lowered herself onto the hallway floor. She felt in her pocket for the result slip she'd brought home from the hospital, stamped with a plus sign and the word 'POSITIVE' in capital letters. How different life had seemed for those few hours, before this cruel new twist. She turned the slip over and looked at the names she'd scratched on her way back: William for a boy, Annie for a girl.

The blood began to throb in her temple and she pressed the bridge of her nose, willing the headache away. Alexa's sparse handwriting was spread across the paper in blue ink, taunting Beth with the thoughts she'd not dared to think about Charlie's late nights. She clambered back onto her feet and pushed the study door. On Charlie's desk she saw a pile of photos – publicity shots for a book jacket – and staring up at her she saw a girl she knew must be

Alexa, with long red hair and white skin, her blue eyes cold.

Beth toyed with the idea of travelling against the tide of home-bound commuters, struggling into Soho to meet him from the office. But it would be too public and Charlie would be putting on his workplace act. She would wait until he arrived home, even though that meant he'd have been drinking. Most evenings now he spent at parties or launches or dinners where alcohol flowed freely from expense accounts. *Networking*, Charlie called it. But that night he came home sober, carrying a stack of typescripts in his bag and a paper package of fish and chips under his arm.

Beth stepped into the kitchen, where Charlie was unwrapping the steaming newspaper. He looked up at her and held out a two-pronged wooden fork. 'Fish supper?'

'Charlie.'

He noticed then her unsmiling gaze, the crossed arms, the clenched fists. 'Beth, love, is everything alright?'

'Charlie, what's going on?'

His face paled. He put the chip fork down. 'With what?'

'With Alexa.'

'I – I'm not sure what you—'

Unfortunate as it was, Charlie had a nervous habit of laughing when he was uneasy, and a strangled chortle emerged as he struggled to think of how to reply.

Beth sucked in a lungful of air and slapped the note in front of him. 'Are you – or are you not – having an affair with Alexa Godfrey?'

The sunflowers floated in the centre of her eyes, yellow blooms in the midst of green, tears gathering below. He knew he couldn't lie. He sat down, closed his eyes, and told her everything.

She struggled from the chair gasping for breath, slamming the bedroom door in his face. What hurt most was not that he had slept with this woman. It had been a dreadful year, the loss of Annie and Limpet still circled their lives, inescapable as the boarded-up pub they passed on the High Road. In the face of so much loss, she could understand the reckless carnal urge. But the deep deception and secret intimacy, these were violations so sharp it made it hard for her to breathe. All those moments that belonged to another woman. An ugly ball of hatred rose inside her and she held onto it for long enough to picture pushing Alexa underneath a train, then felt sick with shame. Why do the women always get the blame? The person at fault here was Charlie. Oh Charlie. All those months she'd spent in Montpellier and he had stayed faithful – which was more than could be said for her. Although, to be fair, one drunken night with a student from Marseilles didn't really measure up to this. Why did he have to prove her parents right? They'd always been uneasy about him – she'd thought that it was because he wasn't Jewish, but now she wondered if perhaps they'd seen something else. An unsteadiness of the soul? His burgeoning drinking problem? Well, whatever it was, she didn't want their sympathy, but she did want somewhere to go so she could work out what would happen next.

After she'd left, her clothes stuffed in an old army rucksack, a cab waiting outside, Charlie walked to the off-licence on the corner. He bought twenty cigarettes and a bottle of whisky, steadily working his way through both until his eyes would not stay open. Too unstable on his feet to walk to the bedroom, he laid his head on the table next to the untouched fish supper and slept. When he woke, a cold chip had stuck to his cheek. He peeled it off and ate it, glancing groggily at the clock above the sideboard: 8 a.m. Bloody hell. Heaving himself out of the chair he walked stiffly to the bathroom and turned on the shower to get ready for work.

The rumble of the Tube felt like an earthquake and the heat seemed to be closing in on him. He could sense that any minute disaster would strike, a giant explosion, a fireball, a burnt-out train wheeling through the station carrying only blackened bodies. The alcohol had blurred the edges of the world, but left his mouth sticky and foul-tasting. He concentrated on feeling sober. The train rocked and he tried to focus on the grubby copy of yesterday's *Evening Standard* that he'd lifted from beneath his shoes, but the words just wouldn't stay still. Already he could feel it, the creeping disgust. He stared at the reflection curving in the Tube window opposite him, the pale skin and black-ringed eyes, sickly beneath the yellow carriage light. Across from him a woman with braided hair polished her shoes with a paper hanky, a leather briefcase on the seat beside her. Further down, three young men sat with their elbows on their knees, rubbing their faces and muttering in low undertones, the occasional laugh breaking free from their huddle. It was hot in the carriage and the sobriety Charlie had felt on the walk from his flat had gone. Now he was muzzy with alcohol, sleeplessness and the disorienting pulse of incipient nausea.

*

Luckily for him, Genevieve had a morning meeting at a publisher's office on the other side of town, so the only people to raise an eyebrow at the state he was in were the two other junior agents with whom he shared an office.

'Heavy night?' Annabel had asked with a wink, tucking her black hair behind her ears.

'Something like that,' croaked Charlie.

Andrew screwed up his nose, waving his hand in front of him. 'Eugh. I can smell you from here, mate. Smells like you've been pickled in rum.'

'Whisky, actually. Is the coffee on?'

'Tell you what, Charlie,' Annabel yawned as she stretched her arms above her head, 'I'll get you some. Andrew? Fancy a cup?'

'Yeah – thanks, that'd be great.'

After she'd gone into the kitchen, Andrew lowered his voice. 'Woman trouble, is it?'

Charlie looked at his face, at the sly slant of his eyebrows, and knew that he knew about Alexa. How many of them had figured it out? he wondered. But he couldn't bring himself to ask. 'Just a rough one, Andy – nothing juicy here . . . Would you pass me the Rolodex? I've got a few calls I need to make.'

Andrew stared at him for a few seconds longer and Charlie shrugged, pulling a clownish face. 'I know, I know, I look a right state. Now would you be a brick and chuck it here? I think I'll keel over if I stand up too fast today.'

After a couple of drinks that evening – *'Hair of the dog, mate, it'll sort you right out!'* – Charlie left Andrew and Annabel in the pub and headed back home. The light was beginning to fade as he emerged from the Tube at West Hampstead and he was surprised by how unsteady he was on his feet. The shop fronts glowed as people moved around one another on their way home. Everywhere he looked people were going back to a place they knew they belonged, a place where they were rooted, one strand in a system of many lives. He pushed his front door open and picked his way across the filthy hallway. The fridge was almost empty and the plates were all still in a festering stack, but he found a packet of cream crackers and some meat paste, which he ate standing over the sink.

He dialled the number of his in-laws. Beth must have hated having to turn to them, but he knew she would never have allowed herself to be vulnerable in front of her friends. Strange how women are like that, Charlie thought. Kind to each other and yet always sniffing for blood.

His wife's familiar North London voice answered. 'Hello?'

'Beth?'

'Charlie. What do you want?'

'Oh Beth, don't, please. Can we talk?'

'Charlie, I – I don't want to talk to you now.'

She spoke with a new hardness and as he pleaded for forgiveness he felt a sudden bolt of bleakness spread inside. *I could really lose her.*

She sighed. 'Charlie this isn't just about Alexa. It's about everything. Your drinking – the lies – it's no way to live a life and it's certainly no way to raise a child.'

The line hummed and Charlie could hear his breath echoing back at him. 'Beth, what are you saying? You're—?'

Her voice was thick with tears. 'Yes, Charlie, I'm pregnant.'

'But Beth, that's wonderful! A baby! – it's – I can change for the baby, honestly, you'll see.'

On the other end, Beth stayed silent.

'Beth, I love you,' Charlie pleaded, the words slurring as his voice grew louder. 'Please, you've got to come back.'

Her voice, when she answered, was cold.

'I tell you what, Charlie. Let's talk about this when you're sober.'

He tried to object, to explain, but he could hear Beth's anger flaring with each attempt and he knew that it was pointless – dangerous even – to lie.

Beth sighed, then cleared her throat. 'Another time, Charlie,' she said. And then the line went dead.

There was an expression that his mother used to use when her patience (never known for being very long) was growing thin. *You're sailing close to the wind, Charlie-boy.* He knew he was too close for comfort now. He crouched down on the floor, waiting for the angry chatter to begin in his head, the ongoing critique of his life as he lived it. Charlie drew his knees tight into his chest and pressed his fists against his eyes, trying to push away the images that passed behind them.

In her parents' house in Belsize Park, Beth set the receiver down as gently as she could, but the quiet chime of the ringer was enough to bring her mother into the hallway. Jenna Colman was a well-preserved woman in her fifties, who prided herself on doing things in the right way. She was constantly on the move, talking ten to the dozen and always busy with family, friends and food. Respected and well liked, she was proud of her children. Her two sons had married well, but Beth – ah, what a mess that had been. Typical Beth, the youngest child, always wanting to be different, to push the boundaries. The fact that Charlie wasn't Jewish, that they could live with. But this drunkenness? This betrayal? It was beyond acceptable. She looked at Beth, who was hunched on the bottom stair. Every fibre in Jenna's body strained with the desire to say something to make her daughter better. She could feel the words jostling to come out, but she bit her tongue. With a deliberate slowness, as if she were approaching a frightened animal, she moved towards the staircase and lowered herself to sit. She took Beth's hand and kissed it. Leaning against each other, the two women sat in silence, listening to the creak of the old house as inside Beth a cluster of cells continued to divide.

At lunchtime the next day, Charlie walked two streets away to use the phone box. It had a piss-stained floor, with post-cards tucked around the walls. *Sexy red-head loves good time . . . Have you been a bad boy? . . . Busty model at your service.* He dropped in a coin and dialled Beth's parents' number, but nobody answered. The coin clattered out and he slotted it in again and dialled Alexa.

She answered in her calm clear tone and Charlie felt a flood of panic pass across him.

'It's me.'

'Oh. Hi, Charlie.'

There was a pause. Charlie felt the smell of urine catch in the back of his throat and a trickle of sweat run from his armpit. 'I needed to speak to you – it's just – well, Beth knows. She found out about us.'

'OK.'

The words were coming fast now, and in her silence they seemed to rush ahead of him, beyond his control. 'And so,

Alexa, I think it's got to end – I just – I can't – the baby, you know. Oh God, I'm sorry – this is – well, not how it was supposed to go.'

'OK Charlie. I understand. If that's the way it has to be, then I accept that.'

He marvelled at the smooth coolness of her voice, her quiet confidence. 'Alexa – I'm sorry.'

Silence. The slightest breath.

'Alexa?'

'Thank you, Charlie, for everything. I have to go now.'

Charlie felt the sickness lurch within him. He leaned his head against the glass panes of the phone box. 'I . . .'

'Goodbye, Charlie.' She hung up.

Alexa's letter arrived a week after he'd broken things off. He tore it open late that night, after an evening that had started with a civilised post-meeting drink and ended trawling the bars in Soho long after closing time. With one eye shut, he read her sparse writing. She'd sacked him as her agent, of course; no more than he deserved. He sighed and felt for his cigarettes in his jacket pocket, pushing the front door shut behind him. Stumbling, he lurched along the hallway and into the kitchen, turned on the gas and filled a saucepan with water to boil. He scraped the hard crust of instant coffee from the bottom of the jar and shook it into a mug, then rolled the letter into a point and held it to the blue flame on the stove until it flared orange. The black smoke billowed upwards as bright tongues snaked along the whiteness, blackening the paper before it was consumed. He held it up to light his cigarette, then dropped the final burning scrap into the sink.

4.

NON-LOCALITY

1979–1986

Even when separated by an arbitrarily large distance, entangled particles cannot be described independently: measuring the quantum state of one particle instantaneously defines the other, despite the distance between them.

McKearnan, L. Quantum Entanglement. Paradox Publishing, 1982 (p.75)

4.1

April 1979

On her way to the Royal Institution, Stella saw them: a tall man with a loping stride and a backpack; a young woman with gold-streaked hair and a pile of books beneath her arm. Even from that distance the buzz of pheromones was tangible, a chemical gauze between their world and hers. Stella tugged at the gusset of her tights, imagining how ungainly she must look, her dress stretched tight across her post-baby bosom, wobbling in the high-heeled shoes she never wore, her hair falling from its pins. It was so recently that she and John had been like that young couple: free to walk in the London twilight, talking about research plans and high ideals, drunk on one another and cheap student beer. And now she was here: the formless helpmeet to John's rising star, uncomfortable in an old velvet dress, on her way to bear witness to his latest triumph: the Fitzpatrick Medal for Physics.

In the light of the ballroom chandelier, a string of baby-mucus shimmered on Stella's sleeve. Around the room John's colleagues stood poised in evening dress, champagne glasses already on their second or third refilling. John was

leaning against a wall in the far corner, a slender woman
in a navy ball gown standing slightly too close, her head
tipped to one side, a strand of chestnut hair falling onto
her face. He glanced up and touched the woman's elbow
to excuse himself, weaving through the room towards
Stella. Relief and anger grappled as she watched him nod
and greet his colleagues, a fraternity to which she could
never belong, even if she'd wanted to.

When she thought back to that time, Stella preferred not
to remember the rows and the sniping, fuelled so often by
the biting sense that she was disappearing from the world
while John pushed on and made his mark. That evening
could easily have bloomed into a fight – her feet were
twitching to run away, the blood rushing in her ears as she
watched those people so full of purpose talking about their
work. But when John reached her, he leaned in close and
whispered 'Shall we go?' and as he spun her around and
out of the door into the chill spring night – well, what could
she do then, but laugh?

'But John, your medal!'

John shook his head and slung his arm around her shoulders. 'It's just a medal, Stels. It's the work that I care about.
And besides, when was the last time we had a night out?'

They walked across Green Park and along the Mall,
hurrying through the chaos of Trafalgar Square – 'A glori-
fied roundabout overrun with pigeons!' said John, as they
turned onto the Strand. A flight of stone steps took them
down to the Embankment and they leaned against the river
wall watching the filigree lights of London reflected on the
water.

'So, Stels . . . what's it to be?'

'What d'you mean?'

'A drink in the pub? . . . a walk in the park? . . . the world is our oyster for one night only.'

Stella thought of Hope in her striped pink and purple sleepsuit, the fuzz of her hair, the clasp of her plump little fingers.

'Can we just take the Tube somewhere?'

'Where?'

'I don't know . . . Anywhere . . . let's just go down into the warm. I'm bloody freezing in this dress.'

He smiled and set off towards the station, the red, blue and white of the Underground's roundel glowing like a beacon in the darkness.

For two hours they sat, knees touching in the rattle and warmth of a brightly lit carriage, sharing a corned beef sandwich washed down with swigs of whisky, as London came and went. At South Kensington, a rabble of students tumbled in, sucking on cigarettes and shouting to each other about politics. At Gloucester Road, the grey-haired man who'd been sitting opposite stood up and extended an arm for his wife, and she looked at him with such tenderness that for a moment Stella could see the young woman she had once been. The students piled off at the following station and Stella watched them as they swarmed across the platform, still arguing. She closed her eyes, resting her head on John's shoulder as the train rattled on around the Circle line.

Surfacing later at Kilburn Park, opposite a row of neglected Victorian villas, John wrapped his jacket around Stella's shoulders. A little way ahead, a dark-haired man stumbled out of an alleyway. His feet fell in an uneven line across the pavement, an empty bottle swinging from one hand. When he reached the boarded front of Biddy Murphy's, he sank to his knees, resting his head against the peeling bill posters that had been pasted across it. Stella turned away from the bombed-out front, not wanting to remember. John squeezed her shoulder as they passed the drunken man, who had begun to mutter at the wall, a litany of names and fragmented thoughts, reaching a crescendo at last with a howl that echoed behind him and along the empty High Road. *I'm sorry, I'm sorry, I'm sorry.*

When they arrived home, Stella's mother was asleep on the pull-out bed in the living room, Hope tucked in alongside her. Watching her mother and her sleeping child, Stella tried to take a photograph with her mind: to commit that evening into memory, as a keepsake of its simple joy. John's arms reached around her waist, pulling her into their bedroom, where lime leaves cast their shadows against the orange streetlamp glow, the floorboards creaked underfoot and everything for just that moment seemed exactly as it should.

4.2

June 1979

A wash of sunlight from the undrawn curtains woke him. Charlie sat up, leaning across the nameless kohl-eyed girl he'd brought home from the launch party to pour himself a drink. At the back of his throat he caught the smell of whisky residue and unwashed laundry, and with a slow press of discomfort he realised what he'd become. The callow skin, the trembling hands, the fug of drink beneath his aftershave. Beth still loved him, she had said so the other day, but she saw all this too. He remembered how her eyes had darted away, her hands clasped around the swell of her belly, and he knew that he would lose her and the baby if he carried on like this. He put down the glass and pulled on his clothes, leaving the girl asleep in his bed. He walked as the sun rose higher, hazy above the dirty city air . . . Finchley Road, St John's Wood, Abbey Road, Regent's Park. The day grew hot, his head ached and his guts turned, but something inside him had shifted, a tiny crack of light. He knew what he needed to do.

A few days later, he sat between an old soldier and a young housewife at his first meeting, aware of the distant sound of his own voice as he said the words out loud. *I'm an alcoholic.* Afterwards, he sat in Queen's Park, feeling the red warmth of the sun against his closed eyes as he listened to the sing-song stream of words of a mother talking to her child. Blinking at the glare, he turned and saw the young woman, her light brown hair glinting gold as she swung the toddler into the air. A man called out and loped over to her, ice cream melting from the cones he was carrying. The toddler shrieked with delight and they sat in a tiny circle of three, oblivious to the busy park around them. Charlie thought of Beth, of the baby that was due in a few short weeks and felt it again, the infinitesimal shift inside. As the young family left the park, he closed his eyes and made a promise to his unborn baby. *You will have the best of everything.*

As they walked the few streets to their flat – Hope sticky with ice cream – Stella thought of the summer that they had ahead of them and smiled. Hope would grow, and their family would too. They were finding their way together.

Later, when John was cleaning the chocolate smears from Hope's face, Stella heard him shout.

'What?' she snapped from the other room, irritated by his distaste for bodily fluids, or muck of any kind, a discomfort that led to frenzied swabbing of breakfast-time spillages or intimate autopsies of the soles of dog-fouled shoes.

In the kitchen, John was sitting in a sunny corner, his face pressed against Hope's wispy hair, his skin pale as wax. 'Stella, something happened.'

There was a slur to his voice, a dreamy quality, as if he

had just woken up. Taking Hope from him, Stella tried to find a gentler tone, grappling with the shrillness rising inside her. 'What is it, love? Are you OK?'

'Something strange has happened. Things – they don't feel right. I'm making strange connections in my head. It's hard to explain. I don't know. It's wrong, though, Stella. Something is wrong.'

'Breathe, John. Slowly now,' Stella said as she stroked his arm. He drew a breath and she composed herself, speaking in a voice that didn't feel like her own.

'Can you tell me more? About these connections?'

He stayed still, eyes squeezed shut, and said nothing.

'Are you seeing things? Hearing voices?'

John's eyes widened. 'Stella. I'm not going mad . . . it's physiological.' *Typical scientist*, she thought, *it has to be a material flaw.* 'Something's misfiring – like synaesthesia but more, I don't know, random. The smell of petrol belongs to the texture of bricks, that cloud sounds like Jimi Hendrix's wah-wah pedal.' He stopped talking and looked at her, his blue eyes sharp. She touched his shoulder.

'Come and lie down for a bit. I'll make you a cup of tea.'

An hour or so later he was reading to Hope as if nothing had happened. Stella watched from the doorway of the bedroom, the small girl enfolded in her father's long limbs, both of them staring with deep concentration at the pages of a picture book. He'd always been a bit of a hypochondriac, she thought, and felt herself begin to relax a little as she started cooking the dinner.

But that night, she woke to John's moans. Soaked with sweat, he lay tangled in the bed sheets.

'John?'

He jolted upright. 'Stella! Where am I? Where is this? I don't – I don't know where I am!'

'Shh, love, shhh – you're here, in Kilburn – in our flat. Shh, it's OK.'

Time passed. The light crept in through the half-shut curtains, sketching the room in pencil tones, while Stella slipped in and out of a jagged sleep. At 6 a.m. she called the doctor. The baby was still asleep when he arrived, a kind-faced man with thick white hair swept low across his black-rimmed glasses. He sat in the wicker chair by the bed and spoke in a soft Northern Irish accent, listening to the sounds that John was making, sounds that seemed to Stella to belong to a time before words.

The doctor turned to her and started to speak. 'These things are hard to diagnose, Mrs Greenwood . . .' he began.

John believed that up to a point everything could be explained; that every action has an equal and opposite reaction; that what goes up must come down, subject to the gravitational force upon it. Forces were not mysterious or unseen, they were the connections essential to life – the cables and power on which we all run. Circuitry, not wizardry, that's what life boils down to. Find the connections and the answer will follow. Humanity, he never tired of saying, was so self-important that it refused to accept that there were things that, though predictable, simply could not be understood. That you might discover the how, but never know the why. But this not-knowing is OK – it's fine! It's perhaps the ultimate state of truthfulness. To suggest, as a scientist, that some truths were unknowable, rarely won him friends. But John was adamant that one day he would find the language that he needed.

For a moment in the aura before the seizure, John met a Frankenstein's monster of taste, smell and sentiment. The tangerine flavour of a midsummer's day, the sensation of his mother's arms about him, the scratch and snag of a boiled sweet swallowed whole, it all rushed in Technicolor behind his eyes as he writhed and sweated in his delirium, convinced that he had found the formula for his unknowable truth.

But when he opened his mouth to speak, it was Stella's name he heard. 'Stella? Stella! I need you!'

John stared with frightened eyes at the white-haired doctor in his cardigan and tie and gripped the older man's hand. Then, with a sudden spasm, his eyes rolled back in his head and his body started to convulse. A trickle of blood ran from his mouth as his teeth bit down hard upon the soft muscle of his tongue.

With the calmness that comes only from a lifetime of practice, the old doctor turned to Stella and spoke in a gentle voice. 'Don't worry, my dear, I'll make sure he's OK – we just need to wait until the fitting has stopped and then we'll make him comfortable. On you go now and call us an ambulance.'

She could hear Hope starting to babble as her shaking hands pulled at the numbers. Each rattling return of the dial seemed to take longer than the last.

The paramedics carried John out in a seated stretcher, like a sedan chair. His eyes had opened, but he had staggered like a newborn foal when he tried to stand up. The doctor

drove Stella and Hope in his car, tailing the ambulance
through the quiet early-morning streets and up the big hill
to Hampstead. From the ambulance, John was lifted onto a
trolley and wheeled into the hospital, while Stella ran behind,
clutching Hope to her hip. Dog-eared posters hung from a
noticeboard as the bed was rolled along the corridor beneath
the erratic blink of striplights. Further along, Stella saw a
woman standing with her head against the wall, her hand
on the shoulder of a thickset man who was slumped on a
bench, his chin propped on his mottled pink hand. They did
not move as the trolley rumbled past.

On the ward, white-aproned nurses and unsmiling doctors
paced from patient to patient. In the bed opposite, a tiny
old lady with white hair standing up in clumps was propped
up on pillows. Her covers had been thrown off to reveal a
torn white nightgown with a bloodstain on the hem and
the crêpe-like skin on her arms swung as she stabbed her
finger at the middle-aged woman – her daughter, Stella
assumed – who sat at the end of her bed. The younger
woman stood and rattled the drawer of the bedside cabinet.
She shook her head, said something to the woman who was
probably her mother, and walked out, her hands balled into
fists.

A kind-faced nurse took Hope and placed her hand on
Stella's shoulder, speaking in quiet Caribbean tones. 'Have
a minute with him, sweetheart. I'll mind the baby.'

Sitting in the plastic-coated chair, Stella touched John's
clammy hand. 'John – it's me.'

His eyes snapped open, intense but somehow empty.

'It's Stella – John? Do you know who I am?'

His face creased with confusion and then dropped back

to blankness. He shook his head. 'I – I don't know. I don't know you.'

'John? It's me, Stella, your wife.'

'Am I called John?'

His face was so fearful and childlike that it took a moment for Stella to register the rising horror in her own chest, the tears that were running down her hot cheeks. She leaned in to kiss him, but he flinched and moved away. Her fingers brushed his cheek and she turned and walked back to the nurse who was holding their child.

A virus, the neurologist said, had caused swelling in the brain.

'But how?' Stella wanted to know, and what, and when did he catch it?

But the doctor shook her head. 'It's hard to say. A common virus could have gone to his brain – it's rare but it does happen. I'm sorry to say, Mrs Greenwood, it's just very bad luck.'

'But he will get better, won't he?'

The doctor paused and Stella saw her fingers pressing tighter around John's notes.

'We'll have to see,' she said. There were scans and tests that needed to be run, anti-virals to administer and time was needed. Only time would tell.

Sitting by him as he slept, Stella listened to the ward: the quiet voices, the creak of springs, the rustle of sheets. At one end of the small ward, there was a trolley with a sighing urn of tea; at the other, a small sink with a dripping tap. How quickly John had become an inmate of this vast institution, sucked forwards and back, like flotsam on an indifferent tide. The pinprick of a repeated shriek drew Stella back from her thought-flight into the ward.

'No – no – no!'

The ragged voice of the old woman opposite reached a crescendo and then broke into a pitiful lowing, met by the squeak of rubber shoes across the plastic floor. Stella watched the rise and fall of John's bare chest, the slow drip of fluids into his arm, the flicker of his closed eyes and for one treacherous second she felt the chilling fingers of a thought she'd never met before. *What if he dies?*

4.3

July 1979

On his twenty-ninth day sober, Charlie was woken by the phone bleating in the kitchen. He stumbled to answer it, catching his toe on the table leg as he did. 'Bloody hell!'

'Charlie?' came the voice from the other end of the line.

'Beth? Sorry! Sorry, I – well – never mind. Are you OK?'

'Charlie, I'm in labour.'

'Oh! Oh my God!'

'Contractions since last night – it's been hours now—'

'Should I . . . ?'

The question hung on his lips. For the last month, Beth had met him twice a week and each time was a little easier than the last. A hair's width, a finger's width; with each day that passed, Charlie had felt the chink inside him widen, heard the hardness pass from Beth's voice. But it had all felt too fragile to bring up what would happen when the baby arrived. She had not said that she wanted him there.

There was a long pause, then a groan.

'Mum and Dad are going to take me to the hospital. But I . . .' Another pause, another groan. 'I thought you should – kn – oh!'

'Beth! Beth! Are you OK?'

'No, I'm not – it fucking hurts!'

'Do you – shall I—?'

'What are you talking about?'

'Shall I come?'

'Yes, Charlie. Come to the hospital! I've got to go, they're coming fast now.'

The line went dead.

'Fuck!' Charlie shouted into the phone's receiver.

Their baby was coming, a tiny piece of life, a tiny piece of hope. Charlie got in the shower and washed and shaved. He put on clean clothes and ran out of the flat. The day seemed to spin around him. Where were all these people going? A double-decker bus nosed its way along the curve of the road, a small girl's face pressed against the window. A crocodile of schoolchildren walked in front of him, a line of clasped hands and warbling noise. Everywhere, people were oblivious to the crack running right through his centre, the flood of lightness that was lifting him above all this everyday life. It is unimaginable that this could be an ordinary day for anyone, he thought, as he jogged down the hill to the station.

He emerged from the train at Hampstead Heath and walked along the tidy row of shops, stopping to buy a net of oranges from the greengrocer and a paper from the newsagent next door. Around the corner, the hospital loomed, a stern cube on the side of the hill.

Lights blazed along windowless corridors shiny with new plastic flooring and Charlie tried to appear confident as he strode towards the lifts, oranges and newspaper tucked under his arm. He pressed the button for the third floor and saw a man in a beige sports jacket step out of the neighbouring lift, a salt-and-pepper-haired woman on his arm – Beth's parents. He jabbed the button three times in quick succession and when the doors clanged shut he realised that he'd been holding his breath. Even the lift seemed to sigh with relief as it heaved itself upwards.

Charlie hurried through the blank angles of the hospital corridor to a desk where a young nurse sipped a chipped mug of pale coffee, a pile of thick patient notes beside her. From behind a closed door came a guttural moan.

She glanced up wearily, her eyes dark-ringed. 'My first since 7 a.m.,' she nodded towards the insipid-looking drink. 'Can I help?'

'I'm looking for my wife. She's having a baby.'

'You don't say?' The nurse smiled, but Charlie's heart was pounding too hard for him to notice. He stuttered on. 'Her name's Beth – Elizabeth – Kenny.'

The young woman ran her finger down the list beneath her coffee mug. 'Aha, here you go. She's in Room 3. You can go in, but not for long – and better make sure Sister doesn't catch you or there'll be trouble.'

Charlie thanked the young woman and walked to the door marked 'No. 3'. Beneath the scent of bleach and starch the room smelled of earth and something metallic. Beth was asleep almost upright, her dark hair tangled across the many pillows pushed behind her, one arm stretching towards a small plastic box on a stand in which he could see a bundle of white, a crumpled face closed in sleep. One tiny wrist poked from the blanket, a plastic bracelet around it, and he saw the words: 'baby girl Kenny'.

The tears came as a shock; fat and unexpected, his body

speaking where he had no words. In her face he saw the trace of all those faces before, a newly minted piece of the puzzle of existence. Beth, Annie, himself, his mother, even perhaps the father he had never known, all there in her newborn sleeping features. But he understood now that it was unfair to bind this baby to any story but her own. She needed to write it for herself, wrapped safely from the violence of other people's needs, their expectations, their understanding of the world as it is. He knew then, more than anything, that she must forge her own way, that every step she took must be in a direction she had chosen.

Charlie took Beth's outstretched arm between his hands and knelt down beside her, listening to the soft sound of her breath. He pressed his lips to her forearm, tasting sweat and the faintest hint of coconut.

'I'm sorry, Beth,' he whispered.

Her eyes lifted heavily. She smiled, her lips pale. 'Charlie.'

'She's amazing. I can't – I don't know what to say.'

'The man of literature lost for words,' Beth's voice was hoarse, but her eyes shone against her sallow cheeks and Charlie smiled back, kissing her arm again.

'How are you feeling?'

'Like I just pushed a baby out of my fanny. Sore. Tired, mostly.'

There was a brisk rap at the door and a wide-jawed woman walked in.

'Awake then, Mrs Kenny?' Her eyes fell on Charlie and her face narrowed. 'Visiting hours are over. You'll need to leave now so Mother here can rest.'

Charlie nodded and leaned over the baby, kissing her

gently on the forehead. She snuffled and let out a single cry. Charlie stepped away in alarm. The nurse scowled.

'Can I – I mean, is it OK if I come back later?'

Beth's eyes had closed again. 'Yes, love. Come this afternoon.'

'Visiting hours are from 9 and 11 a.m. and 3 and 7 p.m. Kindly come between these times, Mr Kenny.'

'Yes, Matron – uh, Sister – Ma'am,' Charlie stuttered as she shepherded him out of the room.

'Just one last thing. . .' Charlie could tell that he was pushing it now. The older woman was walking towards him, looking like she meant business. 'Do we know what she's called yet?'

'Euphemia, after my Granny Effie . . .'

'Euphemia?'

'Effie for short.'

'Effie. Yes, Effie. That suits her.'

'Charlie, I think you need to go.'

'Oh yes, sorry – sorry. Bye, Beth. Bye, Effie.'

'Bye, then. See you later.'

'Goodbye, Mr Kenny.'

The door clicked behind him as he walked back into the corridor, past the young nurse at the desk, who smiled a tired farewell, down in the lift and back out into the warmth of the midday sun.

He arrived home after visiting hours that evening to a riot of sunlight, filling the place with a sense of new promise. In the box-room office, he pulled the cover from his typewriter, wound in a fresh piece of paper and began to type.

*

Every evening for a week, Charlie visited Beth and Effie on the ward, sitting with them until visiting hours ended, awed by this thing that she – that they – had made. He was overwhelmed with the need to put things right, to make her happy, and rushed about fetching pillows and cups of tea.

'Charlie!' Beth had laughed eventually, as he'd helped her from the bed towards the toilet, 'I've only had a baby – I can walk, you know.'

And there it was, that teasing tone he recognised, a mixture of affection and exasperation, with the slightest hint of pride.

'On you go then,' he grinned and patted her bottom.

She waggled her finger. 'Enough of that sort of thing. That's what got me into this mess in the first place.'

Leaning against the doorframe, he watched her walking down the ward, the cord of her open dressing gown trailing on the floor. He walked back into the room and sat down beside the crib where his baby daughter was sleeping.

When Beth and Effie were ready to come home, Charlie accompanied them in a taxi to Beth's parents' house, insisting on a speed of twenty miles an hour or less for the whole journey. The taxi stopped outside the grand white front and Charlie climbed out to open the back door of the car, offering Beth his arm, which she shooed away with a click of her tongue – 'I'm not an invalid, silly!' – though she smiled as she said it. A curtain flickered and moments later her mother came clopping down the front steps, letting forth a stream of incomprehensible monologue. She spoke so fast that Charlie found it impossible to follow what she was saying, which led to unnerving silences that his mother-in-law filled by speaking even faster. Charlie heard the words *darling, safety-pins, milton fluid, chicken and dumplings*, but could make no sense at all of what she was asking him. Feeling a rising awkwardness, he looked at Beth's mother whose face beneath her lacquer-solid hair was turned to him, expectantly. What did she want him to say? He glanced at Beth hoping for a prompt, but she was busy with the baby. He was on his own.

'Um, sorry Jenna, I'm not sure – that is, I didn't quite catch that.'

The older woman exhaled sharply and took a step towards Charlie. Her perfume was dense around him, a scent that reminded him of decaying lilies and caused him to mouth-breathe.

'Charlie, Charlie,' she said as if speaking to a foreigner or a small child, 'do pay attention, dear. I was asking if you would be staying to dinner.'

'Well, that's a very kind offer, but I just need –'

'Actually, Mum, Charlie. I'm ready to go home.' Beth's face was set with determination, but her voice was soft and off-hand; she knew when not to pick a fight.

But to her surprise, her mother's face brightened and she stretched out her hand to Charlie, clasping his fingers in hers.

'Well, I'm very pleased to hear that, but have something to eat first, at least. Come on in you three.'

Charlie glanced at Beth who shrugged and kissed their baby.

Beth's father stood in the doorway. Though slight and short, he was a man of ferocious will, fizzing with volatile power that was both mesmerising and terrifying. He raised his hand slowly to Charlie's and shook it, staring hard into his son-in-law's eyes as he spoke.

'Do not fuck this up.'

Charlie felt in his pocket for the disc he had been given last week when he had reached thirty days sober. He ran his fingers over the words stamped onto the metal: *To thine own self be true.* It had been thirty-six days now, lived through a moment at a time. Just this minute, then the next. He looked up and held the old man's gaze as he replied.

'I won't.'

A short distance away, on the other side of the High Road, Stella sat at John's bedside, her fingers resting on the outline of his hand beneath the covers. Outside, the city glowed with summer as the lime leaves swayed by the window. John's chest rose and fell, his face unchanged in sleep, while in the dark folds of his brain, scar tissue thickened across an invisible massacre of memories and connections. And yet, with each day that passed, there were tiny changes, as a fine slow web grew unseen around the damage. Stella closed her eyes and drew in the stale bedroom air. One day at a time. Just this breath, then the next.

4.4

December 1979

John's hand shook with the effort of holding the pen. Across the page, he traced the letters in a wobbly childish hand. Stella sat beside him, silent and unmoving, knowing that, although he wanted her near, there was a shame for him too, in these primary school worksheets. But his determination was fierce and she knew that he would keep on until his writing flowed once more. Every day they sat together like this: Stella silent as John copied pages of words at the kitchen table.

In the silence between them Stella heard a litany of questions. Would he work again? Would they have more children? Had something in him – in them both – changed for good? John's face – yes, it was his. The same sandy hair, a little too long. The same lopsided smile. But when he looked at her, his eyes were somehow different. And though his was the voice she knew, its cadence now was slower, lower and only able to sustain a few words at a time, his speech fragmented like a badly tuned radio. Cognitively, the doctors had said, he seemed to be functioning well, but his memory loss had been dramatic; there was so much he would need to re-learn. At first she'd thought that they'd meant his

research and the names of his colleagues. But one drizzly
morning when he hadn't known the word for rain she realised how far back he'd have to go to start to learn himself
once more.

After he had fallen ill, both sets of their parents had
rallied. Travelling to Kilburn from Bristol and Finchley in
rotation, they'd visited John on the neurology ward, taken
care of Hope, washed, cooked and shopped, while Stella
had ricocheted from home to hospital, each day becoming
more aware of what she stood to lose. It was a strange
unpeeling: with every ounce of strength he'd gained, she'd
seen more clearly how hard it was for him to find the words
he wanted. One hot day, when the ward had seemed almost
airless, she'd sat at his bedside watching the movement of
his chest beneath the T-shirt she had helped him to put
on. His lips had been slightly parted, his closed eyes moving
in his sleep. A young doctor carrying a packet of notes had
walked up to the bed. A pen had leaked in the pocket of
his white coat and Stella had found herself mesmerised by
the uneven spread of blue as he'd checked John's notes and
the anti-virals on the drip. She'd tried to imagine the inside
of John's body as a battleground – the army of white blood
cells and their synthetic reinforcements coursing through
him, pursuing the fierce virus that had rampaged across
his brain. But however hard she'd tried to picture his body
winning the battle, she couldn't escape the echoes of that
plaintive voice she'd never heard before – *Stella* – *Stella, I
need you.*

Memories of his family and his life had started seeping
back while John was still in hospital – *a wife, a child, a flat
near Kilburn Park* – little shards he'd slowly strung together.

One morning he'd leaned forward and asked, 'Stella – where is – Hope?' and she had cried with exhausted relief. Since he'd come home, his improvement had been vast. So good in some ways that, from time to time when she felt a flash of anger as she lugged the rubbish downstairs, Stella had to remind herself that he was still recovering, that he needed to rest. And for his part, as well as re-learning the fine motor skills for writing, John worked with a focused calm at piecing back together the lexicon of everyday life, carrying with him at all times a leather-bound notebook in which he inscribed his rediscovered word-hoard – *paradox, violin, Tube train, thesis.*

As the days turned over into weeks, then months, John began to come to terms with the fact that his research had moved on without him. His colleagues had been bereft at first – John was their undisputed leader, a brilliant and clear thinker with the unusual ability to push forward his ideas without making enemies. But when it had become clear that he would not be able to come back to work, they had called a meeting and appointed a new project leader. John's good friend Liam had taken the post with a strange mixture of elation and guilt, which he expressed privately in a short, clearly worded letter. It was a kind gesture, and somewhere inside himself John had felt a sensation that he would later learn to name again as *gratitude.* But as he'd struggled through the carefully chosen words, he felt as if his world was being flattened, leaving only a wasteland in which he stood alone.

Stella could see the bleakness that had been uncovered within him, his movements growing stiff and slow. Even in his writing practice, she sensed the new-found strain. He laid down the pen, reading over the page of his clumsy scrawl.

'John?'

He looked up and saw her face was curving – *smiling.* She must be feeling happy. Her voice, he noticed, was softer than usual and when she touched his arm he felt a spread of warmth from where her fingers lay.

'John, I've had a thought.'

'Y-es?'

'Well, I think it would be nice if we were to go away. A holiday.'

What would that involve? It sounded quite hard. He remembered piling clothes into big boxes with a handle – *suitcase!* – and then a bus, or train or even, once, an aeroplane. The memory made him feel quite breathless and he clenched his hands into fists. 'I'm – not – sure. Quite a – lot of – things. Maybe – too hard?'

'Well,' Stella chose her words carefully, 'a few years ago we spoke about the seaside. Do you remember? One night when Hope was tiny and you drove me back from Mum and Dad's? You liked the sea because it puts our problems into perspective, you said.'

He paused. There was a sense of movement and of night, lights passing across their faces in the dark. Perhaps music too. But nothing more. 'I don't, sorry.'

She nodded and began to sing.

I must go down to the seas again, to the lonely sea and the sky,
And all I ask is a tall ship and a star to steer her by.

It was a sad tune, he noticed, though he couldn't say why.
'Very n-ice.'

Suddenly she grasped his hand and pressed it to her lips.
The gesture shocked him and he pulled his hand back
suddenly, noticing the way that Stella's face changed when
he did. She rubbed her eyes and tightened her messy pony-
tail. From the other room the baby – *his daughter* – began
to shout.

Stella stood up, smiling once again, though her eyes
seemed tired. 'I'd better go and get her.' She started walking
out of the room, then stopped and leaned against the doorframe. 'John, will you think about it? We could leave Hope
with your parents and take a sleeper train down to Penzance.
It could be good for us.'

He watched her as she stood outside Hope's bedroom for
a moment, her forehead leaning on the white-painted wood.
When she didn't know that he was watching, her face slackened, showing lines at the corners of her mouth and dark
circles underneath her eyes. In the hospital he had not
remembered her at first and it frightened him to think of
how that face had briefly been a stranger's. Stella emerged
from the room carrying Hope against her hip, the darker
strands of her hair falling across the little girl's white-blonde
wisps and her plump red cheeks. John held out his arms
and the toddler started calling, 'Dada, dada, dada'. She had
been frightened of him in the hospital. Something about the
machinery or the smell or the cannula in his wrist. Once
he came home, though, all that had changed; she was these
days what Stella called *a daddy's girl*. Stella handed Hope
over and began to slice some bread for lunch, while John
bounced the small girl on his knee, her face entranced as

she hung on his every word. 'Sit – still . . . Sit – still . . . Sit – still.'

He swooped her quickly towards the floor and she screamed with delight. 'I said – sit – still!'

'Again! Again!'

He scooped her up and began again, her eyes growing wider with anticipation as he slowly said the words, then swung her down and up into his arms.

After lunch they pushed Hope in her buggy to the park, the bare branches stark against the winter sky. An old horse chestnut tree had been felled and John gathered a few small pieces, stacking the wood across the bottom of the buggy's frame.

'What are you doing?' Stella asked.

'It's – for – carving,' he said, looking up at her from where he was crouched by the wheels.

The wind began to pick up and soon Hope's cheeks took on a purple tinge. John clipped her back into the pushchair and wrapped her in his jacket. 'There – you – go.'

Stella walked a few steps behind as he wheeled their daughter home.

'Humpty – Dumpty – had a – great—'

'Fall!' shouted Hope, clapping her hands with delight.

'Cl-ever girl!'

At the gates Stella took his arm and they walked together, a small family unit on the wide Kilburn streets.

'What do you think then?'

He looked blank for a second and Stella prompted him. 'The holiday? Penzance?' He nodded to show he remembered.

'Stels – I – I don't – I'm not—' His knuckles were pale around the handles of Hope's pushchair.

'It's OK,' Stella said, a tiny waver to her voice, 'I understand. You're not ready yet.'

He nodded again and she wrapped her arms around him, unable to find the words to make it better, unable to look him in the eye.

4.5

Bunting zigzagged from one bedroom window to another, cross-hatching the street in red, white and blue. Along the middle of the road, picnic tables, trestles, workbenches and stacked crates were covered in cloths, while women laid out sandwiches, crisps, jam tarts and lemonade, cans of lager and bottles of Liebfraumilch. Pushing Effie in her buggy, Charlie slipped an arm around Beth's waist and kissed her cheek. Children ran from house to house, snapping the elastic of their union jack hats, waving homemade flags and jostling for the cakes.

'Hold your horses, Gary,' said Mrs Shepherd from number 6 as she batted a small plump boy back from the table, 'not until they've said their vows.'

Beneath the white dome of St Paul's and the white gauze of her veil, a young woman stumbled over her lines, bathed in the stark light of iodide lamps, while legions of cameras rolled. In trucks outside, teams of editors and sound technicians chopped between the images: the bride's flushed cheek, the groom's protruding ears, a flickered smile given slightly too late. The pictures passed as a series of pulses beyond the earth's atmosphere, where a satellite bounced them back down again and into the homes of 750 million people across the globe.

In Kilburn, Kinshasa and Chicago, the images played: flushed cheeks, awkward glances, a sea of flags waving. Stella flicked the TV off and pulled a face at her mother, who was stacking books into a crate, ready for the move.

'Bloody load of nonsense. Fairy-tale wedding? As if there's such a thing as a happy ending.'

Her mother raised her head, looking at her daughter's messy knot of hair, her dirty T-shirt, her clasped jaw. 'Do you want a cup of tea, love?'

Stella nodded as she opened another crate and started to fill it with the contents of the dresser drawers. A new home, a new start, an extra Bank Holiday for a royal wedding. There were plenty of reasons to be cheerful. And yet, when she looked outside at the pub draped in flags, all she felt was scorn and emptiness.

On TV sets in Swiss Cottage, Birmingham and West Berlin, the young woman who would never be queen climbed the steps of a horse-drawn carriage, yards of ivory satin spooling after her as she sat beside the future king.

Beth wiped her eyes as the carriage drew away. She always cried at weddings.

'Are you coming out?' Charlie was standing in the front porch, a silhouette against the street scene of neighbours laughing and children running as sunlight glanced from the bonnets of parked cars.

'Just a minute.' She stood up and turned the TV off and the picture imploded to a glowing dot that slowly faded from the screen. From the street she heard cheers and song, a bubble of goodwill rising from the cans and bottles and the extra Bank Holiday. Happiness, she thought, really can be this simple.

Later, with Effie asleep in the buggy beside them, Charlie and Beth sat on their front wall, laughing as two teenage boys threw lengths of toilet roll over the branches of the tree opposite. In the dimming city sky a single star was visible. Charlie looked at its tiny point of light, a lifetime away, and even within the din of other people's drunken revelry he felt a stillness pass through him.

He sipped his lemonade and spoke in a half-whisper. 'It's strange, isn't it? We're all here, just falling through space, heading for oblivion and yet we're singing and dancing and getting excited about a royal wedding of all things.'

Beth took his hand in hers. 'It's really just a matter of will, though, Charlie. Whether you're falling or flying.'

He thought of Annie and Limpet. He thought of his mother. 'I don't know. Maybe. But you can't make things better by force of will.'

She kissed him. 'No, but accept life for what it is and it becomes flight. You've managed to do it. Look at how you turned things around.'

One year and forty-eight days sober. A father. Three new authors on the books. A growing manuscript of his own. Maybe she was right. He reached out to touch her shoulder. 'I love you, Beth.'

Further down the street, people were singing 'Rule Britannia'.

Beth leaned towards him. 'I love you too.'

*

Gradually, more stars grew visible through the orange night-cloud of the city sky.

From where she sat among stacks of boxes, Stella gazed at a bright speck and surprised herself by muttering a long-forgotten prayer beneath her breath.

In the kitchen, her parents were pouring wine into paper cups. Sitting down beside them, Stella made a toast. 'To Bristol.'

John nodded. 'New − ?' he paused, turning to Stella as he struggled for the word.

She took his hand and kissed it. 'New beginnings,' she said, willing her face into a smile.

4.6

March 1983

Stella only cried after Hope and John were in bed. Sitting at the Formica table in the cold kitchen in Bristol, she lit an illicit cigarette and wept, her throat aching with a sadness that ballooned from deep inside her. She moved with heavy limbs through the darkened house, pausing outside Hope's door to hear her daughter's steady breath. Stella knelt beside her sleeping child, laying a hand upon the soft blonde head: a benediction for good dreams, a secular prayer for a blessed life. And though she knew it was arbitrary, that at any moment your rising star could fall from the sky, leaving nothing the same, she felt it was something she must do, to will with all her might a good life for this small girl.

After she had brushed her teeth and plucked the rogue white hairs from her parting, Stella climbed into bed next to John. His face relaxed in sleep, released from the effort of making himself understood. Leaning against the pillows, she looked up at the dark shapes of the unlit room, the wardrobe door with a hump of towel slung across it, the stump of a washing basket writhing with clothes to be sorted. At night it was hard to be hopeful; the emptiness stopped hiding behind a flurry of things to do and seeped out into the dark, clawing at her as she tried to escape into sleep. It had been almost four years since John's illness and she knew in many ways they had been lucky. He had survived and many of his memories had returned; he did not fly into rages as some had said he might and he was grateful to her for her care. She held her breath as though it could capture that thought. But she could not shake the feeling that he had become a stranger in a familiar body, watching their life with the detachment of an onlooker, only ever half there, with only half a memory of what they had once been together. Sometimes, in her hopeful moments, she sensed that perhaps it all still sparked and whirled beneath the slowness of his speech. But on nights like this it was hard to be anything but desolate.

Bristol was supposed to be their new beginning. She had painted the study and piled it with books – his and hers – so that they could share it for their work. Pictures had been hung and the medal John had won for his research had been polished and placed on the Welsh dresser in the kitchen. But then, one day a year after they'd moved, she'd heard a loud crash as she'd arrived back from her morning's work as a receptionist at the health centre. She'd found John in the study. His jumper had been inside out and his hair stood out in clumps around his face. Across the floor in front of him, piles of books had been lying open, covering the room in a patchwork of paper.

He had turned to her, his eyes wide. 'I remember,' he'd said.

Something had leapt inside Stella, a pinprick of light

dancing. She'd kept her voice steady, but he had not seemed to hear her.

'I remember – when I understood – all this. I remember – the feeling – but I don't – understand – any more.'

His face had grown tense and red from the effort of searching for the words and Stella had sat down on top of the books, not caring that the pages snagged, pulling him towards her. That evening she had put the medal away at the back of the dresser drawer.

Months went by and the hope she'd once held began to slip through her fingers, replaced by weariness. Not the wired exhaustion of nights broken by small children, but the monochrome flatness of ground-down repetition, of waking up and knowing that everything depended on her: the food on the table, the folding of the laundry, John's appointments and Hope's packed lunch. Every movement of every day circled around Stella. She carried them all and it sapped her dry.

Since his father's cancer, it had been hard for John's parents to make the journey to Bristol, so each week Stella would call the house in Finchley, picturing the dark hallway and the pad of John's mother's feet in the deep-pile carpet as she reached for the phone and cleared her throat.

'Finchley three-two-six-oh—'

John's father was fading, but his mother didn't speak about that. So Stella would discuss Hope's school work and the woodworking classes John's occupational therapist had arranged, skirting carefully around the gaping black hole of loss sitting in between them. A few days ago, when they last spoke, Stella had noticed a moment when her mother-in-law's voice had cracked. She had been talking about the

Rotary Dinner, which John's father had been too unwell to attend. It was the first time he'd missed the event in twenty years.

Stella had replied with tentative sympathy. 'Oh, Jean, that must have been hard for you.'

For a few seconds there had been nothing but the hiss of the open line, then Jean had clicked her tongue.

'Oh no, it was fine. We've raised a wonderful amount of money, you know. It was a great success.'

Stella had felt the phone warm against the flush of her cheek. 'I'm so glad to hear that.'

She'd paused, listening to the sound of the TV from across the hallway, then carried on with a forced cheerfulness. 'Now, would you like to speak to John this evening? He's just in the living room, I could call him out?'

Jean had given a delicate cough. 'Oh no, no, that won't be necessary. I don't want to tire him out. Well, it was very nice of you to call. Thank you, dear. Do give him my regards and to little Hope too.'

'OK then. Nice to talk to you. Goodbye, Jean.'

She'd hung up the phone and pressed her hands to her face, letting out a slow breath.

Now, in the bed alongside her, John was growing restless. Hope called out and Stella sat up and swung her feet from the warmth of the covers, wincing at the room's chill air. She straightened Hope's duvet and stroked her cheek, then made her way downstairs wrapped in John's blue dressing gown. In the kitchen, she stood looking out of the window at the outlines of the dark garden, waiting for the kettle to boil. She poured the water into the pot and stirred, watching the leaves lift and swirl together, infusing the liquid with amber and gold. It was a loss, but it was also a presence, a black hole in which the weight of life becomes unbearable. Sometimes Stella felt herself unable to breathe beneath the grotesque heaviness of the simplest of tasks. In the altered gravity of this strange new world things became impossible to lift: the books filled with ideas that had once glittered like treasure; the pen that had danced in her hand across notepad and letter paper, catching thoughts in the fine net of her words and spreading them smoothly across the whiteness of the page. Even the act of remembering weighed on her chest like a boulder.

She sipped her tea as she walked into the living room. The street lamp outside lit the room just enough to see the shapes of chairs and coffee table, the television and the shelves above. Her violin's shadow curved against the wall behind and she found herself following its lines over and over with her eyes. She set her mug on the table and reached to take the instrument down. A memory like an ache unfurled within her, of sneaking late into a concert at St Martin-in-the-Fields, sitting in a corner with their eyes closed to better feel (so John said) what the music wanted to them to know. Peeking through her half-closed lashes, she had seen the flickering candles reflected in John's eyes, which were wide open and looking at her with a mixture of confusion and delight.

She placed the violin back on the shelf, drank the last of her tea and climbed the stairs. As she fell asleep listening to John's breathing, she found herself humming a tune she had not heard for years. When she woke the next morning, the music was still in her head.

4.7

The publisher's meeting finished early and, despite Roger's insistence, Charlie declined his offer of a drink.

They shook hands and Roger gave him a pantomime wink. 'But darling, when are you going to fall back off the wagon and join us in the gutter? You're getting boring!'

Charlie laughed. 'Don't I know it!'

Charlie waved as he walked towards the Underground, fast so as not to break his resolve. 'I'll ring you tomorrow. Behave yourself now, won't you?' he called out to Roger who rolled his eyes and tutted.

It had been almost four years without a drink and it was still hard sometimes to walk away. Keeping busy, that was the trick, although even that seemed to take on an addictive tang. The constant rushing to get things done had become a pattern that was hard to break. While Beth dashed between home and school, never feeling as if she gave the best to either, Charlie carried in his head a constant list of things to do and places to be: improvements to their house in Swiss Cottage and a steady flow of invitations from Beth's wide network of friends and family – bar mitzvahs, weddings and children's parties. The only pause came on Tuesdays at six, in the church hall in Queen's Park. In almost four years, he hadn't missed a meeting.

He stayed on the Tube past his stop, emerging at the top of the hill. Across the street, the red-brick school stood against a pale spring sky. A woman at the exit was selling flowers and Charlie plucked a bunch of purple irises from the tin bucket. He looked up to see a swing of dark hair, as Beth left the school, her floral skirt billowing. He called out, but she was too far ahead to hear him. As he quickened his pace, a car pulled up alongside her, the driver leaning across to speak through the open window. Charlie started to jog.

'Beth!'

She should have heard him, really. He was maybe two hundred yards away. But she was laughing as she opened the car door and climbed in without turning around. Clutching the flowers, Charlie watched the car speed off down the hill.

When he arrived home half an hour later, a man he didn't know was drinking coffee in his kitchen, Effie playing on the floor beside him.

'Hello?' Charlie fired the word like a warning shot.

'Hi. You must be Charlie?' His voice was languid and monied. 'I'm Rupert, Beth's colleague. It's great to finally meet you.'

Despite himself, Charlie forced a smile at the intruder at his table. He'd worked too long in publishing not to; the response just kicked in. He stretched out his hand and Rupert shook it. 'Likewise. Where's Beth?'

'She just popped upstairs to change.'

Charlie ran two stairs at a time and burst through the closed bedroom door.

Beth shrieked, clutching a T-shirt to her chest. 'Bloody hell, Charlie, you scared me half to death!' She looked at his glowering face and the limp flowers in his fist. 'What are you doing back so early? And with flowers?'

'I thought I'd surprise you. I came to the school and saw you – but you didn't hear me when I shouted. And then you got into what's his face's fancy car and drove off.'

'Oh Charlie,' Beth was trying not to laugh, 'that's a lovely thought. I'm sorry I didn't hear you.'

He thrust the battered flowers towards her. 'Here.'

'Thank you.'

She was giggling now and kissed him. His hands wrapped around the bare skin of her waist and he pulled her to him in a rush of overwhelming desire.

Beth pushed him away, a quizzical look on her face. 'Are you OK?'

Charlie looked at the floor. 'Yes – sorry.'

Beth pulled on her T-shirt. 'I have to go down – are you coming?'

As she turned, he slid his hands beneath her top, pressing his face to her neck, but she sighed and batted him away.

'Bloody hell, Charlie!'

He slumped on the bed and listened to the clatter of her feet on the stairs and the rising murmur of laughter from the kitchen below.

Weeks later, one evening after Effie was in bed, Beth stopped him in the kitchen as he was drying the dishes.

'Charlie, I need to talk to you.'

He turned to her with a look of shock. He knew what happened in stories after those words were uttered.

They sat at the round pine table in their kitchen and Charlie lit a cigarette.

Beth waved the smoke away. 'Don't you think it's time you quit?'

Charlie took another drag. 'Is that what you want to talk about?'

'No, actually. It's about me.'

A sudden panic rose in his chest. 'Oh God, Beth, are you alright? Are you ill?'

Beth laughed. 'I'm fine, calm down! There's nothing wrong with me. But the thing is, Charlie . . .' She pressed her hands on the table, fingers splayed. 'I don't want to be a teacher, not forever. I need to – well, do something different.'

Charlie felt his whole body lighten with relief. This he could handle. 'You do? Well, that's great –' He reached for her, not noticing how her body stiffened at his touch. 'But Beth, you've never mentioned anything before.'

'Rupert – you remember him? The Ed Psych from school? He thinks I'd make a good psychotherapist – he says I've got a natural insight.'

'Oh, does he?'

The words were bitter, but Beth didn't seem to notice as she listed her thoughts and aspirations, hands moving in the air as she spoke.

'It's fascinating, Charlie, and Rupert says—'

'Beth, I'm sorry, but I really don't think what Rupert says has anything to do with this.'

Her face fell. She sighed and shook her head. When she spoke again it was with a deliberate slowness. 'Well, it's what I'd like.'

Charlie realised how quickly things were running away from him. He started to talk about money, but Beth had already thought of this.

'Mum and Dad have offered to help pay the fees. They're really keen on the idea, actually.'

'They are? You've already spoken to them?'

This time, Beth winced at his tone. 'Oh for fuck's sake Charlie, they're my parents! I just mentioned it when I went round with Effie the other day.'

Charlie felt the anger surround him, jagged, dark and high. 'Oh that's just brilliant. And Rupert? How come he's in on your plan before you've even discussed it with me?'

Beth gave a short, mean laugh. 'Charlie, are you jealous of Rupert?'

'Fuck, Beth, wouldn't you be if you were me?'

'He's my colleague! And unlike you, you sanctimonious prick, I don't sleep with my colleagues.'

Charlie felt his anger collapse into desperation. It was inescapable: his mistakes would follow him forever, never entirely forgiven, nor completely forgotten.

Effie's sudden cry from upstairs derailed their hurtling discord. Leaving Charlie in the kitchen, Beth climbed the stairs to where the small girl sat with her legs dangling between the banisters. She carried Effie into her room and stroked her cheek as she sang her back to sleep. In the darkness of her daughter's bedroom, Beth tried to remember how it had felt before. How Charlie would touch her with reverence; how awestruck and awkward he'd been when he came to see her in the hospital; how for a while their life had been peaceful. But with every month that passed since then she had felt herself dragged lower as the days rolled by in a futile cycle of work and parents' evenings and trips to the hardware shop. Was this really the life she'd imagined when she met him? Surely, she thought as she listened to her daughter's quiet breath, there must be more than this.

4.8

June 1984

The house reverberated with the sound of small children running. Every so often there would be a thud overhead as someone jumped from bed to floor, making the ceiling below them shake. Stella and John were sitting with Liam and Niamh at the kitchen table, the remains of lunch spread before them. Leaning forward, Stella tipped the dregs of a bottle of red wine for herself, gesturing to Liam to open another. He poured generous measures into the other glasses and John glanced at Stella, a thin line of red staining the dry skin on his lips, aware that he should have stopped drinking half a bottle before. But Stella was deep in conversation, so he lifted the glass to his mouth.

There was another thump from above, then a thundering down the stairs as the children came rushing into the kitchen. Anna and Ellen, Niamh and Liam's red-headed girls, were five and seven. Stella loved having them there, most especially for Hope, whom she knew now would never have a sibling. Her reluctance to think about another child after John's illness had solidified as the years had passed, and despite an unsuccessful foray into baby-making a year ago, she'd found herself growing ever more resigned to the idea of Hope as an only child. Besides, John had all but given up trying to touch her these days and Stella was more or less OK with that. Sure, sometimes she felt the tug inside her, the tense hunger of desire. But the moment John was near, her body become a tight clench of rejection. It hurt, sometimes, to think of the heat they had once known: the dizzying abandon of two bodies together, powerful enough to make another life. It hurt, too, to know that she would never hold again the compact weight of a newborn, or feel the plump press of a toddler's arms around her. She didn't like to think of Hope so quiet and alone. Not, she reminded herself, that Hope seemed to mind too much, given as she was to becoming absorbed in a book or a project for hours on end. She was a self-possessed child – happy to choose differently from others, but never short of friends. Anna and Ellen were particular favourites of hers. Their visits were a hallowed treat: a touch of wildness, helped along by the relaxing of the usual rules, as both sets of parents sat in the kitchen or the garden, drinking wine and smoking the thin fragrant cigars that Liam always carried in his breast pocket.

Bounding to the table, the children coughed loudly, waving the smoke away as they swarmed around their parents, opening drawers and piling snacks into Tupperware boxes.

'We're having a midnight feast,' Hope announced, her voice half a pitch higher than usual.

John swivelled in his chair. 'But – it's only – lunchtime?'

Liam and Niamh looked away from him as he spoke. Despite having visited him often over the years since he'd been ill, at first they always saw the same old John, still expected him to speak with his former quiet precision. It took people a while to get used to the slowness of his speech;

to understand that, despite his lost memory and fractured delivery, John had not lost his ability to think or to understand.

Shifting in his seat, Liam gave a short laugh and raised his glass, speaking slightly too loud. 'Always thinking about their stomachs, these two!'

Anna and Ellen were staring at John. Hope could see their confusion at his speech – she always forgot that to other people her dad's way of speaking sounded odd.

'It's just his brain,' she explained to the other two girls, dismissing their stares with a wave of her hand, 'it makes him speak a bit weird.'

They walked towards John, their faces concerned. He shot out a hand, wiggling his fingers towards them. 'Tickle works OK, though!'

All three children screamed, making the adults flinch, then laugh, as the girls ran back upstairs to Hope's room, clutching their boxes of food.

Later, when they were washing up, Niamh asked Stella about her studies. 'So, what's going on with your PhD, Stels? When are you going back to finish it? I really think you should, you know – you always loved the work.'

It was easy for Niamh to say, of course. She didn't know how much it still took for Stella to get through a day; how long the application form had sat in her dresser drawer; how scared she was to send it. *What if they say no?* She didn't want to cry, but the tears came anyway.

'Stels, what is it? Are you OK?'

Niamh wiped her hands on a tea towel and drew her weeping friend into an embrace.

'Oh shit, I'm sorry, it's embarrassing to be like this. I'm fine – it's fine – I really am.'

'Stella, you're clearly not fine,' Niamh said, noticing now the sunken cheeks and dark circles beneath her friend's eyes, the way her clothes hung too sharply on her body, the fine etchings around her mouth and on her forehead. 'Are you and John – you know – OK?'

Stella sniffed. 'It depends, really, on what you mean by OK.'

'Oh?'

'Well, we don't argue. We get along. But it's just there's something – I don't know – something, kind of gone.'

'What do you mean, gone?'

'Well, some nights I don't even want to sleep in the same bed as him.'

Niamh narrowed her eyes and put her forefinger to her lips. 'You need a shag.'

'I beg your pardon?'

'A bloody good shag – that's what you both need. You know the kind – a proper fuck, sweaty-like, none of your gentle stroking. You want to be grabbing at each other a bit, humping, that sort of thing.'

Stella started to laugh, messy and red-faced. 'Humping!'

'What are you laughing about? It's science. You need those chemicals, girl. Get a nice bit of oxytocin on the go and everything will seem better.'

'I hope you don't teach this in your O-level classes, Mrs McKearnan.'

'I do not, indeed – I'm a very respectable science teacher in a very respectable Catholic school, I'll have you know. As far as those girls are concerned, only rabbits have sex.

Ah, Stel, but seriously, how about Liam and I look after Hope sometime and the two of you go off for a dirty weekend?'

Stella stared out of the window, watching Liam and John in the garden. The wine had warmed up their conversation and she could see that Liam had found the rhythm of John's speech now and was comfortable in its altered tempo. She felt something loosen inside. 'You know, I think that would be really good.'

'Excellent, that's settled then. We'll find a date and you can book a weekend for your sexfest.'

Stella flicked a tea towel at her friend. 'Urgh – stop it, you perv!'

Niamh laughed and started singing '*Ah, je t'aime*' as she walked out into the garden.

They decided on the August Bank Holiday weekend. The bags were all packed a day before they were due to leave, the tickets for the sleeper train and maps of Penzance and the surrounding area zipped tight inside a leather folder. Hope had spent an entire evening discussing plans for what she would take to London, but as the weekend approached, Stella noticed that John was taking longer to find the words he wanted, and speaking less and less. The Friday night before they left, they sat together in the living room with the television on.

She reached for his hand and saw him startle at the unexpected touch. 'Are you sure you want to go, John?'

'Hmm? What?'

'To Cornwall, on the sleeper train. We don't have to go if it's making you uneasy.'

His face grew red as he turned towards her. 'I'm – fine.'

Afterwards, she wondered whether she should have challenged those two little words; she'd known even then that they iced the surface of the truth. But, she reasoned, what would it have achieved? It was a fragile lie to cling to, but it felt like the only way they could survive.

Niamh and Liam waved them off from their house in Finsbury Park, where Hope had already disappeared upstairs with her friends. The sun-baked streets and the dusty heat reminded Stella of the first summer of their marriage, when Hope was a baby and John was lost in the world of his research. John took her hand. His palms were slippery with sweat.

She turned towards him. 'How are you doing?'

Without looking around he answered, 'I'm – fine.'

She tried to ignore the tension that had bloomed across her shoulders, focusing instead on the beat of their feet along the pavement, the glint of parked cars in the sunlight, the heavy pull of the London air about her. It was only when they had stepped onto the Tube that she let her chest expand at last, breathing in the oil and metal taste of the underground air.

They ate dinner in a Persian restaurant just off the Edgware Road, drinking beer and tearing pieces of flatbread as the waiters moved about them and the music blared.

Stella leaned towards John to be heard above the noise. 'We were lucky to get somewhere at such short notice. It's supposed to be very nice, this B&B, the travel agent said. I'll bet they do a good breakfast too.'

John felt the world pulling back from him. It was as though he was watching from another place, audience to a play in which nobody knew they were actors. He tried to swallow, washing the bread down his tight throat with a swig of warm beer. He'd thought about trying to explain what he was feeling; about the fear of not being able to sustain himself through the pitying looks when people heard him talking for the first time; about the change in their voices when they replied; or how they would turn from him and direct their questions to Stella instead. Why couldn't he tell her? He knew she would understand. He turned to face her. She was looking at him, her hands clasped tight in front of her.

'John?'

Below him the truth rolled vast and dark like an ocean. He took a breath. 'Stella, I—'

The skin across her knuckles whitened as her hands clenched tighter. 'Yes?'

He let the air out from his lungs, a beery, bready blast. 'I'm – fine.'

As it grew dark, they walked slowly through the warm streets to Paddington. Around them, night-time London was awakening. Office workers, freed for the long weekend, drank and shouted outside a brown-tiled pub. A bus rolled past with a pack of big-haired girls and flop-haired boys smoking out of a top deck window. A tired-looking woman walked slowly down the steps of St Mary's Hospital, a rucksack slung across her shoulder. John carried the suitcase in one hand, striding two steps ahead as Stella trotted to keep up behind him. The sleeper train was waiting at Platform One when they arrived at the station. Above, the long hand of the clock above clicked to the hour.

'11 – perfect.'

Stella could see that despite his reticence, he was pleased with their exact timing.

She smiled and turned towards him. 'It's not due to leave for an hour, but I think we can board now, if we want to.'

He nodded. 'OK.'

They stepped on board and followed the narrow passage alongside the sleeping compartments.

'This is it,' she said, 'Number eighteen.'

John placed their bag on the top bunk and shuffled around Stella in the cramped space so that he could lean against the door to take off his shoes. Lifting up the ledge by the window to reveal a small metal sink, Stella ran warm water and washed her face, while John unfolded his newspaper. Stella rummaged in the suitcase and produced a half bottle of champagne and two paper cups. She poured two warm glasses and they drank them side by side on the bottom bed.

'It's – a bit – squashed,' John said as he struggled out of the bunk.

Stella noticed his hand was shaking as he placed the half-empty cup in the sink.

'I'll – sleep up – here,' he said.

Stella closed her eyes and felt the world grow leaden. 'OK, then.'

'Stella? Are – you – alright?'

A sense of urgency rose up within her, words she couldn't see but needed somehow to make him hear. She felt their shapes around her and tried to reach for them, but they slipped away, leaving only an echo. *There's nothing I can say that would change anything.* 'I'm fine, John. Let's go to bed.'

The train pulled out of the station and rolled west with a gentle rocking that Stella followed all the way to Taunton, when she finally fell asleep. The sun was rising as they passed Plymouth and from his top bunk John watched the light creep red-gold through the crack in the bottom of the blind. Stella's face was soft in sleep and he reached down to touch her cheek. John felt the flicker of something strengthen in him. *Perhaps I can do this. Perhaps it'll be OK.* The train juddered and clacked, whirring onwards like a heartbeat.

Over tea and bacon sandwiches in the restaurant car the next morning they watched St Michael's Mount pass against the brightening sky. Stella sighed when she noticed John had left most of his breakfast, but said nothing. They packed their bag and sat next to one another in the lounge, watching the morning reflected in thousands of fragments across the surface of the sea. John felt himself begin to sweat, beads that trickled into rivulets along his hairline and across his back.

When he stood to leave the train at Penzance, his knees buckled beneath him and he fell to the floor with a quiet gasp. A rustle whisked along the carriage as people turned in their seats, unsure of what to do. A young man, who turned out to be a medical student, knelt beside him as Stella lifted his knees.

'I'm – OK,' John said in a small voice.

'You may have hit your head, you sound a little disoriented. Best if you stay lying down,' said the medical student, as he took John's pulse. 'Do you know where you are?'

'I'm – on the – floor,' John gave a lopsided smile but neither Stella nor the young man smiled back.

'Your speech—' the medical student began, but Stella interrupted.

'He has speech issues – brain damage after a virus.'

'Oh – gosh – right,' the young man was blushing now. He let go of John's hand and checked his watch. When he spoke again, his voice was higher and slower, as if he was addressing a child, or someone very old.

'Well, your pulse is nice and normal again and I don't think you've hit your head. No bumps that I could feel. So, when you feel that you're ready, you can stand up nice and slowly. OK?'

'Thank – you.'

'No problem. Remember nice and slowly, OK?'

John's eyes had narrowed, but Stella answered for him.

'Thank you, doctor. Most appreciated. We'll be fine from here.'

When they reached the B&B, John lay down on the waffle-knit bedspread.

'I'm – sorry,' he whispered as she helped him off with his shoes.

'It's OK, love. It was too soon for us to go away, that's all.' She kissed his head and walked down to the hallway, where she dropped a coin in the payphone and dialled Niamh's number. After a short conversation and Niamh's insistence that she would drive Hope back to Bristol the day after they'd returned, Stella hung up and walked out into the morning streets, the seagulls crying overhead. At the train station she reserved seats on the next day's departure for Bristol, slipping the tickets into her handbag as she walked down to the front. In the distance the sea stretched out until it met the sky and Stella marvelled at how solid this horizon seemed, despite being only illusion.

It was late evening when they arrived in Bristol. The taxi from the station took them along Stokes Croft, where crowds of people spilled out onto the road, moving together in an undulating mass, a dance of sorts that awoke in Stella the sensation of being eighteen, of celebrating after her A level results. *A clean sweep*, her form tutor had said with a wink as he'd handed over the envelope to her. She had laughed when she opened it – with relief and with joy for her three bright As and the whole world unfolding before her. That evening she had gone out with classmates to celebrate and Stella remembered how that night the streets of Bristol had already become tinged with something like nostalgia. Were the young men and women now walking past the taxi counting down the days as she had, imagining that life would soon officially be starting? How long, she wondered, until they figure out that no one blows a whistle; that if you don't pay close attention you could spend the whole time standing on the starting blocks.

John hadn't spoken much after they'd passed Plymouth. He stared now at the confluence of people outside the cab, his eyes following their movement. Stella touched his knee and he squeezed her hand, letting it drop on the seat beside him as the taxi sped along the Gloucester Road. The house when they walked in felt so empty that she wished she'd told Niamh to bring Hope back today. John planted a haphazard kiss on Stella's cheek and crept up the stairs, his shoulders bent like an old man.

Sighing, Stella left the luggage in the hallway and went

into the kitchen, where she poured a glass of wine. With a sharp tug she pulled open the dresser drawer, taking out a wide brown envelope. She tipped it up and a fan of papers fell onto the table, covered with a page headed '*Stella Greenwood, PhD proposal*'. She touched the application, feeling the old satisfaction of a page full of words she'd written. For a moment she stood, watching the second hand flick its way around the clock. Then, almost absent-mindedly, she pressed the paper into a ball and threw it into the bin. She ran the tap for a few seconds and filled a glass with water, sipping it as she walked up the stairs and into the spare room, where the empty bed was waiting.

4.9

Beth's psychotherapy training began in a tall house in Hampstead. Early each morning, Charlie would watch as she clipped on her earrings and buttoned her square-shouldered jacket, trying to fathom as she sighed at her reflection just what it was that displeased her so much about her body. To him, she was perfect. In their many hours apart, he still longed for the soft abundance of her flesh. After they kissed goodbye, he would listen for the crunch of tyres as she pulled away. He knew the car was an extravagance. Who needs a car in London? But he was a little proud of it – a sleek old Saab they had bought for a song.

Effie was stirring in the other room. He could hear her talking to her various toys, deep in her own world of make-believe. For a while, they had talked about a second baby, but since Beth's training had started everything was so busy; there was no way, she insisted, that they could manage another child. Besides, Charlie reasoned, they were happy with things as they were. Life was comfortable: busy, predictable, rooted. The bedroom door swung open and Effie ran in, a flash of blonde hair and flowery pyjamas. She leapt on the bed and Charlie moved his coffee out of the way just in time.

'What you doing, Dad?'

'Drinking my coffee, Eff. It's time to get up now, though.'

She grinned at him, front teeth missing. 'Race you?'

'OK. Ready, steady – hey!'

With a thumping of feet and a cackle of high-pitched laughter, Effie ran out of the room. Charlie smiled to himself and picked up his mug, leaning back on his pillows for just a little while longer, reluctant still to open himself up to the day. It was not always easy to navigate the world without the soft landing of drink. At work parties he'd discovered how much harder it was to skate from one conversation to the next without the wake of wine and high spirits to carry him along. But in this bedroom, in this house, he was safe. Here, he knew exactly who he was supposed to be.

At 7.10 a.m., in a room that smelled of damp and beeswax, Beth lay on a blue velvet couch and talked to a steel-haired woman in her fifties about – what? Charlie couldn't imagine.

'It's not anything specific, I just feel – stuck. Ordinary.'

'Tell me what you mean by ordinary?'

Beth thought for a minute, noticing the throb of her disdain. Ordinary. Hadn't she always expected to be something more than ordinary? Once Charlie had seemed to be the answer – so free of all the ties that criss-crossed her daily life, the many binds of her family's expectations. But lately she'd begun to wish for something of that old order. The clues and customs of a comfortable existence, where words like 'serviette' didn't exist and people knew without asking the proper moment to take your hat off at a wedding. People who talked about opera and psychology, the way Rupert did when they ate lunch together in the staffroom.

The grey-haired lady remained impassive. 'So by ordinary, you mean – ?'

'Common, I suppose,' said Beth.

The room stayed silent. Beth felt the blood flood hot across her body. 'I'm not a snob; it's just a question of feeling like things are – you know, proper.'

'Proper?'

'The way they're supposed to be.'

'And how are they supposed to be?'

There had been a time, not even that long ago, when Charlie had been everything she wanted. She still remembered the chemical rush of being near him, how her hands had shaken and her teeth had chattered. It was there, just out of reach, and the memory made her ache with longing. Desire is a cruel master, she thought. Once fulfilled, it shifts to a new object, always wanting what it cannot have.

'I think I miss feeling as if I'm not in control,' Beth sat up from where she was lying on the couch. 'Yes, that's it – which seems pretty odd, but then perhaps I just want someone who can sweep me off—'

The therapist interrupted Beth mid-sentence. 'That's all for today.'

Outside it was raining. Beth scrambled in her handbag for her car keys, her fingers brushing across the creased spine of the paperback that Rupert had handed her the previous day at lunchtime. 'It's about the nature of desire,' he'd said, holding her gaze for a fraction longer than was polite.

Sliding into the driver's seat, she glanced at the time: 8.07. Running late as usual. She opened the book, tracing the biro underlinings that Rupert had left across the pages, wondering what he saw in those words. A piece of paper fluttered to her knee.

Sitting in the parked Saab that evening, Beth watched the rain melt her view of the world outside. In her hands she held the note. Eight words in blue ink. Was this all it took to make the world seem bright again? *Dear Beth, Drink at 5? The Old England? Rx.* How could those few scratched markings make her body feel like this? Her stomach churned, her hands shook and somewhere deep inside she felt the long-forgotten swell of her desire. Slipping the note inside her jacket pocket, she paused. She could still drive away, back home to the life she knew. Through her windscreen the world grew clearer as the sun emerged, and Beth knew that somewhere there must be a rainbow. She got out of the car, breathing in the freshness of newly fallen rain, turning around to see if she could catch a glimpse of colour in the sky before she stepped into the plush dark pub where Rupert was already waiting.

4.10

Stella picked up the book as they were leaving Liam and Niamh's house. *Quantum Entanglement* it said on the cover, with Liam's name – Professor L. McKearnan – beneath it. She slipped it into her handbag as she shouted goodbye up the stairs.

'See you this evening,' Niamh called back, leaning over the banisters.

When they got on the Tube, John and Hope found a seat together, but Stella had to walk a little further down the carriage. She took out the book. What was fascinating about entanglement, she thought as she read Liam's well-chosen words, was how the act of observation could change the way in which things behaved. You had to accept that the very act of observation would alter the system being measured; and yet you couldn't assume that any property you observed would exist in a certain state when you weren't measuring it. In fact, entangled histories could only be understood by gathering partial information, because if you have too much information it produces a paradox in which the more you know about one property, the less you can know about the other. What this means, Liam's introduction concluded, is that we have to accept that physical systems don't have definite properties until they are measured – that the moment of watching might, in fact, be the point at which something comes to life.

Stella stared at the blackness outside the carriage window. It wasn't just the idea of being two things at once: that, she felt, she could understand. But the idea that properties might only exist when they were observed was a strange and liberating idea, as if at any unseen moment, everything might be possible. When they reached South Kensington, she put the book back in her bag, holding hands with John and Hope as they struggled through the station crowds and into the tunnel that ran to the museums.

Beneath the vaulted ceiling of the main hall of the Natural History Museum, the three of them stared at the Diplodocus's skull.

John pointed to the swooping vertebrae behind it. 'The long neck – was for—'

'For eating from the trees – I know, Daddy.'

John shrugged at Stella and pulled a face. 'She – knows already.'

He is no different, Stella thought, until he talks. John's hands were resting on Hope's shoulders as he listened to her reading from an exhibition board.

'Daddy, how long is one hundred and fifty-four million years?'

'Very – long.'

Hope rumpled her small forehead, already interested in the next thing. 'Can we go to see the blue whale now?'

*

They ate their lunch on the lawn outside, the August heat
sealed into the gritty air. The wind picked up, carrying a
straining bass note from the west.

John's face lightened. 'Carnival,' he said, smiling.

Stella nodded, remembering the crush of people, the ceaseless flow of bodies moving, rum punch and home-styled
sound-systems balanced in open windows. A sense that
anything might happen.

Down Westbourne Grove the drums beat a restless rhythm
that pulled the crowd along. A float rolled by, swinging with
palm trees made from crêpe paper. Balanced on the back, a
man in tight white shorts with a whistle around his neck
called changes to the drummers as they walked beside. From
her perch on his shoulders, Effie shouted into Charlie's ear.
He couldn't make out a word of what she was saying, but
he felt her body shake with laughter as she rose up in delight
with every float that passed. She was still too young to feel
the anxiety of being hemmed in on all sides by people, or
to know about the dangers of so much moving flesh. As
long as she was with Charlie, she knew that she was safe.

Later, in a small area of green, Charlie bought jerk chicken
and they sat down to eat it on the grass. It was still too
loud to talk properly and so they leaned together, wordless
amid the noise, and Charlie felt the quiet joy he almost had
forgotten of watching Effie when she was content. She
looked up at him and smiled the big-toothed grin of a girl
still growing into her face.

'Like it?' he mouthed, pointing to the tinfoil tray that
held the remnants of the chicken.

'Mmm-hmm,' she nodded.

He put his mouth close to her ear so she could hear him. 'Shall we take some back for Mum? To help with her studying?'

Effie shook her head. 'No, this is just for us, Dad.'

They pressed against each another as the carnival throbbed around them.

Across the square Effie saw two policemen, looking hot in their heavy blue uniforms. Behind them a sound system was pumping and they swayed in time to the fat, rolling bass, their faces red and glistening. She pointed them out to Charlie.

'Can we give them some of this?' she asked, holding up a bottle of lemonade.

Charlie nodded, picking chicken from his teeth as Effie ran over to the two men and held out the drink. They passed the bottle between them, grinning and mouthing their thank yous. The beat changed and they put down the bottle as Effie grasped their hands, pulling them into a circle, swaying one way and then the other as bass vibrated through their bodies.

Charlie watched Effie as she waved at the policemen and ran back to him. She held his arm, taking it all in. Nothing particular happened after that, but nevertheless the memory settled somewhere deep at his core – a moment of simple coherence to which he would return many times in the difficult years that followed.

4.11

March 1986

In Florence Road, Brixton, Charlie stared at the empty walls of the flat, replaying the conversation on a loop, as he had done for the past three weeks. Over and over he saw Beth's pale face, her back against the closed door, and those quiet words: *Charlie, I'm sorry, I want a divorce.*

He supposed he should have seen it coming; there had been signs if only he'd been paying attention. It had been months since they'd eaten a meal together; they were always so busy. On the evenings they were both at home, they would be working: Charlie typing his own manuscript or reading someone else's; Beth writing up notes for her training or marking school books. It was a rare night that they made it to bed together and, even then, sex was silent and perfunctory. But it hadn't occurred to him that Beth might have been planning this.

'Can't we talk?' he'd asked her, but she'd shaken her head.
'My mind's made up.'
She'd not been able to meet his eye.
'But can't we at least try and figure out what's gone wrong?'
At that moment, Charlie had felt nothing but confusion.

It was only later that desperation would kick in, bringing with it the old demons. He would realise then, of course, that things hadn't gone wrong – not for Beth. It was only he who was wrong.

Eventually, he stood up from the sofa, pushing up his shirtsleeves and digging to the bottom of a bin-liner full of his belongings until he found his typewriter. A gang of kids was shouting in the street outside. A window above banged open and someone called out, angry words he couldn't quite hear. Carefully, he rolled a sheet of paper into the battered machine and typed until his eyes started to droop, then he crawled into a sleeping bag on the bare floor and slept.

The following Saturday he took Effie to Swiss Cottage pool. Her questions had grown more urgent each time he saw her. *When are you coming home? Why do you not want to be married any more?* He had even practised in a mirror, so as not to get upset when he talked to her. *I've got a new flat now. Mummy and I love you very much, but we don't love each other any more.* (Except I do! I do love Mummy. She just doesn't love me.) He watched her as she floated in the water, her feet draped across the edge of her rubber ring, arms trailing wide on either side, blonde curls bobbing. He swam around her and ducked below. When he surfaced from the water, Charlie's hair was plastered into dark points around his face. Effie was pointing to the small bright medal on a chain about his neck.

'What's that necklace?'

'It's my St Christopher. It was a present from my sister, your Aunty Annie.'

'The one who died?'

'Yes, that's right.'

'In the bomb near the shops?'

'That's the one. She would have loved to have met you. You look a bit like her, you know. Same yellow hair.'

'Swim under again!'

Charlie loved the way a six-year-old could close the door on a conversation like that. No more now; back to me. He dived under the water again, into the thick silence below the surface, smooth and effortless. Flipping over, he looked up at the pale pads of his daughter's feet above him, the shiny underside of the rubber ring, her small bottom protruding through the middle. Sunlight burst across the water, blanching his skin a deathly blue-white. He spun again and glided up, back to the echoing din of children's shrieks, grabbing Effie's foot and whizzing her round and round as she cackled with delight.

As they walked up the hill, Effie took his hand and pressed it to her crisp-oiled lips. 'When are you coming to live at home again, Dad?'

Oh Effie, Effie, he thought, where do we go from here?

'Effie, love, your mum and I have spoken to you about this, haven't we? We both love you very much, but we've decided that it's better if we don't live together any more – that we don't stay married.'

'Is it because of Rupert?'

The name felt like a body blow, knocking the wind from him so that for a moment Charlie could not move.

'Rupert?' he croaked. 'From Mummy's work?'

Effie nodded, her eyes were wide with fright; she could

sense her mistake, though she didn't know quite what it was.

Charlie spoke with a deliberate quiet. 'Why do you think it might be because of Rupert?'

'I don't know.'

Charlie picked her up and pressed his face to hers. 'Eff, it's OK – I'm not cross with you. Please, love, don't cry.'

But she couldn't help it, the tears just came and though she squeezed her eyes shut, she couldn't make them stop. She burrowed into her father's familiar smell of coal-tar soap and tobacco, and wept for the world she had lost.

As the weeks passed, Effie's questions grew listless, her laughter less frequent. When he took her to the pool, Charlie noticed how she clung to him, no longer interested in leaping with a shout into the pool or swimming underwater. A few Saturdays later, Beth called Charlie into the kitchen and began speaking in sharp-edged whispers.

'What have you been saying to her?'

Charlie bristled with irritation. 'What do you mean?'

Beth ran her hands through her thick hair and he ached to see the smooth skin of her elegant neck – so familiar and yet so distant from him now.

'She's always unhappy after she sees you.'

Charlie swallowed as his longing turned to anger. 'I am not the one who broke up this marriage.'

'She's just so sad, Charlie. She cries for hours after you leave.'

A throb of fury passed across him and he squeezed his eyes shut until it subsided. It left him feeling hollow and heavy. 'OK – OK. Whatever she needs to make it better – I'll do whatever she needs.'

Beth stared at him and a look of pity flickered across her face. 'Right. Well, good.'

Charlie rubbed his face. 'I'll just go and say goodbye.'

The living room was full of books and piles of magazines. A brass pot of dried flowers stood in the empty fireplace, reflecting the jerking lights of the television onto Effie's pale face as she sat on the floor, knees hugged tight to her chest. Charlie sat down next to her and she grabbed his arm, her eyes still fixed on the screen. In the dim light he could see the glossy cover of a brochure on the coffee table. He picked it up. It was an application pack for St Katharine's, an independent day school that Beth's parents had petitioned at length for Effie to attend, but which Charlie had rejected, despite their offer to cover the fees. The decision had enraged Beth's father, who had called Charlie a pig-headed fool. But he had only smiled and thanked his father-in-law for the offer of the money; in part because he had known that his serene response would have needled the old man even further.

Charlie spoke to Effie's profile. 'St Katharine's, eh?'

Effie's eyes moved towards him, glinting lights within the shadow of her face. 'Yes,' she said hesitantly, 'we went to visit on Thursday.'

With silent effort, he found a nonchalant tone. 'Oh. Well, you'll have to tell me all about it on the phone this week. Good night, Effie-chops. See you next Saturday.'

'Bye, Dad.'

He waited to breathe until he was in the hallway, inhaling deeply to try and still the anger as it returned.

His voice shook when he spoke. 'You want to change

her school? Without telling me? How can we even afford it?'

Beth stared at him, a look of distaste creeping into the corners of her mouth. 'It's not "we", Charlie. You don't get to – anyway, I'm getting some help from Mum and Dad with the fees.'

'Help? But why didn't you ask me first?'

'Oh, don't be ridiculous,' her tone held a haughtiness that he'd not heard before, 'what could you have possibly offered?'

Charlie nodded and pressed his hand to his mouth. Beth took a step backwards, her eyes darting to the clock on the wall beside her.

'I'm sorry, Charlie. I had planned to tell you, but everything's been so . . .'

Charlie felt the familiar twist of his despair, the senseless anguish that rose each time he remembered that life would never be the same.

Beth looked at his face, pinched in pain. She knew she had to tell him the other news too. But not now, when everything was still so raw. Not yet.

After he'd left, Charlie felt the first prickle of disquiet. Something wasn't right, but he couldn't quite place it. He heard it again in the screech of the wheels as his train drew away from the platform. *Something unseen, something unheard, something unsaid.*

In Vauxhall, Rupert packed away his squash racket, laughing as his former school friend – now a foul-mouthed, chain-smoking journalist – told a string of filthy jokes, punctuated by a harrowing series of coughing fits.

'You're going to have to give up the fags, newsman,' he said, handing his friend a tissue.

The other man grimaced and shook his head. 'Fuck that for a laugh.'

They shook hands and slapped backs by the station. Rupert descended into the warmth of the Underground, heading north to the house in Swiss Cottage where Beth was waiting; the house that since last Thursday had become his new home.

4.12

October 1986

John knew that if he said it aloud it would sound as if he was going mad, but the word was definitely *kind*. The wood felt kind as he turned it in his hands. And his work, he thought, was a kind of mastery (noticing how the word had changed its meaning, though it kept its sound), different to the mastery of numbers and thoughts that he had known before. The course leader had said he had a gift for precision and he knew it was true. He could see the beauty in the angles and the planes of the things he made; could feel the cellular perfection of a once-living piece of timber when he held it, sensing its power and its purpose.

Stella had seen the change in him; the lightness that had returned to his movements as he worked for hours in the garage, the radio murmuring in the background. It didn't seem like much: a weekly class in a run-down education centre, but for John it was a way of coming back to life. It had brought them all a new kind of life. Not the life they'd had before, but a path to follow where once there had been nothing. Her epiphany had come one morning, finding her hands running across a familiar shape, the smooth curve of wood, the gentle tension of long untuned strings. The violin was old, untouched for years, but it retained the beauty she remembered. Stella turned it in her hands, examining the patina of the aged wood, remembering the sounds that she'd made from this worn old instrument. She'd hated to admit it, but her mother had been right: she did need something more than her part-time job at the doctors' surgery to get her out of the house. It wasn't until her dad had suggested the orchestra, though, that she'd pulled the violin from the dusty shelf and discovered, beneath the high rafters of Hope's school hall, that the music was still there within her.

On the days that Stella worked, her parents would collect Hope from school and bring her home to John, who would appear at the sound of Hope's bright chatter, sawdust clinging to his clothes. Stella's parents were always careful not to make too much of staying around, though John knew it was no coincidence that he was rarely left in charge of Hope for longer than an hour. But even while her grandparents were there, Hope would drag her father's arm and lead him back into the garage, asking him to show her what he'd made, collecting offcuts to use in her doll's house – a block of wood to cover with cloth and call a dining table, a handful of sawdust to fill a tiny cushion.

He held the wood and thought of what he'd make next, of how he'd fit together the pieces of a felled tree into something new. His eyes strayed to the photograph with curled edges that he'd pinned to the wall, its colours fading: a constellation of blown confetti, Stella's red dress billowing behind, her head thrown back in laughter; a man he recognised as himself looking on with an expression he decided must be wonder. A picture frame – that could be just the thing. He'd give it to Stella as a gift and maybe she would laugh again in that vital way that he only half-remembered. Maybe she would look at him properly, or even share his bed again. He missed the feel of her against him at night, but when he imagined what he might say to explain it to her, the words dissolved on his tongue.

That evening, as he lay alone, he thought about the delicate grain of the wood, the memories that had grown clearer as he sanded it, seams of thought whose shape had emerged with each stroke. *The spin states of two entangled particles along the same axis will be exactly opposite to one another. When a pair of entangled particles is observed, the entanglement will be broken.* John was certain that he had never known how a particle could tell when it had been observed, or what lay at the heart of this instantaneous communication – a sub-atomic sleight of hand that had tormented his colleagues with the prospect that they might never have all the answers. In the stillness of his bedroom, the memories rose in brief flashes of illumination before sinking back into the darkness of his brain and into sleep.

Stella arrived home from work the next day to the smell of sawdust and fallen leaves, the bite of autumn in the air. Strains of music spun tinnily from the garage, in between the rasp of sanding. She thought about the night before, of the orchestra's conductor who had placed his callused fingers on her hand after rehearsal; of the stale smell of his bedroom and the sour taste of his disappointment as she'd left, heart jack-hammering beneath her shirt. Last night, when she'd got home, she'd stood in front of the hallway mirror, expecting to see the guilt marked across her face. But the reflection that met her was not what she'd expected. Between the fine creases around her eyes and the gentle drop of her chin, she'd seen a spark of something coming back to life.

And perhaps now, as John looked up from the bench, he saw it too. Setting down the sanding block, he walked over to Stella, his eyes widened with an unspoken question as Hope ran into the garage, bursting with stories of school.

'What you making, Dad?'

John winked. 'Present – for your – mum. Shhh!'

The spark glowed and Stella felt the memories sharpen into focus. The first time she'd seen John in the pub on Gower Street; walking together in Bloomsbury; pressed together in Hyde Park; cradling their newborn daughter on the bathroom floor. He was all these things and yet more too; the person he'd become, she realised, was a person she had yet to know. He took her hand and she let herself be drawn towards him.

From the kitchen window, Stella's mother watched as Hope clambered in between Stella and John, tugging at their legs until they hooked her up and into the middle of their embrace.

That evening, while Hope slept and John fitted the first pieces of the frame together, Stella wrote a letter to the conductor, sending her apologies for the rest of the term. I'll find another orchestra, she thought, as she sealed the envelope. In the garage, John tacked the photo back onto the wall and laid the wood down on his workbench, noticing how the imperfections in the grain were what gave the work its beauty.

4.13

December 1986

The silver discs lay side by side: the St Christopher medal from his sister, the punched metal chip from his AA meetings. One for protection, one for sobriety, though neither one had kept its promise.

Charlie reached for the bottle on his bedside table, knocking the discs onto the floor beside a stack of unread submissions. Since Beth had told him about Rupert, several months before, he'd found that he could no longer read for any length of time; the words had become impossible to follow along the page. He'd become overwhelmed by the piles of manuscripts months ago and had taken to bringing them home in the hope that they'd be forgotten, that no one at the agency would discover how out of hand his workload was getting. Geraldine had been watching him more closely than usual, appearing by his desk first thing as if to check he'd made it to the office on time. As if she sensed that something was unravelling. His first drink hadn't seemed like much after three nights without sleep. A nightcap, that was all. Medicinal. But now, sinking a glass of whisky before he even made it out of bed, it was hard to tell himself that he was alright.

He had sensed himself beginning to vanish one evening in August. It was hard to pinpoint the moment he first felt it; it may have been when he saw that a silver BMW had taken the place of their old Saab, or when he heard the sharp new voice in which Effie said *MumandRupert* as one word. It may have been the way in which Beth had not been able to meet his eye or the fact that he'd had to gulp from the bottle of vodka in his pocket after he had left Effie on the doorstep. As he'd walked south, past the stuccoed façades of St John's Wood and Regent's Park, Charlie had felt the traces of his old life fading around him, as if he'd never really been there at all.

When, a few weeks ago, Beth had invited him to celebrate Chanukah in the house that had once been his, Charlie had declined. The thought of lighting candles and sharing food with the man who'd stolen his wife was more than he could bear. He would take Effie for an afternoon in Camden market instead, he'd said to Beth on the phone, only half joking when he added, 'to show her how the other half live'. Beth hadn't mentioned his drinking, though she'd smelt it on him more than once. She'd wanted to avoid the confrontation until she was certain it was true, she'd said to Rupert, who'd nodded and said he would support her, but that she had to think of Effie. Beth had been furious. Upstairs, Effie had hidden under her bed and cried until her mother had stopped shouting.

Now, Charlie wondered why he hadn't just gone along and smiled through the prayers he didn't understand. He could have put on the pretence for Effie. At least if he had done that he wouldn't have ended up losing her.

*

It had only been a minute. Fifty-six seconds, to be precise, the time it took to duck behind a stall and swig from the bottle that would calm the tremor of his hands. But when he'd turned back, Effie was gone. He'd searched everywhere, his cries growing ragged and more desperate, until a policeman had stopped him, suspecting drunk and disorderly. On hearing the story, he'd radioed from the car, then driven Charlie back to Swiss Cottage, where Beth had opened the door and stared at him with a look of cold fury.

'How could you?'

Over her shoulder he'd seen Rupert speaking to a policeman – the policeman, it transpired, who'd noticed an unaccompanied seven-year-old walking down Camden High Street and brought her home. Charlie had shaken his head, his hands pressed to his mouth. It had all happened so quickly, he'd said, really just a matter of seconds. The market crowd had been so thick, he couldn't find her when she darted off. Beth had stared across the threshold at her ex-husband, noticing the smell of him and the way his eyes couldn't hold her gaze. And though she'd known even in her anger that one day she might regret it, she'd let the rage hiss out, leaning close enough so no one else would hear as she'd whispered in his ear. 'Do you know what, Charlie? She'd be better off without you.'

After the policeman had spoken with them all, Charlie had gone in to the front room, where *Blind Date* was blaring from the television. He'd sat beside his daughter, who was curled beneath a blanket on the sofa, and taken her hand. 'How are you?'

Effie had pulled her hand from underneath his and tucked it around her middle, scowling. 'I'm fine.'

He'd touched her shoulder. 'Effie, I'm really sorry. Was it very scary?'

She hadn't turned around again. 'I *said*, I'm fine.'

Charlie had moved to kiss her as he stood up from the sofa, but she'd ducked away, leaving him leaning awkwardly.

In the hallway, Rupert touched him on the arm, but Charlie could not bring himself to look at the man whose calm tone disguised the hammer-blow of his words.

'You can't see her until you've sorted this out, Charlie – your drinking, I mean. It's not fair on anyone.'

Charlie had forced himself to look up. 'Get out of my way,' he'd whispered, frightened to raise his voice in case he ended up doing something he'd later regret.

Beth had folded her arms and stood in the doorway as he walked down the road. As she pushed the door shut, she'd made a silent promise that she would never let Effie be hurt by him again.

Now Charlie waited for the whisky to blunt the sharp edges of doubt in his head. He looked at the time: 5 p.m. He had slept for most of the day. On the floor where they had landed, the two discs caught the light and he reached down to pick up the smaller medal. He rolled a fresh sheet of paper into his typewriter and began the letter to Beth, explaining why this would be for the best. He slipped the St Christopher inside an empty cigarette box, wrapping it in silver foil and tying it with a ribbon. *A parting gift.*

The box pressed against him as he walked down Brixton High Street, past muttering drug dealers and shouting drunks, beneath the dark shadow of the railway bridge, the café and car mechanics in its arches. Turning up Stockwell

Road, he walked beside its rows of unloved townhouses until he reached the Thames. His resolve began to falter, the urgency draining away to reveal a limp unstructured fearfulness. *Is this really what I need to do?* A cloud of lethargy eased across him and he sat on a bench overlooking the river, pulling a bottle from his jacket pocket. To the east, he could see a gloaming reflected from the tall buildings and spires of government, but here the river was quieter, darker, easier to get lost in. He stood up and walked on. From the middle of the bridge he watched London layer upon itself, busily spanning back and forth along the water, taxis and buses speeding past, the astringent slap of the wind sharp on his face.

Much later, Charlie stood outside his old front door, the silver-wrapped gift in his hand. Rupert's car gleamed sleek in the moonlight, a thin layer of ice sparkling on its windows. Charlie's heart shuddered and sweat began to gather in the armpits of his jacket as he looked at the darkened windows of the house. It would be best for Effie this way. Beth was right, she would be better off without him. Pressing his hand against the front door, Charlie slipped the envelope and his final gift to Effie through the letterbox. In the cold, his fingers left prints of condensation on the painted wood. He stood and walked away into the anonymous night as the final traces of his touch faded back into the air.

INTERLUDE

New Year's Eve, 1999

In the chaos of Princes Street, a young woman crouches by the steps that lead to Waverley Station. A fine cloud of steam rises as her urine meets the chill air this bitter Hogmanay. Her blonde hair is held in twists by tiny butterfly clips and her eyes are bright with glitter above her silver Puffa jacket. As she pulls up her jeans, she sees above the churning crowds the floodlit castle, high on its mound, and closer to her the dark peaks of the Scott Monument. Thunderbird One, the tour guide had called it earlier; though Sir Walter, glowering from his stone chair, was evidently not amused.

Effie turns around, looking for her friends from her hall in York, but she can't see them. *For fuck's sake,* she mutters, lighting a cigarette. Through the crush she sees a girl in a fake fur jacket, her long brown hair wild as she links arms with a policeman and skips a reel. Without entirely meaning to, Effie finds herself moving towards the scene, where people are laughing and clapping in a circle as the pink-cheeked girl spins the policeman round and round. The clock above the Royal British Hotel – usually two minutes fast – has been corrected tonight. Five minutes to go. She pushes away the thought that Adam should be there and draws hard on the last of her cigarette. Somebody hands her a bottle of whisky and she laughs and swigs and passes it back. A young man pulls her into the centre of the circle and they spin one way and then the other, circling the policeman and the grinning girl, who Effie realises is very drunk. On they spin, faster and faster, as more people join the whirling group of dancers. As the bells begin to chime for the end of one millennium and the beginning of the next, the girl stumbles and begins to fall. She reaches out and, in a moment of freakish drunken acuity, Effie catches her before she falls face-down on the ground. The bells chime – one, two, three. The girl stretches up her arms and wraps them around Effie's neck. Four, five, six. *Hello, I'm Hope. Thank you, beautiful girl.* Seven, eight, nine. *My pleasure. Are you OK?* Ten, eleven, twelve. Around them people are cheering and fireworks boom. Effie knows that neither of them will remember this tomorrow and perhaps that is why she lets the kiss happen, to savour a moment that will never be a memory.

Across the country the bells ring out, a wall of fire dribbles damply down the Thames, while London teems with people clamouring for the bright new world that they think they've been promised. Champagne bottles gather in the gutter as party-goers make their way home on the all-night Tube. As he walks among the revellers, Charlie sees that glass is on the rise – more glass than stone these days – the brittle surface of a new era. London has become a city filled with mirrors. But Charlie does not want to see himself, still less reflect on what or who he has become. The old stone has the benefit of being porous, taking in a little of what the city belches out; but these new towers let nothing past their hard and sleek exteriors.

When he left the agency, they hadn't been sorry. Relieved that he had jumped before he needed to be pushed, his colleagues had wished him luck as he left ostensibly to work on a book. But he knew, as they suspected, that it was an excuse. That his heart wasn't in the world of words any more. And sure enough, though he wrote a little every day, it was walking that became the elixir to tame the noises in his head, to salve the raw cracks in his heart, to keep him slowly notching up the days without a drink.

As he walks, he thinks of Effie, her name like a beat in his head, marking the time that has passed since he last saw her. So many years now. His feet begin to take him north past Regent's Park and St John's Wood; the traffic tearing by on Finchley Road where it is never quiet, even in the wee small hours. A church clock somewhere chimes 3. When he reaches the house, he stands, out of habit, to one side of an old lime tree, sheltered in its shadow, watching the blank windows opposite where once his daughter used to sleep inside.

Inside, Beth wakes with a pang of anxiety. *Where's Effie?* She sits up and rubs her face, as time and space settle around her. *Effie is in Edinburgh, Effie is an adult, Effie is fine.* It doesn't ever really stop, though, does it? she thinks. Once they're born you are bound for life to the potential horror of their loss. She stands up from the bed and walks into Effie's room and over to the window. Beside the tree, Charlie sees her dark outline and steps back behind the trunk. Beth sees a movement and presses her face to the glass, but her sight is not that good these days and she can't quite make it out. She thinks perhaps it was a fox.

In Bristol, John has gone to bed but, still fizzing from the ceilidh she had played at earlier, Stella cannot sleep. In her party dress, she stands in the bright hallway, running her hand along the wooden photo frame that John had made her years ago. Behind the glass is a faded photo taken on the steps of the register office on the Euston Road, her thin red dress blowing in the wind of the passing cars, as John stands watching. She walks along the row of frames – Hope's baby pictures and school photos; the weddings and sepia family portraits; a blurry snapshot taken on a timer in Niamh and Liam's garden, with everyone laughing and pointing as the camera clicked a moment before they were ready.

Her hand rests on a blank space of wall and she feels the tug of sadness, the absence of the baby she never conceived. Even after all these years she still misses him, their imagined son. She sits down on the hallway floor, looking up the stairs to the closed door of the bedroom that she once shared with John. She wonders how Hope is enjoying New Year in Edinburgh. No boyfriend, yet, she thinks, that's good. With a sigh she stands and makes her way up to the small white-painted room at the back of the house, climbing onto her narrow bed and falling asleep still wearing her clothes.

5.

DECOHERENCE

2002–2007

Upon observation, the entangled state ceases to exist.

L. McKearnan, *Quantum Entanglement.*
Paradox Publishing, 1982 (p. 114)

5.1

June 2002

Pages fluttered in the breeze from the open window. Warm wood, dust and wool: the college library was a haven for Hope as she sat behind a pile of green leather-bound books, the gold-embossed lettering glinting in the light of the warm summer's afternoon.

A waft of cigarette smoke drifted through the window from the party of finalists loitering on the college lawn, caps in the grass, half-drunk bottles of champagne by their sides. That their futures hung entirely on the series of two-hour exams they'd taken over the last week was not a concern this June afternoon. Time stretched before them rich and glorious, a bright clear sea reflecting the infinite blue above.

A floorboard creaked, someone coughed, the library door shut with a soft swish. Hope stared at the still-white page before her, biting her nails while a list of twentieth-century writers churned in her mind. Names and voices competed, holding her to ransom in her head. Dear God, she prayed, not the Fear. Everyone knew about the Fear: it was what every finalist dreaded. Paralysing noise that rendered you thought-dumb. Nothing to be done, except pray it struck your neighbour and not you. When there are only two hours to determine your future, you grow ruthless. It's a dog-eat-dog world. And, after a false start that saw her struggle through two-and-a-half years of the wrong course, she was determined that she would not now fall at the final hurdle.

Her father had been a great scholar once, before his illness. There was evidence around the house, peeping out from beneath the notes that he left himself: books full of equations that were like an alien language; a prestigious Physics medal forgotten in the back of a drawer in the Welsh dresser. She had a memory of a story her mother used to tell about how, outrageously, he had not been there to collect the medal when it was awarded. Something about running away from the ceremony together and spending the evening drinking whisky on the Tube. The details were hazy and her mother rarely spoke of it now, though she'd told it often when Hope was small. Perhaps because then they'd thought that John might one day win medals again.

Her mother had been a scholar too, before she'd become pregnant and Hope's father had fallen ill. Certainly, there were many books and dusty mounds of paper piled up in the corner of a room that was still called the study, although the desk had been covered for years in boxes and broken bits of furniture. She tried to imagine her mother's face unscathed by worry and her father with his speech unhindered, but it all seemed quite improbable. Those people whose footsteps had traced the tall white streets and the broad green parks of London didn't exist for Hope; she knew only their ciphers and the clues they'd left behind. It is an exquisite pain, she thought, to see the shadow of something eternally just out of reach. She bit her lip and cast her attention back to the books. Perhaps Gertrude Stein would have something to add.

As the weeks went by, Hope's calls and emails home had dwindled. When they'd spoken the day before, she had spiralled between the high-pitched laughter and galloping anxiety that Stella recognised from those first years in Oxford, when Hope had been so unhappy. Listening to the sound of her daughter unravelling, Stella had dug her nails into the soft wood of the kitchen table, leaving a series of crescent marks along its edge. She had boarded the train at Temple Meads the next morning almost by accident, only vaguely aware of having made a choice to pack her bag and drive to the station after John had reassured her that he'd be fine. It dawned on her at Didcot, while she was waiting on the crowded platform for her connection, that she had not told Hope of her plans. Holding her mobile phone at arm's length so she could read the tiny writing without her glasses, she'd scrolled through the list of names. She'd had the phone for several months now, but it still felt alien to her that she could make a call from almost anywhere. To her surprise, Hope had answered, her voice breathless in between the wind-noise that crackled across their conversation. They'd agreed to meet outside the college library at six. Stella had glanced up to see the clock above the platform glowing 3.02 p.m. 'An afternoon in Oxford, how lovely!' she'd said, and Hope had laughed as she said goodbye. The connecting train had arrived. Hoisting her bag, Stella had climbed

aboard, trying to ignore the uneasiness that made it difficult for her to stand still.

In a different train heading south, Effie curled up in the
cocoon of her seat as the countryside shuddered past, her
hangover giving the wide breaks of green a melancholy
tinge. Hangovers always did that – brought out the sadness
in everything. Effie knew once she had got through today
she would feel calmer. But for now, queasy and bone-tired,
she was tormented with boomerang thoughts from the night
before. The row with Adam, the angry walk past York's
city walls and along the river home – or home, at least, for
one more night. The rising panic as the packing didn't seem
to end (not helped, she now suspected, by the bottles of
Smirnoff Ice she'd kept on drinking as she shovelled her
clothes with growing abandon into her bags). At 3 a.m.
she'd collapsed into bed fully clothed, ignoring the missed
calls from Adam. He must have slid the note under her door
sometime before 7 a.m., because that was when she got up
to finish the packing. When the taxi had arrived at 10, she'd
slipped the unopened letter into her handbag and struggled
out of the door with her three huge bags, while the driver
had watched her from his seat. She hadn't tipped him when
he'd dropped her at the station.

A guard had eyed her with suspicion as she pushed her
bags up into the train, flustered as the whistle went. He
told her that, strictly speaking, she was not allowed to travel
with so much luggage, almost immediately regretting that
he'd spoken as Effie's face crumpled.

'It's OK, love, just for this once,' he'd stuttered, helping
her to shove an overstuffed holdall into the tiny luggage rack.

'Thank you,' Effie had snivelled, her usual poise undone by lack of sleep and a deeper sense of loss: leaving Adam, leaving York, leaving the safety of university. She was setting out into the uncharted real world and as the train drew off she felt a growing certainty that neither her degree, nor the year she'd spent travelling beforehand, was adequate preparation. For an hour she'd slept, the train closing the gap between her old life and her new one, whatever that would be. When she woke, she remembered the letter and pulled it from her bag, recognising Adam's scratchy scrawl on the front. How random, she found herself thinking, to write me a letter in the middle of the night. Just the kind of pretentious thing Adam would do.

She tore open the envelope and pulled out the note from inside, reading it once, then again, as the words – so gentle-looking on the page – came to life inside her. She took the letter in both hands and pulled, enjoying the rasp of the paper as it ripped. How could she have been so stupid? She tore again and again, small fragments of Adam's writing fluttering onto the coarse train carpet. *Sorry . . . time apart . . . travelling.* He'd booked a ticket, of course – not that he'd told her last night; he was too cowardly to tell the truth or even to break up with her in person. She'd argued with him then – why had he taken so long to tell her and (though this was never said) why did he want to go travelling without her? And after all that, this note beneath her door in the middle of the night; a line drawn firmly under the years they'd been together. He'd used phrases like *love* and *the wrong time* and, most sickening of all, *I only wish we'd met when I was older.* But as far as she was concerned, the letter might as well have said: *Off travelling. So long. P.S. fuck you.*

Too empty to cry, she leaned her head against the glass and watched the backs of industrial estates flash past, tin roofs gleaming in the sunshine on the approach into King's Cross.

Outside Oxford, domes and spires appeared on the horizon, a cluster of golden stone bright among the green. Stella ran her hands through her short greying hair and pulled a notebook and pen from her handbag, pressing words onto the page to staunch the flow of whispered fears. *What if, what if, what if?* When the train pulled in, she moved as one with the crowd along the platform and out of the station, where a sea of locked bikes glinted silver in the sun. As she walked along the narrow streets she peered through the arched college entrances, their painted signs forbidding her to enter. Strange, she thought, how a city can stop being yours once you leave it. In a corner of Blackwell's café she gazed through the window at the stone heads around the Sheldonian as the many lives of Oxford intersected underneath them: black-gowned finalists, camera-toting tourists, a sunken-cheeked pickpocket working his way around the crowd. A girl walked past and for a moment Stella was so sure it was Hope that she grasped her purse to run downstairs. But when the young woman turned to face the window, Stella sighed and sat back down. Her hands began to shake. She wondered why she was so nervous about meeting her own daughter. It was true that the last few times had not been easy. At Easter, Hope had grown so impatient with her and John – and their questions about jobs and studies and boys – that she'd stormed upstairs in the middle of dinner. No one had mentioned it later when she'd come down to watch the television, curling up on the sofa next to her father, leaning her head on his shoulder. Her lineless face had looked so sad, but what could Stella have said? She never seemed to get it right. Better to leave it be. And yet her body had brought her here today with a magnetic tug she could not – and did not want to – resist.

When Hope left the library, Stella was waiting. Hope paused at the entrance for a few moments as she watched her mother from a distance. She noticed the gentle stoop of her upper back and how she looked around the quadrangle of the college that had once been hers with a lowered gaze, tugging at the hem of her jacket and pushing at the bag on the ground with her foot. She seemed so small beside the grand limestone façades; but that was the point, of course, of such an elaborate building: to remind each visitor of their place within the scheme of human knowledge. Hope hitched her rucksack higher on her shoulders and sucked her stomach in, regretting the KitKat she had eaten for breakfast as she felt her flesh against the waistband of her jeans.

Stella turned, her face breaking into a wide smile, and ran towards Hope, leaving her bag behind her.

'Mum, your bag.' Hope mumbled into her mother's tight embrace, too old really to be embarrassed and yet somehow still scanning the quad for faces she knew in order that she might hide from them.

'Oh Hope, it's good to see you! You look wonderful.'

Hope rolled her eyes and pulled her cardigan tighter around her middle. 'I doubt it. I've barely seen daylight in weeks. But thanks for coming, Mum. It's good to have you here.'

Stella studied her daughter, noticing the speed of her speech, the jerky movements and retractions of her body, the hunted look in her eyes. In truth, she looked dreadful – her skin was yellow, her hair dirty.

Stella touched Hope's cheek. 'Come on then, remind me where your room is.'

When Effie's train arrived, Beth ran the length of the platform, her loose dress billowing, her wooden necklace thumping on her chest with each step. Effie waved, feeling herself grow heavy and slow even as she wrapped her arms around her mother, breathing her familiar scent of coconut oil and washing powder.

Beth touched her cheek and asked her if everything was OK, but when Effie tried to speak she felt her throat grow tight, so she forced a laugh instead. 'Just a bit of man-trouble, Mum.'

But Beth had seen the sadness slip across her daughter's face. 'Let's talk about it over dinner.'

Relieved to have been granted the time to find her strength (she would not let Adam make her cry), Effie nodded and kissed her mother's cheek.

Effie was grateful for the running chatter that volleyed between her mum and Rupert at dinner. Tales of patients – no names, of course. The predicted war in Iraq. House prices. Who's getting married, who's being cheated on, traumas and triumphs, the gentle boasts and condemnations that weave the fabric of a family. Effie sipped her wine and listened, detached from it all. The world seemed far too vast for any of this to matter. And yet, there was still the question of the rest of her life and what, exactly, she would do with it.

Beth pushed her dark hair from her face. Threads of grey ran from her temples and her make-up had gathered in the creases around her eyes. 'So, Effie . . .' she lifted her glass and sniffed the viscous red wine, then put it to her lips and drank, ' . . . have you decided what you're going to do about a job?'

Effie sighed, the heaviness pushing against her. 'I'm not sure. I was thinking maybe I could take a bit of time out – you know, before I get my degree result – and try and work it out.'

She drew her knees up to her chest, her feet resting on the edge of the chair, and wrapped her slim arms around her legs.

Beth watched her, the bowl of her wine glass cupped between her palms and said nothing. Rupert leaned across the table and pulled the dish of pistachios towards him. 'What's Adam going to do, Eff?'

Beth caught it before her daughter spoke; she saw the drop of Effie's face and realised what had happened.

'We've broken up. He's going travelling and doesn't think we'll manage the year apart. Actually, neither do I. But he was a bit of a prick about it all, to be honest.' Tears silvered the edges of her eyes and she wiped them away, determined to keep her composure. She would not break down because of Adam.

In Hope's college room, Stella sat on the bed watching her daughter as she changed.

'That was my room over there,' Stella pointed out of the open window.

'I know, Mum, you tell me that every time you visit.'

'Oh – do I?' Stella frowned. 'Sorry, love. Anyway, I thought we could go to Green's for dinner.'

Hope nodded. 'Sounds nice. How's Dad?'

'He's alright, actually. He's working on a bench for the garden at the moment, but he's got a bit of paid work coming up and then we're planning to go on holiday afterwards.'

Hope's face brightened for a moment, then disappeared inside a T-shirt. Her voice emerged, muffled. 'God, Mum, you spend all your time planning holidays, but you never seem to actually go on any.'

'I know, I know. But I'm sure we'll manage one day.'

Stella sighed and Hope noticed how tired she looked.

'Sorry, Mum. Are you OK?'

Stella waved her apology away and picked up a book from the side. 'What's this?'

'Oh – some poetry I've been looking at. Actually, hang on – I want to show you something' Hope flicked through the pages, cracking the spine before she handed it back to her mother.

Stella looked down at the dense, fragrant paper and read once, then twice, the beginning of a poem that she'd never seen before.

> *The time will come*
> *when, with elation*
> *you will greet yourself arriving*
> *at your own door, in your own mirror*
> *and each will smile at the other's welcome,*
>
> *and say, sit here. Eat.*
> *You will love again the stranger who was your self.*

'My God, that's beautiful. Who's it by?'

Hope's smile peeked out, a faltering ray of brightness. 'Derek Walcott. I thought you'd like it.'

Stella took her daughter's hand and as she did she felt the slightest lift within the room, something infinitesimally small rising up between them and into the warm college air.

In the dim light of the restaurant, Hope could see her mother's younger face, a mirror of her own features across the table. They ate fish and drank white wine, talking about her finals and her plans for the future. They walked back through the dark streets, small leaded windows alight along the college walls. In Hope's room they sat on the bed drinking instant cocoa, leaning against one another, watching the moonlit quad below.

'Did you like it here, Mum?'

Stella looked at her daughter, who had softened with the wine. 'Oh yes, I had a lovely day.'

'No, I mean when you were a student. Did you like it here then?'

Stella grasped Hope's hand and kissed it. 'I loved it. The books and the ideas. I even loved the gowns and Latin at dinner. All that stuff.'

'So why did you leave?'

'I got a scholarship for my PhD in London – and it was time to branch out, to be somewhere bigger.'

'And you were good at your studies, right? You did well?'

Stella wondered where Hope was going with all these questions. 'Yes – I suppose – yes, I did do well.'

Hope stood beside the window, her back to her mother.

When she spoke, her voice was very quiet. 'So why did you have me?'

Stella felt a flush creep across her face, a rush of adrenalin sharpening the room around her. She reached for Hope and turned her around, feeling the girl's bony shoulders in her hands, feeling how light she had become, as if she was trying to disappear.

'Hope,' she said in a voice that sounded like somebody else's, 'you are my greatest achievement. I've never regretted having you. Not for a second.'

A rowdy group of finalists staggered across the quad, arms about shoulders and waists, clutching champagne bottles, braying indecipherably at one another. The sound echoed between the high walls, then faded away, as Stella and Hope held one another by the window.

'Time for bed, I think,' Stella stroked her daughter's hair.

Hope nodded. 'You sleep on the bed, Mum – I'll go on the floor.'

Hope's breathing slowed within minutes, but Stella lay wide awake in the dark. She reached out from the bed and brushed her hand against the soft skin of her daughter's cheek as the two red dots on the clock-radio pulsed with every passing second. In a few weeks, thought Stella, all this will be over. This cloistered Oxford life, which had been Hope's world for the past six fretful years, would vanish; though not before she had stood in front of a list of names, working upwards from Third Class to the top of the board, where she would meet her own name with a stream of profanity and a rush of relief.

*

A few weeks later, Effie got her upper second – no surprises there. Beth and Rupert took her for an evening at the National Theatre to celebrate, with dinner beforehand and champagne at the interval. Tipsy on the Tube ride home, Effie leaned against her mother, their hair twisting together, blonde and dark, across Beth's shoulder. Rupert watched the two women as the stations flashed behind them, entranced by their unfathomable bond. Apart from the difference of their hair, their faces were uncannily alike: the same aquiline nose, the same long neck, the same wide, slightly arrogant, mouth. And yet, there was something in the way Effie was talking that sparked a sudden image of Charlie. The thought felt sharp, like chipped ice, and it stayed with Rupert until he fell asleep that night.

Beside the river, Charlie passed the National Theatre, unaware that he was walking the same route as Effie, Beth and Rupert had taken earlier that evening. His eyes roamed across the water as London slipped into its night-time self. For no reason that he could name, Charlie felt the flash of a long-forgotten wrong, a doubling blow that knocked the wind from him and flooded the whole world with a cold new light. *She'd be better off without you.* Sometimes he would imagine Effie as an adult. He'd even thought about going to see her, or phoning her up, but after so many years, fear had ossified the intention. It was far too late – now – to go back. His hands clamped tight around the railing, sweat oiling his grip, while the river ran onwards and out into the dark.

The next morning Effie awoke to the smell of coffee and the clatter of her parents in the kitchen. Her bedside clock

said 8.30, but she resisted the urge to pull the duvet around
her like a comfort blanket and, with a loud sigh, swung her
legs out of the warm nest, stretching her toes in the deep
pile of the bedroom carpet. This would be the first morning
that she had emerged before midday. The last few weeks
had been oddly exhausting; the less she did, the more slug-
gish she became. Her parents hadn't said anything, but she
had seen their silent looks across the kitchen table; an inner
communiqué, she was sure, about her.

Downstairs, Rupert and Beth were sitting at the breakfast table, their hair still damp from the shower. A spread
of toast and coffee and fresh orange was laid out before
them, a stack of newspapers resting alongside the cereal
boxes.

'Well, good morning, sleepyhead,' Beth looked over her
reading glasses at Effie.

'Morning,' answered Effie, pouring a bowl of cornflakes
and milk.

Comfortable in the silence and the morning warmth, Effie
was just beginning her second cup of coffee when Rupert
shook his newspaper shut and placed both hands on the
edge of the table.

'So, Eff, listen . . .' he glanced over as Effie raised her
eyes, the coffee cup still at her mouth, 'I've been speaking
to an old school chum of mine – he's a good sort, was a
journalist for years but he runs a PR agency now. Built it
up himself and it's been bloody successful by all accounts.'

Effie put the cup down and leaned back on her chair, her
long legs crossed, her hands clasped across her knee.

'Anyway,' Rupert continued, 'he was saying that they were
looking to bring in a new assistant – someone just out of

uni, smart, organised – and naturally my thoughts turned
to you. . .'

'Naturally,' Effie deadpanned.

'Well? What do you think?' asked Beth.

Effie stared into the middle distance. In York, she'd never
felt compelled to visit the careers service and, as a result,
knew next to nothing about what Beth and Rupert would
have called 'proper' jobs. 'I don't really know anything about
PR – I mean, how do I know if I'd be any good at it?'

Beth fixed her daughter with a therapist's stare. Effie
braced herself as Beth began to speak in a voice that was a
semitone lower than usual.

'Effie, you just need to try. How will you know what you
want to do unless you give things a go?'

Effie felt as though she was being bound with invisible
cords. 'I just don't know if it's the right thing, Mum. What
if there's something just around the corner?'

'Oh Effie, don't be such a fatalist! You make your life
happen; it's not just waiting for you. You've got to work
for it!'

Without knowing how it happened, Effie was on her feet,
the words tumbling thick and unstoppable from her mouth.
'I do work – I did work – and look where that got me! You
say life doesn't happen to you, but it does. I never chose for
Adam to leave me, I never chose for you and Dad to split
up, I never chose to be born, even—'

'Ah, that old chestnut! Effie, come on, you can do better
than that – you're not sixteen any more.'

'Mum! It's not a joke, don't take the piss. You say I can
choose, but I can't – I never have. It's always you that
chooses.' She was crying now, her face blotched red.

Beth held out her arms and Effie sat on her lap, and for a fleeting second Beth had a sense of this skinny woman as the baby she had once been. 'Shhh, Effie, it's OK. You don't have to do anything in a rush.'

Effie kissed her mother's cheek, then stood up, blowing her nose on a square of kitchen towel. She looked over at her stepfather who had disappeared once more behind the pages of the *Guardian*.

'Thanks, Rupert. I'd like to give it a go.'

Rupert looked around his paper and beamed a wide smile. 'That's my girl. I'll get you his number after breakfast.'

5.2

September 2003

Early-morning Brixton, thought Hope, is a place where the past and the present collide. Dilapidated villas stood proud and the quiet streets widened as she moved through them, high heels tapping on the way to her new job. She passed the town hall, the Ritzy cinema, a man sleeping in a shop doorway. Everywhere, life seemed just about to start. It was only that she wasn't sure if she was ready for it. Beneath the soap and antiperspirant she could already smell her own earthiness; the scent of an impostor. She descended the steps to the Underground, pink ticket tight in her hand, welcoming the warming rush of metallic air as she tugged at the hem of her skirt and felt her clammy nyloned thighs chafe against each other.

At Green Park, she saw stacks of deckchairs and early-morning travellers – where had they come from? – sleeping by their luggage. She glanced at the gaudy side-view of the Ritz as she checked her *A–Z* and began to walk towards Buckingham Palace and St James's Park in the direction of her new office.

*

The agency had been founded by a newsman of the old school: heavy drinking, forty-a-day, effortlessly superior. He had built it with military precision and an extensive network of old-boy contacts and as she walked into the quiet hum of the office, it felt to Hope as though she'd set down in another country, with different cultures and expectations and a strange, half-familiar language.

Offices, she soon realised, breed a kind of hierarchy. People moved and talked with hidden meanings she could not fathom, leaving her hot and dry-mouthed with anxiety.

'Hey you, new girl!'

Prickling, Hope looked up from the reception desk where she sat surrounded by rubber-banded piles of post, an ugly beige computer and an audacious arrangement of lilies. A tall blonde woman of about her age looked down at her, her dark eyebrows raised, tapping a pen against her teeth.

Hope raised a hand in greeting. 'Hello.'

'Yeah, hi,' the woman replied, eyes on Hope's forehead. 'Look, I'm going to need you to stuff two hundred envelopes for me by lunch, OK?'

Hope nodded, pulling her mouth into a smile.

'And whatever you do,' the woman continued in a languid voice, 'don't fuck it up. These are for that twat in there—' she jerked her head towards the newsman's door. Hope could see him through the glass, smoking his fourth cigarette of the morning, leaning back in the big leather chair while bellowing down the phone, the cord stretching tight, then slack, as he rocked back and forth, growing redder and more agitated with each inhalation. There was so much anger everywhere. She felt it surge, a foul-mouthed torrent of people's hurt and fear, which seemed to graze her as it passed. Her skin was too thin. She was always afraid.

The blonde girl sighed and tossed her hair, then stretched out her hand. 'I'm Effie by the way.'

Hope forced herself to smile and meet the woman's eyes. *I will not be afraid of you.* She seemed somehow familiar, though Hope couldn't think why.

'Nice to meet you. I'm Hope. That'll be fine about the envelopes, sure thing!' Her cheeks ached.

'Well, great,' said Effie. 'Thanks for that. Not that you have a choice, newbie.' Effie scowled as she saw the newsman look her way, then stalked off.

Hope watched her with a mixture of resentment and awe as she moved across the office, sure-footed and smooth-skinned. It was hard not to feel irritated by someone so certain of herself, with a voice that rang with confidence and privilege. And yet.

Effie circled in Hope's thoughts all morning. She was sophisticated in a way that Hope had never encountered before, an inhabitant of an exotic world shaped by the Londoner's sureness that all of life was happening there. A string of expletives burst across the office. When she looked over, Effie winked and Hope flushed as she carried on stuffing stacks of papers into her pile of envelopes.

Smoothing down her crumpled skirt, Hope scooped them up and made her way over to Effie, who was tapping at her computer, a half-drunk cup of black coffee beside her. 'Hi – Effie? Here you go.'

Hope leaned forward and the teetering pile slid towards the desk. Oh God! She could see what was about to happen:

the coffee cup, the pale denim of Effie's snug jeans. She gasped and shut her eyes, waiting for the disaster.

When, a second later, there was no crash, no scald, no sudden accusatory silence across the office, Hope tentatively opened one eye.

Looking straight at her with a crooked smile and one hand on the top of the pile, Effie took the stack of envelopes and lifted it to her desk. She raised her eyebrows and smiled again. 'Thanks, uh – ?'

'Hope.' Her cheeks were burning and she had a sudden urge to curl tight into a brace position to stop the terrifying sensation of the world somersaulting away. She cleared her throat and raised her hand in a kind of half-wave. 'Yeah, right – well, thanks.'

She turned to walk away, but Effie called her back. 'Hey, Hope.'

'Yeah?'

'We're going for drinks on Friday at the Chapel, if you want to come?'

An invitation! The world stopped turning over and was suddenly filled with warmth – a Technicolor moment that would lead to a Technicolor life of parties and romance and . . . 'Oh, great, yes, that'd be lovely! Is it, I mean should I – you know – bring a change of clothes or something?'

She had started to gabble, she realised, noting Effie's cocked head, her small smile – not quite cruel but with a hardness that brought back the scowls of blonde-permed girls in playgrounds past. Hope stopped speaking, trailing off into a non-verbal sound, tucked her hair behind her ears and walked back across the office, conscious of Effie's gaze against her back.

*

Hope wasn't an accomplished lover. She'd had boyfriends, of course, and though she'd shed her virginity as quickly as possible with the nicest boy she could find at the time, sex had thus far been more of a box-ticking exercise than a carnal awakening. There were benefits, she could see, to a secret world of smell and taste and sensation between two people. But she had never seen any sign of coloured lights flashing, never felt herself become a starburst of sensation and nothing else at all. At the age of twenty-five, Hope was certain she was the last of her kind.

There had been plenty of attempts, though. Paolo, the jet-haired musician, who'd whispered obscenities in Italian while he bucked inside her. Or Mali, with his lustrous eyelashes and curly brown hair who loved her, but loved himself more. Or Timothy, a beautiful image of pink-cheeked perfection, who cried when he came and then fell promptly asleep. Or Nick who didn't wash often enough and whom she'd only fucked when she was drunk. None of them ever once made her come; she had relied on herself for that once they'd left or passed out. A wave of warmth rose through her and, looking up, she saw that Effie was staring at her, her eyes lingering for a second before she turned away. Hope noticed how the line of her nose gave her face a regal profile, the gentle curve of her belly peeking taut and brown from the cropped edge of her T-shirt.

How do you stop looking, once you know someone is watching? It became a kind of game, one that offset the boredom spliced with panic that passed for Hope's job as the newsman's new assistant. It's grossly unfair, she thought to herself, how much potential for disaster there is in the most junior office role. Mistimed mailings, mislaid cheques, missed minutes, mis-booked lunches. Over the next five days Hope was shouted at eleven times (she kept a tally). And with each mishap and reprimand the likelihood of further errors increased as the nestling almond of her amygdala sent waves of adrenalin crashing through her body: a roaring flood to dampen hunger, quicken her heartbeat and tighten her muscles ready to run. But where to run? The grey pods gazed back blankly, the computers hummed, someone spoke in a falsely bright voice on the phone. Nowhere to run. Nowhere to hide. Nothing to hide from, in truth, except the painful thump of her own fight-primed body.

Her hands shook, spilling coffee, dropping papers. Her mind raced, leaving blanks and blurs that gaped whenever anyone asked even the simplest of questions. The discomfort was intense, yet invisible, like an ill-fitting pair of shoes. But solace came in the story that she'd begun to tell herself in moments of daydream. A lover, an adventure across late-night London, dark-lit bars with maudlin singers plucking at badly tuned guitars. Then dancing and sunrise and sophisticated breakfasts, with papers and coffee, passing the colour supplements, which spiralled brightly before her eyes and . . .

'Hope? Hope? Are you OK?'

The office snapped back into focus as Effie leaned towards her and touched her shoulder in a waft of ginger perfume. Her hands were smooth with long perfect fingers, short clean nails and delicate nodes of wrists, encircled with chinking silver bangles. Her slender neck wore a tangle of silver chains: a cross, a small bird and a flat round St Christopher pendant nestled against her skin.

'Pack up, newbie, we're off to the pub!'

*

Three drinks in and it seemed the obvious topic of conversation among the group of ambitious young women. Bethany
from Marketing recalled a cold forest floor, Claire from
Consumer a bunk bed in her second boyfriend's bedroom,
Anna from Accounts a pub toilet. Intimate details were
shared in lurid, competitive descriptions. Effie sat with a
wry detachment, a flicker of a wince passing from time to
time across her otherwise placid face. The noise was rising
now, the drinks flowing, a warm hum of bonhomie and
titillation rustling around the table. Drunk and buoyed up
with a sense of new beginnings, Hope reached for another
drink, leaning heavily against Effie as she did.

'Oops, sorry!' she shrieked above the din.

Effie looked faintly amused and placed her hand on Hope's
forearm, her fingers pressing lightly on the warm flesh. Her
lips brushed against Hope's ear. 'That's quite OK, newbie.'

She leaned back and gave a broad, full-toothed grin,
slender arms behind her head. 'So what's your story, then?
Anything outrageous to share?'

And maybe it was the beer or maybe the fierce rush of
blood that had passed through her at the other woman's
touch, but whatever the reason Hope found herself telling
Effie about all the men she'd slept with: from the weeping
cherub to the never-sober fuck buddy.

Effie nodded and gave a small half-smile. 'Impressive. But
there's something missing, right?'

'No, that's pretty much everyone,' laughed Hope, conscious
of her cheeks growing hot. Effie touched her burning skin
with cool fingers.

'D'you know what I think, Hope? I don't think that
anyone's ever hit the spot. All those men desperate for you,

but they gave you nothing in return. I reckon you deserve more, a beautiful girl like you.'

To her horror, Hope began to cry, fat unbidden tears coursing trails across her cheeks. She swabbed her face with a paper napkin and looked away.

'Hope? I'm sorry, I – I didn't mean to upset you.'

Suddenly the poise was gone and Effie sounded like an actual person, someone finding her way like the rest of them. The wry smile dissolved as she placed her hand again on Hope's arm. The shame abated slightly, and Hope tried to smile and knock back the concern that had made Effie suddenly real. But that touch had unleashed an irreversible reaction: there was no going back now. The two girls looked at each other. A new order had been made.

They laughed on the busy streets of Soho as they stumbled down the stairs of a smoky cellar bar, away from the tawdry group of girls from the newsman's team. The night passed in flashes of lucidity: a cigarette stolen from a handsome dark-haired man; a fourth drink, a fifth. Cocktails for the road. Laughing at Hope's impression of her bucking foul-mouthed Italian. Fingertips touching. A sharpness in every corner of her body. Heat pulsing in her thighs. Running hand-in-hand, car headlights dancing. A stumble. Leaning, breathless against a wall. Something urgent being said. And then.

In the dimness of the impending dawn they lay entangled on the mattress that served as Hope's bed. In the distance, they heard sirens and, below them, the sounds of Hope's neighbour, a young man she wouldn't have recognised if she'd passed on the street, but whose bathroom habits she knew almost by heart.

5.3

April 2005

London at night was another city, one that Charlie knew
well from his long walks to and from his job at the homeless hostel. This was the world of the young and the
streetwise, but look closely and you'd discover the under-
class: the lost, the vulnerable, the shadows from another
time. In the dark spaces between the tall glass buildings
you'd see them, curled up on cardboard beds, or moving
slowly through the streets, quiet as ghosts. In the café by
Brixton station that locals called 'the greasy', Charlie sat
with his tea, tired and cold after another long night,
watching the flow of people on their way to work. In the
daylight dominion of suits and Starbucks, Charlie knew he
was invisible. He belonged to the underbelly of this gleaming
world of commerce and waste. There, his story was one of
many – voiceless in the daytime, unheard within the noise
of people in a hurry.

That evening he wandered back to the hostel, passing
through the strange intimacy of city life. The blue-white
flicker of a TV, T-shirts hung in the window to dry. Further
on, a bay window, an old man sitting beneath a bare bulb,
a cityscape of piled-up books around him. When had it

begun, this need to walk? Charlie listened to the sound of his trouser-legs rubbing and his feet as they hit the ground. At Vauxhall he crossed the road and slipped into the dark of the railway arches, watching unnoticed as sweat-slick men emerged in pairs from the bass thump and smoke of the club across the street. Battered by the crosswind on the bridge, he hugged his arms about himself, tilting his head down and following the white toe-caps of his trainers as they swung in and out of his vision. In the middle, he stopped and looked east, letting his arms hang by his sides. The wind whipped at his coat and his eyes shut tight against the blast of bitter air. But even behind his closed eyes, he could see the view before him: the lit-up arches of Lambeth Bridge, the flicker of the water below, the stately thrust of the Houses of Parliament, the low dark trees along the curve of the river. Almost every night this ritual was the same, save for the bite of the wind, which grew kinder in the summer. He heard old words echo back across the centuries, flitting along the river from Westminster Bridge, an afterglow of the bright moment in which they came to life:

> *Ne'er saw I, never felt, a calm so deep!*
> *The river glideth at his own sweet will:*
> *Dear God! the very houses seem asleep;*
> *And all that mighty heart is lying still!*

At four in the morning, after he had finished his shift at the hostel, he stepped out into the near-deserted streets of Victoria. Onwards and upwards, he whispered to himself. Onwards and upwards and into the secret world of the city in the night. Near Embankment he sat by the water and took a sandwich wrapped in tinfoil from his pocket. As he ate, he watched the curves and minarets of government buildings take shape against the lightening sky. On the neighbouring bench a homeless man shouted in his sleep. Charlie stood up and followed the river east, the rising fingers of Canary Wharf blinking in the distance.

Later, his path curved back along the river and south again to Brixton. He walked on as the sky glowed red, then orange, then pink behind the black regiments of chimney pots and heard, once more, Wordsworth whisper in his ear:

> *This City now doth, like a garment, wear*
> *The beauty of the morning; silent, bare.*

As the last night-buses brought the first tide of the daytime – the cleaners and security guards, baristas and sandwich-makers – Charlie was heading back to his flat. He was tired from his night's work, from carrying the weight of other people's chaos and despair: the anger of the people he'd turned away when the hostel was full, the fear of a refugee family who'd arrived exhausted and with nothing, his own disgust at the debris that the addicts left behind.

He crawled onto his bed and listened for the soft sounds of the young man who lived above, but this morning he heard nothing. Had he moved on? It seemed to him that people shifted so quickly these days; he could barely remember how many had passed through the rooms above him in the many years he'd lived there. They blurred now into a montage of late-night door-slams, noisy sex and rattling pipes. But it brought its own kind of comfort, that anonymous intimacy. It could distract him from the chaos in his head, the replayed conversations with Beth, the constant whispering desire to drink, just as writing once had. Years ago, he would write for hours after he had walked the dark streets, measuring his life out in typescript on paper. But he no longer had any words to write; his feet had traced his story all across the night-time city. The pages lay on a shelf in the living room, waiting, though he wasn't sure for what. Behind his closed eyes his mind turned over thoughts of the night before, their ceaseless flow undercut by a murmur of older, darker memories.

It was midday when at last he fell asleep. In Brixton, shoppers bustled, busy with lunchtime errands, while a few miles north, Hope queued in the supermarket in Victoria Street to pay for her lunch. The day felt heavy as she walked back to the office, counting the hours until it was time to go home. What does it take, she wondered as she lifted her lunch onto the desk, for us to stop pretending? A death, perhaps, or a birth? What would crack my world open so that I could start again?

She looked at the supermarket sushi lying flaccid on her work desk, strip light glinting on the plastic packaging. Around her, the air was filled with the electric hum of monitors and the smell of last night's supper being microwaved for lunch. What was this, this false place? It was not a place of comfort or ideals. This whole office, these many rushing emotions, they were all nothing more than an illusion, a mirage created by mysterious market forces that she didn't understand. Here, she thought, and all across the city, armies of people were shackled to the harsh blue-white light of their screens, incarcerated between ceiling tiles and commercial-use carpets.

Kate from Accounts was striding between the desks and booths, her synthetic grey suit crackling with static, her high heels still with a price label stuck to the sole. As Hope watched her, she realised that this was the moment. Glancing across the office to Effie, she picked up her bag and walked out, tossing the sushi into the bin as she passed.

The call came at 5.32 p.m. The green screen glowed, Effie's name spelled out across it in small black squares. Her voice was so loud that Hope had to hold her phone away from her ear. 'Oh – my – God!'

'Jesus, Effie, you don't need to shout.'

'Fuck me, what a drama! All hell broke loose after you left. The phone was ringing off the hook and the newsman – well, I thought he was about to have an aneurysm.'

'Did he?'

'No. More's the pity.'

Hope laughed. 'I just couldn't take it any more.'

Effie snorted. 'So we gathered. Ha! Look, I need a drink after all that. Shall I come over?'

Hope looked about her room, the CDs stacked in piles along the skirting board, the cheap poster of Matisse's *Icarus* she'd bought as a student, the collection of empty wine bottles on the sideboard. 'Sure, yeah, come over – oh, and would you pick me up a copy of the *List*? I guess I need to get job-hunting.'

'You totally do. See you in a bit.'

*

The next morning as she was getting ready for work, Effie sat on the edge of the bed. 'Don't you think it's time you told your parents about me?'

And that was how Hope ended up on a train to Bristol on the first day of her unemployment, listening to people in suits making important calls. *Hi, Dave, it's Piers.* And being cut off from them. *Dave, can you hear me? Hello? Dave? Forfuckssake.*

Stella cried out in delight when she came home and saw Hope in the garage with John.

'Who fancies a cuppa?' said Hope, voice wobbling as her pulse thudded in her throat.

When the kettle was boiled and the tea was poured, Hope told them about Effie. The silence was thick with a weight of its own as Hope stared at the three cups of tea on the table and waited for one of her parents to speak.

'Hope.'

Her head jerked up at her father's laboured voice: slow, tentative, a parody of the agile young man she'd never known.

'Do – you – love her?'

Hope nodded. 'I do.'

Stella looked at her daughter's smooth face and recognised the beauty of someone who doesn't realise how beautiful they actually are. It was remarkable how, when she really looked, she could still see the traces of the baby that she'd swaddled in her one good bath towel; the small girl who had cried for her daddy, then cowered when she saw him blank-eyed in his hospital bed; the teenager with the frizzy hair and over-sized clothes; the wild-eyed finalist with trembling hands, whose soft cheek she had stroked in her sleep.

John's hand reached for Stella. 'Your – mother – and I—' Silence broadened as he burrowed for the words. 'We're – proud – of you. We—'

Stella pulled her hand from John's and clasped her daughter's wrist. 'We love you, Hope. And we would love to meet Effie.'

The cold tea slopped onto the table as the three of them leaned together in an angular embrace. Stella breathed into Hope's shoulder, relieved that even in the washing powder and perfume she could still find the scent of her child.

The following weekend Effie took Hope to meet her parents at their house in Swiss Cottage.

Effie and her mother argued loudly in the kitchen, while Hope sat rigid on the edge of a fraying velvet chaise longue, looking around the over-stuffed living room. She took in the Persian rug, the Guatemalan wood carving, Malian drums and wall hangings from India; rich paraphernalia of a well-travelled life.

'I don't agree!' she heard Effie shout above the clank and sizzle of dinner being prepared.

'More parmesan perhaps?' Rupert was asking no one in particular as he stirred the risotto, a glass of white wine in hand, his thinning grey hair grazing the collar of his brushed cotton shirt.

Beth stretched around him, placing her hand on his shoulder, a thick silver cuff around her wrist. Pulling the wooden spoon from her red-stained lips she frowned. 'More wine and salt – definitely.'

Effie caught her mother by the waist and twisted her around. 'But Mum, how can you think that? He doesn't even scratch the surface of what it is to be alive – I mean, for God's sake, what about people like me? Am I stuck in some sort of arrested development because I don't want to be fucked by a man?'

Hope felt her cheeks flame, but Rupert went on stirring, undisturbed.

Beth laughed and hugged her daughter. 'You are such a firebrand, Effie! And no, I don't think that. I know it's contentious, but we do need to look at the cultural context a little here. I mean, when he was writing—'

'When who was writing?' Rupert asked, peering around from the stove.

'Freud!' both women shouted at once.

'Oh, right,' Rupert shrugged at Hope through the doorway as he turned back to his pan.

Beth carried on speaking, one arm stretched out in front of her as though she was conducting. 'Anyway, if you tease out the bones of the argument, what you get to is that our sexual selves are an important part of who we are, but it's our experience as an infant that shapes our understanding of the world, our capacity for love and our sense of worth. And I like to think that, even though your dad wasn't about much, you were always sure that you were loved. That I loved you so much it took my breath away. Still does, actually—'

Effie grinned and kissed her mother on the forehead. Beth went on. 'And the fact that you're sure enough of your own heart to know who you love and to share that with Rupert and me – well, that feels like the opposite of arrested development, actually. I think that's the sort of maturity we're all aiming for, Effie.'

Hope watched the ease with which mother and daughter moved around one another, how comfortable the shift from heated argument to affectionate lull. There seemed to be no barrier between them: they flowed together to create something purely theirs – their words and non-words, the unspoken sense in which they seemed to know each other's meaning. How intensely they heard one another, unwinding ideas between them with enchantment on their faces. What must such openness feel like? A little bit terrifying, perhaps, she thought.

The light caught the small silver medal on Effie's neck and Beth reached out to touch it, then drew her hand back as if the metal had burned her. 'Oh – it's his!'

Effie's face angled slightly, her nostrils flared. Hope wasn't the only person who could see she was angry. Rupert caught Beth's hand, but said nothing, wise enough to know that this was not a fight for him to join.

When she replied, Effie's voice was hushed. 'Yes, Mum, it is. I always wear it. You know that – it was what he left me.'

'Of course. I'm sorry, Eff. I just – I don't know – I forgot, I guess.'

'It's all I have, Mum.'

Effie frowned, but Beth pulled her close. 'Oh Effie, darling, it's OK.'

Her mother's arms about her, Effie touched her finger to the silver disc with its worn outline of a man carrying a small child on his back: St Christopher, the patron saint of travellers. The picture was rubbed quite smooth, faded almost to nothing. Effie thought of all the places this thin metal token had travelled with her father and then with her. She turned it in her finger and thumb, looking at the places where it had been worn down by touch, piece by tiny piece, lifting away invisible traces of their lives and carrying them out into the world.

5.4

July 2005

Hope looked up as the lights along the carriage blinked off then on again. Three weeks had passed since the bombings – three underground and one on a bus, its sides blown open like a flower in bloom – and still her body ran cold at every flicker or bang on the Tube. She sighed and leaned in closer to Effie.

'The thing with Dad is that it just takes a lot longer for him to get the words out because of the scarring on his brain from when he was ill – oh, hang on, isn't this our stop?'

'No, next one. Hope, we've talked about all this before. It'll be fine, honestly.'

'I know, I know, I just – basically he's using a diversion, if you like, so talking to him can be a little bit painful, if you're not used to it. You need to be patient.'

The Tube screeched once again and a busy platform slowed outside the windows.

Effie took Hope's hand in hers. 'Come on, silly thing. It's all going to be fine.'

A flood of people rushed across the station concourse: a copper-haired old lady and her Barbour-jacketed daughter, a straggle of teenagers with their bags and shoelaces trailing, a white-knuckled mother clutching at her pram. Hope and Effie moved against the tide towards the trains. At the far end of the platform a tall, thin man and a short, sturdy woman moved towards the scrum of Saturday shoppers and day-trippers. Stella tugged at John's arm and pointed to where Hope ran across the station, clutching the hand of a tall girl whose blonde hair streamed out behind her.

'There she is – oh!'

John opened his arms wide as Hope jogged towards them, her face alight. They encircled her with an arm each, a small family unit locking into place. Effie stood a few yards back, watching. Her skin prickled with a nervous heat and her stomach felt as if it were turning inside out. Hope kissed her parents and started talking so fast that she didn't seem to take a breath.

She pulled them over to Effie, blushing as she took her hand. 'Mum, Dad, this is Effie.'

'We're very pleased to meet you, Effie,' Stella said in a voice clipped short around the edges.

'Likewise,' Effie replied. 'It's – I've been really looking forward to meeting you both.' She forced herself to look straight at Hope's father, expecting to see some abnormality, something that would mark him out as different. Her eyes tracked across his face, taking in the shaggy grey-brown hair, the slight fall of his jowls, the crenulations of his ageing skin. He smiled, deep folds radiating from the corners of his eyes and across his cheeks.

'Hello – Effie.'

'Good to meet you, John.'

Hope linked arms with her mother and led the way through the swarms of people. They descended the escalators, down and down again, into the airless warmth of the Underground. Amongst the rattle of the ageing Tube trains, the foursome pushed and quickstepped their way through the crowds and tunnels and emerged, relieved, at Piccadilly Circus. Stella and Hope led the way onto a side street and into a dark-fronted restaurant where they sat down at a bare wooden table in the window. Stella put on her reading glasses to study the menu.

'We came here as students,' she said as she looked around, taking in the dark walls, the chrome counter.

John nodded. 'Yes – but – it was – different then – shabby.'

Effie was surprised by Stella's throaty laugh.

'Yes, it was a right old dive back then! – I seem to remember that the actors from the theatres over on Shaftesbury Avenue used to come here for a cheap dinner before their shows – that's what John told me anyway.'

John turned to Hope and nudged her, a triumphant half-smile forming. 'She – thinks I – don't' – a pause caught him and they waited for him to untangle the word – 'remember!'

Stella turned towards him, a strange expression on her face. Her features seemed to Effie to have softened and it took a decade from her. 'You do?'

John took her hand and kissed it. 'Naturally.'

The two girls looked at the older couple, waiting for an explanation. Hope handed her mother a napkin and she dabbed her eyes.

'This is where . . .'

She paused and John finished the sentence for her.

'. . . your mum told – me – that she – was expecting – you.'

Stella told the girls of her return to London in the late summer before the term began and the hazy evening that John had come to meet her from the train. As she finished talking, she took John's hand and when Effie saw the look that passed between them, she turned her eyes away.

The waiter who came to take their order was so beautiful that Hope had difficulty forming her words. How did anyone even manage to speak to him, with those cheekbones? Those eyes?

Effie prodded her in the ribs. 'You're gawping, Hope,' she murmured, amused.

The handsome waiter left them and the girls began their story of the newsman's office. Hope's parents laughed at Effie's impression of the bluster and hysteria, though Hope was relieved that she'd toned down the language. The thought of her mother hearing Effie's vigorous workplace swearing left Hope feeling slightly sick. The conversation moved on to Hope's plans for a new job. (The mother definitely didn't approve, Effie remarked to herself, impressed at the older woman's self-restraint, but disliking the change in atmosphere around the table and the return of Stella's clipped tone.)

'Charity work? Will that be paid?'

'Yes, of course, Mum. It's a proper job. It's just in-house, which means I'll get to really understand the work the charity does. Plus the people will be nicer.'

Effie looked at Hope, eyebrows raised.

'Well, most of them will be nicer. Not all agency people are as bad as the newsman, of course.' Hope nudged Effie with her knee, and the two young women grinned.

'And how about you, Effie?' Stella's voice was beginning

to thaw again as she sipped her white wine. 'How did you end up working at the agency?'

Effie told them about Rupert's connection to the newsman and how he had set her up with a job with his old school chum a few years before.

Stella probed further. 'So where did your dad go to school then, Effie?'

'Oh no – not my dad. Rupert's my stepdad. But he got together with my mum when I was six and my dad – well – I've not seen him since I was seven. So, to all intents and purposes, Rupert is my dad, I guess.'

The older woman looked pained. 'Oh well, that's – I mean – do you have any idea where he might be?'

'Well, I think he may still be in London, but I've not tried to find him. I figured that if he's not interested in seeing me, then why should I go looking for him?'

Hope watched her mother as she considered this answer and Stella was conscious of her daughter's stare. But she could see the pain that spun out of Effie in silent waves and she knew she had to try to make it better.

'Do you wonder if, maybe, it might be worth hearing his side of the story?' Stella asked in a quiet voice.

'Mum!' Hope's tone was harsh, but Effie stopped her.

'It's OK, I don't mind. I have wondered about it, yes. Lately more than ever. I keep remembering things, little flashes that I haven't thought of in years.'

Stella nodded, waiting for more, but Effie stopped and looked down, her hair closing like a curtain about her face. Then she sighed and straightened up, a smile stretching into place, 'But anyway – I'm sorry! This wasn't supposed to be about me and my baggage.'

Hope laid her cheek against Effie's shoulder. 'I'm sorry,' she whispered in her ear, 'she just can't help herself.'

But Effie shook her head. She had warmed to Hope's mother and her brave questions. Beneath Stella's brittle patina, Effie could see the fault lines of someone whose life had been torn and reformed, hardening like a shell around the tender centre of her dreams.

After lunch they walked out, shading their faces as their eyes adjusted to the afternoon sunshine. After the wine, Piccadilly felt highly tuned, traffic and people turning in a kaleidoscope of red, black, blue, grey.

When they reached the green expanse of the park, Hope caught her father's arm. 'Dad?'

'What are – you – after?'

'What? How do you know I want something?'

John smiled and Hope laughed. 'Oh, OK! I've passed these deckchairs so many times and never had the chance to sit in them. Can we stop here for a while?'

They set four chairs together in a circle, heads in the centre, legs pointing outwards to form a star. One by one, they leaned back against the green and white stripes, turning their faces up to the bright spring sky above.

'See that cloud, Mum?'

'Which one, darling?'

'The one that looks like an upside-down snail.'

'That's not a snail, darling.'

'It's not?'

'No, certainly not.'

'What is it then?'

'It's a phallus.'

Effie and John began to snigger.

'Mother!'

'Well, honestly! Where's your imagination?'

An aeroplane crossed the sky, too high for any noise to be heard. Hope watched the vapour trail as it slackened and broke, receding gradually back into the blue.

They said goodbye at the statue of Eros. Stella and John descended the steps to take the Tube north, back to Paddington, while Effie and Hope crossed the road and went into the bookshop that had once been Simpson's department store. Effie loved this place, not just because of the books, but because everywhere she could see the shapes and traces of a forgotten world: the elegant turn of the revolving door; the marble corners of the staircase, its banister unnervingly low; even the lit-up numbers above the lift. It all seemed so full of hope, remnants of a time when people believed that they had fought the war to end all wars. Stepping into the wood-panelled lift, Effie and Hope held hands and laughed, and Effie wondered how she might have survived a life in which she would have had to keep her love for Hope a secret. Perhaps, she thought, things are a little better now after all. The doors hissed open and they walked towards the bar. A scowling waiter brought their drinks to a table over-looking a cluster of slanting rooftops, and Effie smiled to see its rare view of a wide London sky.

'They're amazing, your parents. They seem so in love.'

Hope paused, twisting a strand of her thick brown hair around her finger. 'It's strange, Eff. I've never seen them like that before.'

Effie took her hand. 'Well, cheers to them, I say.'

Hope looked out across the rooftops of the city. 'Yes, you're right,' she turned back to Effie and clinked her glass, 'cheers to Mum and Dad.'

The rain had battered Bristol while they'd been away and the drive home from the station was a washout. Even in the short run from car to house they'd both been drenched. Stella fumbled in her purse to find the key, her clothes clinging to her, her hair sending currents of water down her face. She felt a pressure about her waist and looked down to see John's arms around her. His face was wet with rainwater and as they kissed a crack of lightning flashed, the thunder rumbling straight behind.

'It's right above us!' Stella gasped.

She turned the key and they dashed into the hall, peeling off wet clothes as they did, laughing at the sight of themselves both standing in their underwear. It was like being caught in time, thought John – this place, these bodies, this sudden need – it was so infinitely familiar, yet so very distant.

'I've – missed you – Stella.'

She laid her head upon his chest as they embraced in the hallway, a puddle seeping from the wet clothes at their feet. 'I've missed you too, John.'

They kissed again. The windows rattled. He grasped her hand and led her upstairs to the bed they had not shared in almost twenty years.

5.5

In the flames of the Chanukiah, Effie saw herself as part of something greater, a mesh of lives that spanned generations: the same words uttered, the same lights lit. She heard the familiar prayer intoned by Rupert and her mother and felt the ancient words in her own mouth. Across the room she could see Hope's face, soft in the candlelight, her expression somewhere between self-consciousness and awe. Afterwards they ate, of course. Creamy soup and latkes, roast chicken and potatoes which Beth piled high on their plates, and organic wine, the origins of which Rupert described at such length that Effie rolled her eyes and prodded him in the side.

'Just pour it out already, Rupert!'

Hope marvelled at the warmth of it, the way the conversation flowed unhindered, words cast lightly without effort or fear. Years ago she had gone to a salsa evening – someone else's idea – and she'd hated every awkward second until she'd partnered with the teacher. With him she danced like someone else, his minute touches guiding her until she was fluid against him. It was like that here: Beth and Rupert, confident and accomplished, gently prompting her into being sure of herself, drawing her into their dance. It felt so new, so easy, so free that she didn't dare to ask herself whether any of it was real.

When the plates had been cleared and Rupert and Beth were washing up, Hope and Effie sat with their coffee by the open fire. Effie leaned her head against Hope's shoulder, blowing twists of Hope's brown hair from where they fell against her face.

'You're so lucky, Eff.'

'Hmm, what's that?'

'Having parents like these. They're so open – you can say anything to them. They didn't bat an eyelid when you came out; they're always talking about sex and drugs – practically telling us about their own experiences—'

'Believe me, they do share their own experience given half a bloody chance—'

'Oooh, gross!'

'Yup.'

Effie picked at the skin around her thumbnail. 'It's not all straightforward happy families,' she said softly, 'you know that.'

Hope moved closer to Effie, who had folded into herself, arms wrapped around her knees. The night she'd told Hope about her father she'd done the same, pulling herself into a tight ball as if for protection. It was not long after they had first been together and Hope had been unsettled by Effie's empty sobs, unsure of who this broken person was.

'Do you – do you ever think about finding him?'

Effie unfolded her legs and sat back, turning to look at Hope. 'Well—'

'Hello, you two!' Beth came in carrying the cafetière and a plate of homemade truffles.

Hope held her stomach and made a groaning noise. 'God, Beth, I can't possibly eat another thing, but thank you.'

Effie stretched long, like a cat. 'Give them here, Mum – I'll have a few.'

Beth laughed so that her earrings shook. 'That's my girl,' she said.

Christmas in Bristol a few weeks later was a quiet affair. Midnight mass, with its congregation of fair-weather Catholics and drunk people (which, noted Hope, was not necessarily a mutual exclusion). Stockings left outside their room on their return – 'Mum's tradition,' explained Hope. 'Anyone here on Christmas morning gets a stocking. One year she even did one for the cat.'

On Christmas Day, after turkey, stuffing and a slew of terrible cracker jokes, they took their wine glasses into the living room, where John pored over a copy of the *Radio Times* marked up in pencil with the schedule of his festive viewing. During a polite impasse over what to watch – there was a period drama that Stella had suggested they put on, but then had insisted she didn't mind not watching it – they flicked onto an old black and white film that Hope had never seen before, to the horror of her parents and Effie.

'What do you mean you've never seen *It's a Wonderful Life*?' shouted Effie from the kitchen, where she'd gone to fetch some water. 'Stella? John? Look at the gap in your daughter's education!'

John tutted and Stella laughed. 'I guess that settles it, then,' she said.

When the film had finished Stella and John excused themselves. Hope poured two more glasses of wine and settled onto the sofa next to Effie, listening to the churn of the boiler and the creak of the floorboards as her parents got ready for bed. Later, tipsy, the two girls switched off the TV and made their way upstairs, where the door of the main bedroom was shut. In the bright light of the bathroom Hope stared at the toothpaste foam as it gathered in the sink. Something was different, but she couldn't quite put her finger on what.

'Oh – wow. Well I never.'

'What is it?'

'Mum and Dad are in the same room. I've never known them share a room before. Something must have –' Hope paused, cringing at the thought.

Effie gave a quiet laugh. 'It's great that they're happy.'

'Yes,' said Hope, spitting another glob of toothpaste into the sink, 'I guess it is.'

Effie kissed her, sliding her arms around her waist. Leaning back, Hope turned to look in the mirror, noticing her own sturdy body, the brown hair that would never be tamed, in sharp contrast to Effie's tall, blonde poise. And yet, here they were together, tiptoeing into her childhood bedroom and curling into one another in a makeshift double bed on the floor, next door to her parents who had somehow found each other again.

*

They travelled back to London the day after Boxing Day, full of food but deflated, their festive jollity gone. As the train cut through the green rolls of countryside, Hope leaned against the window. In the distance, the smoking towers of Didcot appeared and she thought of all the times she had descended from the train here to catch a connection to Oxford. How temporary it all had felt, ricocheting between two cities every eight weeks. In the glass she could see the reflection of her eye, the smooth curve of her cheek and, in the background, Effie's profile: the strong line of her nose, the high edges of her cheekbone. She tried to pinpoint when the shift had happened; when home had become where Effie was. Perhaps it had been when they'd moved in together and made a space of their own. Or perhaps it was not a moment as such; not a point that could be pinned down, but an accumulation of time that gradually gathers until it takes on a shape and momentum of its own.

A little later, Hope reached for Effie's hand and they moved closer together. 'I've been thinking, Eff.'

'Oh, yeah?'

'Well—' She paused then, not for effect, but with a sudden realisation that asking this might change everything, like a mistimed turn or a hole in the road.

'Hope? Are you OK?'

'I just think, perhaps, we should get married.'

Effie's face was blank.

Hope waited for a few seconds, but no answer came. 'Effie? Are you not going to answer, at least?'

The industrial outskirts of West London flashed past,

bleak and empty in the dimming winter light. Hope tightened her fists and turned to look out of the window, but
Effie clasped her shoulder, pulled her back and kissed her,
hard and salty with tears.

'Yes,' she said in a voice so quiet it was barely a breath,
'yes, let's get married.'

5.6

On the seventh floor of the Tate Modern, Effie walked into the Members' Room with her parents.

Stella felt her head begin to throb, aware of a sudden sense of tattiness, of the loose hem of her skirt and the snag in her tights and of the way in which John was staring at the beautiful woman with grey-streaked hair and the man who walked beside her with quiet assurance. Rupert looked like the man that she'd once imagined that John might have become, his white shirt crumpled, his smile warm but reserved.

Beth held out her hand. 'Stella, John, so pleased to meet you at last.'

Effie noticed how her mother's vowels were rounder as she introduced herself, the threads of her North London accent tidied away for the time being.

Beth and Rupert knew, of course, about John's speech and Hope was grateful for the gentle way they spoke with him, neither tensing as they waited for his answers, nor slowing their speech as they asked questions or told stories. They are good people, she thought, as she watched her mother warming to them too.

Across the river, the dome of St Paul's rose between the glass of tall new buildings, a familiar city stretching its limbs, still buoyant on a worldwide bubble that had not yet burst. The skyline shaped their conversation as they remembered the wedding underneath that dome of a woman who had never become queen.

'It was the day before we moved to Bristol,' Stella was saying, 'I can remember the street party outside as we were packing.'

Beth, though, remembered the funeral better. The sweat on the foreheads of the soldiers carrying the coffin in Westminster Abbey, the tremor of their steps beneath its weight as they moved across the black and white tiled floor. The card among the white wreaths that bore one heart-breaking word: *Mummy*. Beth had never been a royalist – here Stella and John nodded vigorously – but as those two boys walked beside the crowds of weeping strangers she'd felt a rush of compassion and a compulsion to keep watching that she hadn't been expecting.

Hope and Effie talked about their wedding plans between the snatches of their parents' reminiscences, a patchwork of memories that would be their new shared history. Hope slipped her hand inside of Effie's as they let their parents speak, the familiar stories played back from different angles. Hope watched the cathedral opposite as time and people passed and the curved edges of the dome darkened against the sky.

Later, when they'd left Hope, Effie and her parents at Paddington, John watched from the train window as the back-views of houses sped past in the fading light. Here, he thought, were the untold stories of countless lives reduced to the briefest of glimpses. And he and Stella too, he supposed, became glimpses; their faces unseen in the train's swift flash of metal, a brief punctuation mark in the interleaved existence of inner-city lives.

Stella took his hand. 'I was thinking that we should go away for a holiday sometime, just the two of us.'

Their legs touched. He looked at her face and saw a brightness that seemed familiar. He couldn't quite reach the memory, but there was something in the way it glimmered in his chest that made him suspect it was a good one.

'Did you see the poster in the station for the Night Riviera? The sleeper train to Cornwall? I thought maybe we could try again.' She started to sing quietly, '*I must go down to the seas again, to the lonely sea and the sky,*' and then stopped and looked up at him, 'I don't suppose you remember that, though, do you?'

He didn't remember the song, but the idea felt warm and light inside him. He took her hand and pressed it to his lips. From another carriage they heard voices rise in song, '*Bread of Heaven, feed me til I want no more*'. The rugby's over then, he thought, not entirely sure how that connection had been made. The music tumbled in rich waves along the carriage, lifting its listeners and carrying them along, as compelling and irreversible as the train itself.

Stella drove them home beneath the orange lights of the dual carriageway, windscreen wipers slapping back and forth as the shadows slipped across John's face.

He turned to look at Stella. Her eyes were fixed forward, hands tight on the wheel. 'Why – the sleeper, Stel?'

He could remember wanting to leave the city, the sense of being overwhelmed by noise and motion. He could feel the memory of a song that he had sung to Hope as a baby, the words about the sea and the sky. The car slowed for a traffic light and Stella glanced at him.

'It's the sleeper train. I'd love to do it again, but without the stress of the last time. I've always loved the idea of falling asleep and waking up somewhere else – just dreaming our way through the tedium of the journey. It's almost a kind of time-travel.'

'Um.'

'Oh, now don't go getting all physicist on me. I know it's not actually time-travel. It's just – well – a bit magical.'

'Stella, you are – funny.'

They drove on in silence through the backstreets, turning left into their row of sleeping terraces. A fox froze in the road in front of them, its eyes glowing with reflected light. For a minute it stared at the waiting car, then sauntered off towards some bins.

'I'd like – to go.'

Stella pulled up the handbrake and switched off the engine. Still looking away from him, she reached a hand across to his thigh and let it rest there. 'I hoped you'd say that.'

John held her hand and pressed it to his lips. 'Yes. It's been – a long day. Let's – go to bed.'

Beneath the smooth chill of cotton, John lay listening to Stella in the bathroom. In all the years they'd been together, he'd never quite worked out what it was that she did in there to take so long. He'd noticed it more when they'd started sharing a bed again a few years ago, pleased at the return of this familiar ritual. He must have dozed off because her cold limbs jolted him awake as she climbed in beside him.

'Sorry, sorry, I don't know why I get so cold.'

He stretched his arms out and she basked in the warmth of his long body, which radiated heat. They used to joke that was how he stayed so thin, burning all his energy like a human primus stove. 'Better?'

She gave a low noise of approval, pecked him on the lips, then rolled over. John leaned back on his pillow and turned out the light, pressing himself against the cool curve of Stella's spine.

In the darkness of his room in Brixton, Charlie sat up in bed. There was always a moment as the memories faded when he felt at peace with the system of this whole vast city around him. And then, with the flicking of a switch, it disappeared. His eyes adjusted, taking in the magnolia walls, the dirty carpet, and he remembered. *It's not as if I had a choice.* But in some unspoken place he knew that was not the truth. There was always a choice. Sometimes it would be a snap decision, a single point that changed everything. And sometimes it would be a thousand tiny acceptances, settling in layers until the world became a place that you no longer recognised.

5.7

February 2007

Perched on the edge of the bath, Effie's hand shook as she pressed the mobile to her ear. 'Mum?'

'Hello, love.'

'I need to ask you something.'

'What is it, Eff? Are you OK?'

Effie paused. She could hear Hope clattering in the kitchen across the hall, oblivious to the Pandora's box that was about to open.

'Well, what with the wedding and everything, well, I'd – uh – I'd like to try and find my dad.'

Her mum was silent at the other end of the line. The phone went dead and Effie stared in horror at the screen with its five bars of reception. She knelt down on the floor and bent her head low, her heart racing. In her hand, the phone lit up and started to ring and she stabbed at the buttons, her hands trembling. 'Mummy?'

'Effie, I'm sorry, my signal went. You didn't think I'd hung up, did you?'

'No, no, not at all,' Effie lied.

'Oh, Eff, you did! I can tell from your wobbly voice. Silly girl, I wouldn't do that.'

It was impossible to lie to her mother. Over the years Effie had discovered that this was both a blessing and a curse. Beth carried on speaking, her voice a quarter-tone higher than usual. 'Darling, of course. I understand.'

'You do?'

Beth had expected this would happen one day, but even so she was shocked by the ugly surge of guilt that rose from somewhere behind her stomach, a visceral reminder of the part she'd played in Charlie's absence. The cruel words had flown from her that day, but she had been right. Effie had been better off without him. Where Charlie had been colourful and volatile, Rupert was muted and steady, calmer and more reflective because he was parent to someone else's child. He had given them both a life they'd never have had with Charlie.

'Mum?'

'Yes, Effie.'

Effie could hear the click of her tongue against the dry roof of her mouth. 'Do you have anything that might help me find him?'

Another silence flooded the line, but this time the phone stayed connected. 'I'm not sure, to be honest. I'll have to have a look and let you know.'

In the bathroom of her flat, Effie pushed her face into the palm of her hand. 'Oh Mum, do you think—'

Beth saw now that Effie would never forgive her role in keeping him away, her acceptance – encouragement even – of Charlie's belief that Effie would be happier with Rupert as her father. She would never understand that it had been for the best. But Effie wanted reassurance that looking for Charlie was the right thing to do and, relieved, Beth told her yes, it was. For a moment, she considered a caveat – *but don't expect too much from him* – or even a warning – *he may have fallen off the wagon again, and he was never a very nice drunk*. But as they talked, she began to see that Effie needed to be free of the stories of the past. Besides, Beth told herself, Effie had grown into a formidable woman, she'd be able to handle anything that Charlie threw at her.

Just as she felt the fear begin to lift, the question came, touching on the nerve of her raw guilt.

'Why didn't you try harder to find him, Mum?'

'Well, why should I have? He chose to disappear.' Beth's tone had sharpened; attack as her chosen form of defence.

'But didn't you ever wonder why?'

'Effie, I was trying to look after you. I did the best I could!'

Effie gripped the side of the washbasin and heaved herself to her feet. There was a gap somewhere in what her mother was telling her, she could feel it. Easier just to roll with it, though.

Beth promised she would look in her files and send anything she found that might help with the search. Effie said goodbye, conscious of a widening chasm between them.

Hope was slicing onions, her eyes streaming. Effie wrapped her arms around her, pressing her face into the messy topknot of frizzy brown hair. The yellow walls and the tall window of the kitchen were beaded with condensation from the pans that rattled and steamed on the hob. Hope was an enthusiastic chef, always trying new recipes, though often too impatient to read them in the proper order. She would skim the list of ingredients, making approximations and adjustments. She loved the precision of slicing, blending and browning just-so. But often she found herself so absorbed in chopping an onion into perfect slivers that she would forget the rest of the dinner until she smelled it burning. Perhaps the worst – and certainly the messiest – had been the eggs that she'd boiled until they exploded. Despite her best efforts, a faint gritty residue could still be seen across the kitchen ceiling when she'd moved from her Brixton flat two months ago to live with Effie in Kilburn.

Hope put down the knife and turned around. 'What's the matter?'

Effie wondered how Hope always seemed to know before they spoke that something was wrong. They didn't even have to be in the same room. It was as though she felt it on the air, the vibration of sadness or anger, like an aerial picking up radio waves. 'I'm going to try and find my dad.'

'That's brilliant. What's the plan?'

That was the other thing she did: turn thoughts into action. *It's not enough just to say it – you've got to* do *something about it!* Hope preferred to live like there was no time to waste.

'Oh God, I'm not sure yet. But once my mum's gone through her files I should have a better idea.'

It seemed unlikely they would yield anything significant – 1986 was a long time ago. But still, they would have to wait and see.

Hope narrowed her eyes. 'But there's something else, right? You're cross about something.'

Effie smiled a little, lifted by the rare pleasure of being understood by another person. 'I just don't know why she didn't try to find him.'

Hope let the thought settle, aware that there was nothing she could say to make it better.

After a while, Effie spoke again. 'I mean, Rupert's a great bloke, but Charlie's still my dad.'

That evening, as they were eating their dinner, Effie's mobile chirruped. The small grey screen shone orange with a message from her mother. She hadn't entertained much hope that Beth could help, but when she saw that she'd sent an address, Effie found she could no longer swallow. She thought of all the times that she'd wondered where her father had gone, of the exotic life he must have left her for. Anything that might have justified him never coming back. And yet he was living in Brixton, and neither he, nor her mother, had thought to tell her until now.

She pushed the plate away. 'Sorry, Hope, but I need to go for a walk.'

From the living-room window, Hope watched Effie walk towards the main road that would take her south towards the city.

The next day was Saturday. They woke early, dressed and left without eating breakfast. In the Tube they sat in a near-empty carriage, changing at Oxford Circus and travelling south all the way to the end of the line. They emerged in the dusty morning sunlight of Brixton, buffeted by the shuttle and return of people going about their weekend business. Across the street, Morley's department store was already busy, and up the road, Hope knew, the market would be bustling. She remembered the first time she'd gone there on a Saturday, watching with disbelief as a giant snail extended from its shell. *'It's alive!'* she'd gasped to the man who was selling the snails alongside plantains and tins of ackee and he'd laughed – *I think he wants to give you a kiss* – and held it out towards her, its white underside damp and ruffled at the edges.

Turning up Acre Lane, they passed grand old houses long since turned into flats and a leafy square with a squat grey-fronted pub in one corner. They turned right onto Florence Road and walked up to the black-painted door of number 42.

'Shall we buzz?' asked Hope.

Effie nodded.

When there was no answer, Effie scrawled a note and pushed it through the door.

Lying, sleepless, on his bed, unaware that the doorbell was broken, Charlie heard the snap of the letterbox.

On the doormat in the shared hallway he lifted up a folded scrap of paper, pulling down his glasses from his head to read the small neat handwriting.

One word – *Effie.* He saw her name and the string of digits that must be her phone number. *Effie.* Dear God. Could it really be?

He had wondered so many times what this day would be like, whether it would ever come. How could he even begin to explain? How could he make her see that everything he'd done had only been with her best interests in his heart? She'd been better off without him. He knew that from the pictures that Beth sent him each year, as they'd agreed she would. He found his mobile in a drawer, tried to turn it on, then swore as he realised it was out of battery. He walked up to the payphone on the corner of the street, slotted in a pound coin and dialled with shaky hands.

After they had spoken, he leaned against the glass panels of the phone box, watching the street outside blur in the mist of his breath. A woman with a pram walked past, her gaze darting from him as her pace quickened, but he'd seen in her eyes as they'd briefly met his that she had been afraid. Charlie felt the bite of panic in his gut. *What if Effie is afraid of me, too?*

At the top of the road two young women turned the corner. He didn't realise at first, even though the graceful movements of the taller woman made him think almost immediately of Beth. It wasn't until he saw her expression that he knew who she was. He watched them pass on the other side of the street, their arms linked as they walked towards his flat. For a moment he thought about leaving, of heading off in the other direction. He imagined going to the greasy caff by the railway arches, where he was still only on nodding terms with the owner after twenty years – except at Christmas when they'd exchange gruff season's greetings with one another. He could send Effie a text, explain it had all been a mistake. He glanced back down the street and saw her nearing his front door, her long hair ruffled by the wind. She pulled her coat tight about her and as she turned he realised how much she looked like Annie. He stepped out of the phone box and began to walk.

Charlie looked at the two young women who stood in his living room. They were luminous in their youth: their smooth skin, their white teeth, their movements fluid and unselfconscious.

She introduced her brown-haired companion as Hope.

'Good to meet you, Mr Kenny.'

'Oh, Charlie, please.'

It was strange to play the grown-up, the father figure. It felt pretend, the words not quite his own. It was as if he was playing a part in one of the TV dramas he sometimes watched in the evening before he left for work.

Effie looked at her father, taking in what he'd become. His skin was toughened around the jaw with patches of white stubble; his nose lumpen, his eyebrows wild. But this was definitely her dad. She recognised the tenor of his voice, the way he cleared his throat before he spoke and the down-wards turn of his mouth at rest – a default setting of sadness so deep-rooted that it shaped his whole being.

Charlie watched his daughter's face as she looked at him, deep in the dialogue of her own thought. Remarkable, he thought, how much happens silently within a mind.

She leaned towards him and her voice cracked as she spoke the words he'd been waiting for. 'I just need to know why.'

It was the question he'd asked himself over and again. But how could he explain to her the fear that stood between him and the world like a wall of glass? The nights he'd walked north from the river and on past the park, through the backstreets of Mayfair and further up until he reached, at last, the ever-busy rush of Finchley Road. The nights when he'd stood in the shadows across the street, watching the dark windows of the house that had once been his, willing a chink of light that never came, wishing for the strength to become someone worthy of her love.

'I don't – I don't know where to start with this.'

The words came out sharper than he'd meant them to be and she looked startled at his tone, her forehead folding into creases. It was so long since Charlie had spoken like this, with anything at stake. He felt a surge of adrenalin spike through him with a burst of flood-lit clarity.

'I want you to understand Effie, I left because I love you. I—'

His mouth was gluey as the words faded into whiteness. His hands started to shake.

Effie looked at him and pushed her hair back roughly with both hands, screwing her eyes tight shut. 'That doesn't make any sense!'

'You had Rupert and your mum – you were better off without me.'

'Better off without you? What the fuck are you talking about?'

'Effie.' Hope's voice was a gentle warning tone, her hand on Effie's forearm.

Effie turned. 'What?'

'Give him a chance.'

Effie paused, mouth slightly open as though she was about to reply, but had thought better of it. She sighed, then pressed her lips to Hope's. Hope wrapped an arm around her. Charlie wondered how he hadn't realised before that the two girls were lovers.

He pressed the heel of his hand to one eye and then the other. Light flashed across his vision and he blinked, hunching over as he waited for the contrast to settle. When he spoke, his voice had a slight tremor. 'Oh dear, I think I should have offered you a cup of tea or something, shouldn't I? I'm sorry – can I get you a drink? Tea? Coffee?'

He left the room and the two girls sat in silence, looking at the shabby surroundings. The walls were bare, the glass-topped coffee table filmy with dust and unidentifiable spillages. Newspapers were stacked by the wall, a half-drunk bottle of orangeade on top of them.

Hope turned to Effie. 'Are you OK?'

Effie shrugged. 'I think so.'

The door brushed across the rough blue carpet and Charlie re-emerged carrying three mugs. 'I'm sorry they're chipped. I don't have many – I'm not really used to visitors.'

He handed them each a mug of grey-brown instant coffee. 'And, uh – how is Beth? Your mum, I mean.'

Effie raised her eyebrows and sipped her drink. 'She's well – she and Rupert have a practice just up the road from the house. She plays golf, volunteers with the Rotary club, goes on holiday quite a lot – that sort of thing.'

Charlie winced at her privileged voice and her version of the world, a daytime dweller's London.

She carried on speaking. 'And what do you do? You know, for work?' She chewed on a fingernail, looking suddenly nervous. Charlie felt a rush of tenderness, relieved that she was gentler than her voice let on.

He told her about the homeless shelter, how he'd started working there fifteen years ago and all the changes he had seen across those years – the new influx of homeless families, people clinging on by their fingertips. 'I man the doors, mostly.' He didn't explain, though, how the work reminded him that there were people whose lives had worn thinner than his own. Nor did he say that, sometimes, when someone beat the odds of their desperate circumstances – a council flat here, an employment scheme there – the bright glimmer of their new hope could set something flickering inside him too.

The light caught Effie's St Christopher, throwing a tiny orb of reflected brightness onto the wall above Charlie's head. He looked up and saw the silver medal around Effie's neck and his eyes widened in surprise. 'You still wear it?'

'Yes, I do.'

He saw that her eyes had filled with tears.

'I was so sure that you would come back. But you never did.'

'Oh, Effie.'

Coal-tar soap and tobacco. The scent of her father transported Effie across decades as she sobbed into his shoulder.

'Shh, Effie, shh. I'm sorry, I'm sorry. I thought it would be best. Oh love, I'm sorry.'

She sat up and took Hope's outstretched hand, speaking into middle distance. 'You know, it was barely spoken about, the fact that you were gone. We would talk about everything except you not being there. I think that Mum was trying to protect me, actually. But I don't think it was the right way.'

She wiped her face again and pushed herself forward in her seat. 'Anyway, I think it's time we went.'

Charlie cleared his throat and laced his fingers together. 'Effie, would you – consider seeing me again?'

She stared hard at him and he felt the world spin faster, a whirl of pain and hope and time. Eventually she nodded. 'Yes, I think I would.'

After the girls had gone, he sat looking at the three half-empty cups, his proof that they had really been there. From the shelf he took down a large brown envelope and ran his thumb across the thick wedge of paper inside. Then he drew the curtains, lay down on the sofa and slept until early evening.

5.8

Outside Hyde Park Tube, a woman was selling overpriced roses from a wooden cart. Charlie stopped and lifted a bunch – reds and dark purples – handing over a small stack of coins. He waited by the gate, self-conscious in his tidy jacket, the flowers making him feel conspicuous as passing strangers turned and smiled. Were they imagining a lover's tryst, perhaps? But this was no romantic meeting. Charlie waited, watching the cars stream around Park Lane. Behind him, dust rose from the bridleway, catching in his throat and leaving a light coating of grit on his face.

He glanced at his watch. She was late, but who was ever on time in London? Even in the days before mobile phones, waiting was part of any arrangement. Someone was always delayed. He remembered standing for over an hour outside the window of Swan & Edgar at Piccadilly Station ('the dilly' they had called it back then), when he and Beth were first together. When she'd finally arrived, wearing long leather boots and a sheepskin coat, he'd asked her why she didn't seem surprised that he was still there to meet her. She'd stared at him with black-lined eyes and her lips had slid into a half-smile. 'But Charlie, I knew you'd wait.'

And perhaps Effie would be the same today, because he
would wait – and wait and wait – if that was what was
needed. He shifted the flowers to rest in the crook of his
arm – and when he looked up, there she was. Her blonde
hair flowed loose – long and pale just as Annie's had been,
though her skin was olive and her features proud, like Beth's.
It made him ache to see how beautiful she was. He held out
the flowers. 'These are for you.'

She hesitated, unsure of what to do, then took them and
held them to her face, breathing in their faded city-scent.
'Thanks, Charlie.'

The use of his first name made him flinch. He had always
loved to hear her call him 'Dad' – and though he knew he
had no right to claim this title now, the loss of it pierced
him.

They walked into the park together. The roar of the city
made their silence seem natural, but as the traffic noise
began to fade, Effie felt the need to speak.

'How have you, been – uh, you know, since Hope and I
came over?'

Charlie considered the question, unaccustomed to everyday
conversation. 'I'm – um – I've been well, I suppose.'

They walked on, passing the place (though of course they
did not know it) where a single moment of abandon had
begun the long sequence of events that had brought them
to this place. Gradually, Charlie found he could remember
the lightness of touch that had once been his trademark at
literary parties: raconteur, listener, confidant. And, though
he was rusty and anxious, he found a glimmer of his old
confidence, and was grateful for it. Effie was grateful, too,

for the glimpse of the father she remembered. Tentatively, like walking along a path in the dark, they spoke of the years that had passed: Effie's schooldays, her time travelling before university, the job she had grown to enjoy despite her terrible boss.

When he began his story, Charlie started further back, recounting his weaknesses – the drinking, his affair, the moment he realised that Beth no longer loved him. Without meaning to, he spoke a little about Rupert; about how he'd felt he couldn't compete with this man whom Effie had seemed to adore.

That was when she'd cried, both in anger and in grief. 'How could you think that? How could you think that my life would be better without you in it? You were my father!'

She looked at his weather-beaten face, the folds and crags a topography of twenty years of walking the city in all the seasons of the night. His eyes had sunk into the leathery flesh, their whites a clouded yellow, and yet they were still unmistakably his eyes. He was still unmistakably her father: the gentle man who could weave a story out of thin air, his arms wrapped around her in a force-field of her own, safe from the world. She touched his hand, the same hand despite its rough old skin.

'I mean,' she whispered, so soft he hardly heard, 'you *are* my father.'

Facing one another, fingers interlaced, they listened to the world pass by around them: the buses, planes, cars and people, each precious life a mystery of its own. The trees above them rustled and Effie tilted her head, her young neck tanned and smooth.

'A wood pigeon,' she smiled as the bird began its familiar call.

Charlie held out his bag. 'Here – I've got some straw- berries. Shall we sit down?'

The red juice ran over her fingers as she ate and she wiped them on the grass.

'There was something I wanted to tell you, actually.'

'Oh?'

Effie plucked a daisy, not looking up as she spoke.

'Hope and I have decided to get married – a civil part- nership – and, well, I wanted to ask you how you'd feel about being there? Just, you know, attending – it wouldn't be anything big.'

Still holding his strawberry, Charlie stared at the canopy of leaves above them and said nothing.

Effie waited, unsure – she thought – of what she wanted him to say. But when he placed his face in his hands, sighed and spoke the words – *Effie, I just can't* – she felt a hollow stretch inside her like a hole burned in paper.

She reached over and placed her hand on top of his and he looked up at her from beneath his greying eyebrows.

'It's OK, Charlie. I understand.'

'Effie, do you remember when I took you to Camden Market?'

She nodded, afraid that if she spoke her voice would betray the fracture that was creeping from her stomach towards her throat.

'I lost you and a policeman had to take you home. That's when I realised I didn't have what it took.'

Effie looked at him, her eyes steady.

'Oh, Charlie, I—' she began. And then she stopped

speaking. Because, she realised, there are some things that talking can't fix; some things you just have to carry.

Charlie stood up and held out a hand for his daughter, leading her back through the park towards the noise of the city. Their hands stayed linked all the way to the Underground.

As they said goodbye, Effie reached into her handbag and took out a thick cream envelope. 'Here, you should have this anyway.'

Charlie took the invitation and slid it into his rucksack with a nod, noticing the way her voice had tightened, her chin raised a fraction higher than before.

'Thank you, Effie. Can we meet again? Would that be OK?'

She closed her eyes for a moment as she nodded a quick approval. 'Sure. It'll be quite busy these next couple of months, but I'll be in touch.'

They kissed, a brief touch of the cheeks, and he watched her as she ran down the stairs to the Tube without looking back.

At Swiss Cottage, Effie strode through the backstreets towards her childhood home, where Rupert answered the door in his Saturday civvies: rugby shirt, chinos, socks with a hole in the toe.

'Well, if it isn't our Effie!' he said in the special booming voice he used when trying to be jolly. 'Long time, stranger. Come on in!'

Beth was in the kitchen, where the smell of coffee and fresh bread was rising with the steam and sunlight.

She gestured to the wide pine table heavy with food and

papers. 'Darling! Sit down, sit down.' Beth kissed her and led her to a chair, 'Coffee?'

A radio chattered in the background, its words indecipherable – intelligent white noise, Beth called it – drowned out as it was by the clank of pans and the rattle of the kettle.

Plates were clattered onto the table, a pile of cutlery dumped with a crash. Bread and cheese, pickles and salad, water, coffee, glasses, a jar of pickled onions.

'Butter, oh – Beth, don't forget the butter!' Rupert called with a sudden urgency as the table grew even more cluttered with lunch things. Beth rolled her eyes, but brought the butter dish, shifting plates and cups along as she placed it in front of Rupert.

'Thank you, darling,' he smiled up and patted her bottom.

'You lecherous old sod,' Beth shot back, one eyebrow raised. They laughed and Effie felt a comforting sense of life drawing back together, of things returning to their rightful place.

'So how did it go, then?' Beth held a half-eaten cheese sandwich gripped between her thumb and forefinger as she spoke.

Effie swallowed her mouthful. She thought of the dusty flowers in her handbag and of the touch of his familiar hand. 'It was OK.'

She sipped her coffee and spoke again. 'He's not going to come, though.'

Beth put her sandwich down. 'Perhaps, Eff, it's for the best,' she said quietly.

Rupert leaned into the table. 'Are you OK, Effie?'

His greying thatch of hair flopped into his eyes, distracting from the thinning area at the back. He had always been so level, so calm. She had always known where she stood with Rupert; always been confident of his feelings for her. After Charlie had disappeared, it had been Rupert who had sat next to her as she cried for her father. Beth hadn't been able to stand it. But out of guilt or kindness, Rupert had been the one who had stayed with her sadness, waiting beside her until she had no more tears.

She reached out for his hand. 'Rupert – listen.'

His eyes widened a fraction but, as always, his voice was deep and soft. 'Yes, Eff?'

'I want you to know that as far as I'm concerned, you're my dad. I mean, you did all the hard work, right?'

They laughed then, remembering the wilder years, the teenage lies, the time that Rupert had to collect her from a warehouse party in Neasden at 4 a.m. when she'd been in such a mess that she'd wandered away from all her friends.

'It wasn't *all* hard work. I mean, we had some fun too, didn't we, Effie?'

'We did.'

There was silence for a moment around the table.

When Rupert spoke again, both women heard the tremor in his voice, a tender fragment slipping out beneath the therapist's mask. 'Thank you. It means a great deal to me that you said that, because I think of you as my daughter. I really do.'

Effie felt the burnt-out space inside her grow smaller. She sipped her coffee and smiled at Rupert and her mother, contained in the warmth of their cluttered kitchen.

*

A hundred and something miles to the west, Stella and John were also in the kitchen, their table covered with brochures, guidebooks, a laptop and the dog-ends of a plate of cheese on toast.

'Are you – sure – you want – to take – the—' Stella waited as John paused, 'sleeper?'

'Yes, I think so. We can catch it from Paddington after the wedding. The girls have got lots of help for the clearing up – they won't need us.'

'But – the beds?' John used his hands to show one above the other.

'Bunk beds, you mean?'

'Yes. Not – your – uh – usual choice,' he was grinning as he spoke, his expression gently mocking.

'What do you mean? I can sleep in a bunk bed perfectly well!'

He took her hand and kissed it, still laughing quietly to himself.

She pushed his shoulder and tutted, but her face was playful as she did. 'I can't believe you're taking the piss out of me!'

'My – prerogative!'

She laughed and flipped open the laptop. 'So we're settled then? I'll book it, shall I?'

John looked at her as she typed. The gold threads of her hair were silver now, and her face had folded softly on itself and grown tight around the mouth. But she was somehow unchanged – despite everything. He nodded in agreement and smiled his lopsided smile.

With a swipe and a click it was done. 'There we go! We're

all booked,' and then she sang, '*We will go down to the seas again, the lonely sea and the sky.*'

She looked at him, searching for any trace of recognition. John shrugged and Stella laid her head upon his shoulder, looking out of the kitchen window onto their scrubby patch of garden. In the background, the radio pipped and a newscaster began to speak in serious tones; outside a small bird settled on the feeder and a cat padded along the fence. But in that small kitchen, the world was distilled for Stella into the points of pressure made by John's fingers as he laced his hand through hers.

Early the next morning, John walked barefoot into the study and opened a desk drawer. From a brown envelope, postmarked over twenty years before, he pulled a sheaf of papers and laid them on the desk. He ran his finger over the list of printed names on the first page. His eyes settled upon the familiar letters of a name that was both his and that of another person; someone he'd once been but whom he would never know. John Greenwood, PhD. It was good of them to have credited him – right that they should, of course, but still. It gave him a glow of gratitude after all these years to have worked with generous colleagues who'd never tried to claim his ideas as their own. Liam had even tried to get him back on the project, before they'd moved to Bristol. John, though, had shut down every conversation about work, explaining in his fractured way that he had stopped, that physics now was like a foreign language to him. Liam had tried to cheer him up, of course, to brush aside the bitter shards of his withdrawal. But John saw it in his friend's eyes, the pity that confirmed his loss.

The paper lay before him now with Liam's handwritten covering letter. John pushed the envelope aside and lifted up the slim pile of A4: the culmination of all those thoughts that had once consumed him utterly. On the shelf above the desk was a row of carved figures, whittled by his own hand in sinewy gold wood. Next to them, a single folder held his remaining research notes; even after he'd realised how much the illness had taken from him, he hadn't had the heart to burn them all. He took the folder down, carrying it in his spare hand to the kitchen. The early morning light had an edge of cold to it and he tensed at its bold chill. On the table there were stacks of letters and newspapers, magazines and flyers, the laptop and a mobile phone charger. He pushed them to one side and set his work upon the wooden surface. When the kettle had boiled, he stirred instant coffee in a mug, watching the steam coil across the window and settle into clouds of condensation on the glass. Outside the birds were noisy, a cascade of tiny shouts and replies; but inside all was silent, except for the rustling of the pages that he turned, reading the words that once had belonged to him.

An hour later, Stella came into the kitchen and saw him bent over his papers, a column of sunlight falling across the back of his head. She watched him, his brow furrowed in concentration, his lips moving as he read. Hearing her at last – his ears were not as sharp as they once had been – he turned his head, spectacles askew on his nose, greying hair standing out in too-long tufts, dressing gown falling open to reveal his ageing skin and the white hairs on his chest. And yet, despite the changes wrought by time, Stella saw that this morning he was more like his young self than he had been in years. There was something in his eyes that reminded her of the John before his illness.

'Stella,' he murmured, his voice cracking at its first use of the day.

'What's that you've got there?'

'It's my old – work – on quantum – entanglement – and the – paper – they – published after I'd – left – do you – remember?' He looked away for a moment, as if afraid of something – disdain perhaps, or pity.

Stella took some bowls from a cupboard, then some cereal from the sideboard. She moved the piles on the table to one side and set the breakfast things down. 'Looks interesting. What do you think of it, then?'

John took from his dressing-gown pocket a small wooden figure he'd carved last week, turning it in his hands like a worry doll. 'I – think,' he said, his eyes meeting hers, 'I'd like – to read – some more.'

Later, as John showered and she tidied away the breakfast things, Stella picked up another pile of papers. These were newer, tucked beneath the telephone directory and a guide to local recycling services, something she had been working on in the mornings before she left for her job at the health centre. The notes were tidy and clearly structured; it was as though her idea had grown a life of its own, the way it poured from brain to hand to page. It was a feeling she remembered, or half-remembered, from another time, another life. Stella opened the computer and brought up the University Admissions screen, where her PhD proposal sat waiting, black on white, cursor blinking at the end. She took a deep breath and read the title: *Stella*

Greenwood – Speaking the Silence: Illness as a metaphor for motherhood in modern women's writing. Then, before she could change her mind, she moved the arrow on the screen and pressed 'Send'.

REPRISE

4 *August 2007*

Summer blooms in north-west London – discarded ice-cream wrappers, plastic bags and cigarette ends swirl in the tail-wind of passing cars, gathering in drifts along the gutters. Tucking the curtain beneath her chin to hide her nakedness, Hope peers out onto the early-morning street. Today is the day.

Without her contact lenses in, the world is soft, its edges smudged so that the blown rubbish blends into trails of smooth white movement below the high red fronts of the houses opposite. The street is quiet, the sky brightening to a hazy blue. She presses her forehead to the glass, so old that the pane is gently rippled, and mists the window with her breath. Across the room two dresses hang – one blur of white and one of black – and beneath them, she knows the bright blobs to be two pairs of neon pink shoes, perched on top of a pile of papers. 'Wedmin', they've taken to calling it, because getting married seems very much to be like the world of work: the codes of conduct, the politics and planning. Who sits where, who isn't speaking to whom. At least they were saved the pain of working out what to do with Effie's father.

She walks barefoot into the kitchen, a towel wrapped around her instead of a dressing gown, fills the kettle and puts on some toast, flicking the radio on as she passes. The weather will be fine, the traffic is OK; the world is no more terrible than it was yesterday. She pours the boiling water into the mugs, prodding the tea bags with the handle of the butter knife, then stirs in the milk. At the smell of burning toast she swears and pops the toaster, pulling out two charred slices and tossing them into the bin.

'Bloody hell!'

Effie walks into the kitchen, yawning, in her knickers and a T-shirt, her hair a bright blonde tangle, dark rings of yesterday's make-up beneath her eyes. 'Good morning, my love. What's all the noise about?'

In their hotel not far away, Stella and John are sleeping back-to-back, wedding clothes hanging in the bathroom, their travel bags zipped tight at the end of the bed.

On the streets of Belsize Park, Rupert is running, wincing each time his left knee takes the impact of his foot against the concrete. Even with the pro-cushioned, high-impact super-trainers he bought for a sum slightly greater than the cost of his first car, his joints are simply not up to this any more. He stops and leans against a pillar box, bending and stretching his knees to try and ease the pain, then limps to the coffee shop on the corner, which has just opened its doors, and orders a skinny cappuccino and a croissant.

At home, Beth is lying on her broad white bed in their clean white room, staring at a dust tail hanging from the cornice as she recites the names of all the cousins who'll be coming today.

'What's the format for a civil partnership?' her mother's sister's daughter Rebecca had asked last night, as though it were some alien ritual rather than a wedding in all but name. Beth very nearly replied with a lurid fiction just to watch her cousin squirm. But she hadn't. In the end she smiled and answered patiently, choosing to believe that the woman was merely being ignorant rather than malicious.

Squinting in the early morning sunlight as it dazzles on the river, Charlie walks across Vauxhall Bridge, a brown paper package tucked under his arm. He sees the same familiar sights, the boats and grand buildings, and yet today they have taken on new meaning as they set the scene for the beginning of a new chapter.

The registrar is eating breakfast; the caterers are at the fruit market. In London and beyond, wedding guests are emerging one by one from their slumbers and into the day that will bind together in law the two young women who, at this moment, are standing in silence by the high window in their living room.

Tea is drunk and beds are made, showers taken and toenails clipped, time moving ever onwards, all paths leading to the concrete steps and tall pillars of Marylebone register office. Aunties, uncles, cousins and friends plot their way by Tube and by bus, while Hope and Effie zip up their dresses and wait for the taxi to arrive. John and Stella lean against the wall of the living room, looking out at the familiar houses of Kilburn. Beth and Rupert pace in and out of the kitchen asking questions that Effie abruptly dismisses. The hall is ready, it's all in hand.

'For God's sake, just enjoy it!' she yells through the toilet door.

By now Charlie has reached Marylebone High Street and his shoes are beginning to rub. Why he has worn this old suit and hat he can't exactly say. After all, he won't be attending the wedding. Effie didn't argue when he tried to explain; perhaps she was relieved. He hopes that he can make her understand. The street is busy with Saturday shoppers, a wealthier class of people than he remembers from when Annie and Ben were married nearby. He touches the sandstone sills of the pub in which he toasted them some thirty years before. And though the place is now a chrome-sleek gastro pub, he feels Annie's absence there so acutely he has to shut his eyes and press his feet inside his shoes to feel the floor beneath them. He closes his fingers about the smooth brown package he has carried across London, feeling the weight of the words in his hands.

'Are you OK, sir?'

A voice in the darkness. He opens his eyes and sees a young man from the pub, his white shirt crumpled, a spill of something yellow on the collar. He looks concerned.

'I'm fine. Thank you.'

The barman's face is unconvinced. 'Are you sure? Would you like a drink of water?'

Charlie, who is not accustomed to daytime exchanges, does not reply at first.

'Sir?' the young man says again.

'I'm sorry, son. That's very kind of you. I'll sit down here a moment, if you don't mind?'

'Be my guest.'

Charlie sits on a wooden bench and tilts his face towards the gentle morning sunshine. He watches the people on their way to elegant furniture shops and designer boutiques, those dealers in dreams and imagined desires when all other needs are met. The waiter places the water and a paper napkin on the warm wood of the table and Charlie smiles his thanks. He raises the glass to his lips and drinks, drumming his fingers against the package in front of him. When he has finished the water, he pulls a pen from his pocket and begins to write on the napkin, slowly at first so as not to rip the tissue paper, then more urgently, until the white is filled with words.

They walk in, hand in hand, to the room where every face is familiar. There is something unreal about this mismatch of people, the many threads of their lives tangled together in one large room overlooking the Euston Road.

Music plays, words are said and repeated. Effie smiles and Hope squeezes her hand. Rings exchanged, they kiss to whoops and cheers.

Throughout the short ceremony Stella holds John's hand so tightly that his palm grows moist. How could thirty years have passed since they had left this very building, stumbling blind with hope out into the noise and grime, totally unaware of what life would hurl towards them? How could thirty years feel so short and yet so elaborately long? What had happened to all those dreams? They evaporated, she supposes, in the heat and grind of life taking place, those sharp turns and roadside slips that come out of nowhere and leave you reeling, unsure of which way is up.

John looks at his wife, aware from the pressure of her fingers that she is feeling anxious. He remembers their wedding, not in this room but in this building. Of course he does. He remembers the images – Stella's face turned up to his, the flash of her blue shoes as she walked down the steps – and senses, too, the echoes of his feelings: the clench of anticipation, the warm rush of joy.

Around the corner, in the hall where the reception will be held, caterers busy themselves with tablecloths and wine glasses, music singing from the speakers and food laid out along trestle tables. A wicker basket has been placed at the back of the hall with a hand-drawn sign that reads 'wedding gifts'. Among the activity, nobody notices the man who walks into the hall and places in the basket a manila-wrapped package with a small folded card taped to the paper, which reads, *'For Effie and Hope, with love, Charlie x'*. He walks out, back to the brick and metal interior of the pub where he had been before, noticing the smell of coffee and disinfectant that has replaced the fug of cigarette smoke and beer that he remembers from his youth. In a leather-seated booth by the window he sips a coffee and folds a beer mat between his fingers, watching the old skin gather on the back of his hand as the tendons flex beneath.

A movement from outside catches his eye and he lifts his head to see the passing crowd of people in their wedding-best. In their midst, two girls are walking hand in hand. Hope wears white with flowers in her hair, soft beside the sharp edges of Effie's bright diamonds and black taffeta.

Charlie leans back into the shadows, but he is unprotected from the shock of seeing Beth again. Her hair is shorter and stylishly cut, threaded with grey but still dark. She has a subtle double chin and deep lines around her eyes, but it is unmistakably her, beautiful in a tailored purple dress. The pain is breathtaking and raw. He clasps the beer mat tight and drinks his coffee, relishing its scald as a distraction from the lacerating intrusion of the past. Rupert walks by, trim but jowly in his three-piece suit. He turns to speak to the tall thin man and the plump woman in a cream coloured skirt who are walking alongside him and Charlie feels a twinge of satisfaction to see a prominent bald spot on the back of Rupert's head.

The wind catches somebody's hat and it blows back along the pavement. Charlie watches as the woman in the cream skirt trots after it, pinning it with the corner of her foot beside the pub window. On the other side of the glass, Stella catches sight of her reflection and looks away, unwilling to examine the slide of her features, the lines around her mouth, the deep circles beneath her eyes. She doesn't know whose face this is. But Charlie, watching her in profile from his seat, is struck by a sudden certainty that he has seen this woman before. She stands without meeting his eye and walks back towards the wedding guests, hat clasped to her chest. Charlie thinks for a time, watching the street settle again after the party moves on, but for the life of him he can't place her. He stands and walks over to the bar to order himself a sandwich. The food is much better nowadays, he'll say that for the twenty-first century. Back in his day he'd have had to make do with a bag of crisps and some nuts poured over *a bar salad*, Limpet used to call it – and Charlie holds for a moment the bittersweet memory of his friend, who's now been dead for longer than he lived.

When his sandwich is finished, Charlie screws up a used paper napkin and stuffs it into the half-empty coffee cup, watching the seep of the brown as it blurs across the tissue paper. He stands, pulling on his suit jacket and pressing his hat to his head as he steps into the wide bright world of London in the daytime.

The dinner plates are being cleared. Stella smooths her skirt with shaking hands and sips her warm white wine, her throat tightening as the acid rises. A glass chimes as someone taps it with a spoon and a hush falls across the room.

Hope leans towards her across the table, flush-cheeked and radiant. 'Are you ready, Mum?'

From nowhere a memory envelops her of Hope as a baby in her arms. She can feel the weight and warmth of her, her downy hair, the gentle sound of her breath.

'Mum?'

Hope is surprised by the serene expression on her mother's face. She looks quite beautiful.

'Sorry, darling. Yes, ready as I'll ever be.' Stella stands and looks out across the faces turned towards her. She glances down at John, who grasps her hand and straightens the notes, which he has helped to write. She takes a deep breath and begins.

The room swells with collective good feeling and Stella tells a brief story of their small family, John's illness and his abandoned work on entanglement. For a moment her voice wavers and she pauses. John looks up at her profile as she touches her hands to her mouth, then carries on.

'Quantum entanglement, it turns out, is a good way in which to talk about marriage – and this John asked me to say – because when two particles become entangled they remain connected even when they are far away from one another. Einstein called it "spooky action at a distance" because even he couldn't explain why it happened. Loving and staying with another person is a bit like that. It relies on a pinch of the mysterious – of responding to one another even when there is no visible force compelling us; even when it may seem thankless or hopeless. Because it gets results, even if we don't know exactly why.'

Glasses are raised and toasts are made, music and more wine flows. Later on, as people begin to move onto the dance floor, Stella and John kiss their daughter and new daughter-in-law goodbye and wheel their cases out into the dark. John hails a cab and they watch the busy London night flash by around them. Nothing, Stella thinks, is ever still in this city.

Beneath the flyover Charlie strolls, more comfortable now that night has fallen, though his bones feel tired from a whole daytime of being awake. Without thinking, he crosses the Edgware Road and begins to walk along Praed Street towards the rising arches of Paddington Station, past the glinting glass office blocks that loom over squat pubs and the hunched sprawl of St Mary's Hospital. Anonymous within the press of a tourist crowd, he crosses another road and turns down the steep ramp and into the glowing mouth of the station. He sits down on a bench and, exhausted from the day, drifts into a half-sleep. When he wakes, he sees the tall man and the woman in the cream suit from the wedding, sitting on the other side of the concourse with their luggage. The woman's eyes catch his and he feels it again, that stab of recognition, as she smiles at him and looks away.

The manila packet falls to the floor as Effie and Hope are loading the gifts into bags. The name on the card catches Hope's eye and she calls to Effie who is dragging a sack of presents across the floor.

'I think you might want to have a look at this.'

Effie walks over, barefoot and slightly unsteady. 'What is it?'

'It's from your dad.'

Effie stares at the package in her hands, a crease darkening between her eyebrows. She opens the wrapping. 'It's some sort of manuscript.'

The top pages are yellowed and smell of cigarette smoke, but as Effie leafs through the pile the paper grows whiter and the typescript darker. She sits down, the detritus of the wedding party forgotten, and begins to read a handwritten covering note on the back of a paper napkin.

There is only so much you can be for anyone. Ultimately, they have to make things happen for themselves. I see that now, too late. When I left you, it was because I thought that a father had to be a finely balanced compound in the chemistry of a child's life, needing certain properties like money and prestige to do the job properly. I thought if you had Rupert you would be better off than you could be with me, and every time I walked through London and saw the homeless and the hopeless I felt I was right, even if that meant that I had to suffer. I didn't know it was possible to

be so wrong. I know I've failed you again by not being at
your wedding, but I wanted you to know that even though
you didn't see me, I was there. I love you, Effie, and I think
of you all the time.

In Paddington, Stella scrubs at the stain on her skirt, feeling
the beginnings of the bruise beneath. An announcement
echoes across the near-empty platforms. Charlie watches
the couple gather their things and climb aboard the sleeper
train as he stands and walks out of the station.

Sleep arrives, eventually, for everyone: for Hope and Effie
entwined in their marriage bed; for Charlie on the cold
ground of Hyde Park; for Stella and John in the narrow
berth of a moving train.

All across the city the corners of buildings are sharpening
as the night lifts; the roads gleam with dew-fall; the dark
windows blink one by one into life as people are rousing
and making ready for the day. In the middle of the park,
damp with morning mist, Charlie rubs his face and in the
black space behind his closed eyes he sees the shape of two
hands, their fingers interlaced. He lifts his head, surprised
and relieved by the cold and discomfort to find that he is
still alive. Looking up into the pale London morning, he
sees the shapes emerge within the clouds. Two hands clasped
tight, chasing the old image away.

Hundreds of miles to the south-west, a train is lumbering
into Penzance station, its cargo of travellers sitting up,
sleep-eyed and stiff in the tiny carriage berths. Tight next

to John in the one narrow bunk, Stella looks up at the crack
in the curtain and its incision of brightening blue. Her head
on his chest, she listens to the thrum of his heart as it beats
on and on, a miracle within. His arm rests heavy across her
and his breath is warm on her cheek as in a cracked voice
he starts to sing:

> *I must go down to the seas again, to the lonely sea and the*
> *sky,*
>
> . . .
>
> *And all I ask is a merry yarn from a laughing fellow-rover,*
> *And quiet sleep and a sweet dream when the long trick's*
> *over.*

The train pulls into the station and they climb down into
the sharp diesel-scented morning and Stella feels a sudden
quickening as something nameless firms within, gently
rising, a silent bird that lifts her with it higher yet, borne
up on wings that open to a place of weightless light – and
she recognises this feeling as something she has known
before, but had forgotten; a feeling long obscured beneath
the soot of so many arrivals and departures. And with her
hand in John's and the sunlight warm on her face, she dares
to quietly say the word.

Acknowledgements

Thank you, Sophie Lambert, for being an exceptional person and an awesome agent.

Thank you, Holly Ainley, for your brilliant and thoughtful editing. Working with you is a joy.

Thank you, Emma Finn, Jake Smith-Bosanquet, Alexandra McNicholl, Alexander Cochran, Tracy England and everyone at Conville and Walsh.

Thank you, Ann Bissell, Charlotte Cray, Suzie Dooré, Fran Fabriczki and everyone at The Borough Press.

Thank you to my first readers, who were so generous with their time and thought and friendship: Tess Mahood, Jim Mahood, Sarah Matthews, Gerry Heraty, Iona-Jane Harris and Mary-Anna Ryan.

Thank you to Sarah Barker, Sarah Beard, The Bath Novel

Award, Mary-Anne Harrington, Andrew Hewson, Charlotte Mendelson, Alice Morley, Hellie Ogden, Emily Owen, Jayne Shipley and Clare Sturges for wise words and encouragement along the way.

Thank you, George Harris, for scientific inspiration and generous advice. Any errors are, naturally, my own. Thank you, Lucy Clibery, for your wisdom about Jewish tradition and so many other things besides.

Thank you to my friends and my family – Mahood, Stevenson, McHuid, Crowley – for love, support and being bloody good fun.

Thank you, Mum, for understanding with such depth, for love with such strength, for straight-talking and sound-boarding and for showing me that walls are for writing on, not for head-bashing.

Thank you, Dad, for your quiet wisdom, your gentle strength and for telling me when it was time to stop with the head-bashing.

Thank you, Ella and Amy, my precious fierce girls.

And thank you above all to Matt, without whom this story would never have been written.